BALCONY One

STONE EUGENE CLARK

For George and Cynthia Rodinos—

who built Balcony One with their own hands,

and welcomed me like I'd always belonged.

This is not exactly their story.

But it grew from their walls.

And for Liz—

keeper of the bar,

whose presence nudged the idea into motion.

Elizabeth bears her echo, but the fiction is mine.

This book is made of scrolls. scrolls are rooms—spaces that hold memory as much as story.

In Balcony One, the building remembers.

The past lingers in wood grain and glass, in ritual and residue, in what's been kept—and what's been lost.

Each scroll unfolds like breath: the first inhale, the held stillness, the tremor before the fall.

The structure is spiral, not linear.

You may return to the same moment from a different angle.

Each scroll moves through five spirals:

Opening, Outer, Middle, Inner, and Closing.

Within these spirals live shards.

A sound unfinished.

A scent that belonged to someone lost.

A grief that flickers and vanishes.

You are not moving forward.

You are moving inward.

The building does not end.

It deepens.

This is a work of fiction—

but like all old buildings, it holds truths passed down in breath, blood, and rumor.

Some names have been changed.

Some memories have not.

And if you want to be daring—

start at any scroll you desire and let the spiral take you in.

The scroll structure is nonlinear but emotionally cumulative.

The reading it invites is slow.

Spiral if you must.

Attend, but do not hurry.

Let yourself linger.

The story waits for those willing to listen.

Contents

I remember what they forget.

The way footsteps sound before sorrow.

The way laughter lingers in brick.

George, the gypsy, with his hands.

Cynthia, with her eyes.

I was built from their touch—

filled with the breath of others.

They come and go—staff, guests, ghosts.

They may mingle or echo their own memories.

But I keep the blueprint beneath their changes.

At night, the light folds into the stone.

The shadows bloom from wooden beams.

And if you're standing in the right place—

and paying attention—

the front of the building reveals its heart—

through light and shape and time,

remembering how to love.

Some call me haunted. Some call me holy.

I say nothing.

I listen.

One of them is coming back.

She was infused within.

And not sure why—

or how she was pulled into the walls

—into the soil.

She has forgotten who she is.

She thinks the dead forget.

But silence is where I speak.

I was born in their hands.

I remember.

And the breath they left behind

still stirs the dust.

~Balcony One

Scroll:

THE WAITING ROOM

Virgin, Utah – Autumn 1918

The plates—clean. The flatware—weighted. And the door—elegant.

It opened soft and slow, with the hush of a room inhaling—and the waiting room, as everyone called it, always seemed to be breathing… enough to remind you it was alive.

It didn't match the rest of the building.

The adobe gave way to velvet chairs, brass coat hooks, and a Victorian settee too fine for the dust it held. A chessboard sat untouched on a carved walnut table. The pieces were mid-game. No one knew who started it.

Music lingered in the air, but not from any visible source—something stringed, fretless, and faint. A cross between a Greek laouto and a desert mandolin, strung too tightly to name. The instrument itself hung above the hostess stand, alongside a cracked fiddle and a hand-painted bouzouki.

Rosa, the chef's daughter, liked to tell guests it was *a tribute to the gypsy's travels.*

She remembered the sound from somewhere else.

The floors were hardwood, worn thick by cowboy boots and leather soles. There were streaks of turquoise in the distressing that caught the light like veins of stone under skin. The paint near the ceiling flaked where the heat gathered in winter.

The mirror near the host stand was rimmed in raw pine—knotty, unvarnished, secured with hand-forged nails that looked older than the wall they bit into. No two pegs matched exactly. Some had oxidized into bruised copper green. Others were still raw, waiting to stain.

The glass itself warped near the corners where silvering had thinned, leaving shadows that moved a half-second slower than the people who cast them. Reflections never aligned quite right—something about the light refracting from yellow stucco walls, or the angle of the copper fashioning standing guard below.

Guests called it charming. Rustic. A desert relic framed by ocotillo branches and hand-painted signs.

But there was something in the glass beneath the sheen that caught and held things too long. Spirits in the form of residue. Emotion that took shape—and sometimes, teeth.

Some said the mirror was once a window. Others claimed it had been brought from an old saloon in Silver Reef where a man once vanished while tying his cravat. Mateo swore it had always been there, even before the host stand was built.

Rosa said it didn't reflect the room.

Only what the room refused to forget.

Elizabeth never looked in the mirror anymore.

But this morning—as she turned—something shifted.

It wasn't movement. More like a soft distortion, the way hot air wavers above a stovetop. She caught it in the edge of her vision—long enough to register the suggestion of another figure.

Not her own and not Rosa's, either. Rosa was late as usual.

Elizabeth turned her head slightly. The mirror held still.

Nothing out of place.

Except—no reflection.

It showed neither her face nor the room around her. Only black—flat, depthless, quiet.

She stepped forward without meaning to. Her hand hovered near the glass. Still no image. But the scent changed again.

Bougainvillea. And something older. Beeswax?

She almost said her name.

Sophia.

It brushed the inside of her mouth like a dry prayer but didn't come out.

Instead, she reached forward and touched the edge of the mirror. Not the glass, but the textured cantilever of wood George had shaped with his own hands. The mirror hadn't always had a frame. George cracked it once, years ago, with the ring his mother gave him before she died. Said the ring slipped while he was lifting the pane, caught the corner, and the crack bloomed like frost across the silver.

Most people would've thrown it out.

But George never let anything go to waste.

He built a cradle of pine around the break. Tight joinery, hand-rubbed oil, a kind of reverence, making the pine frame mismatched. Now it hung there, still faintly fractured, but steadied. Witnessing.

It had hung in this room before the floor was finished. Before the menu was printed. Before the Zitting brothers ordered their first drinks and made jokes about the "Greek haven in Mormon country."

But George remembered when it first pulsed.

Three days after his mother died—in Greece, 1911.

George couldn't attend, neither could Cynthia. They were swarmed by work at their restaurant in La Verkin—

The Stagecoach Grille.

This is where the mirror first hung.

That night, Cynthia's chair was empty. George—sitting alone, could hear the haunting chants of a Greek Orthodox Byzantine hymn engulfing his mind. A faint scent in the air—pomegranate and bougainvillea—and then the mirror turned black for three full seconds.

That was the first time.

This was the second.

Elizabeth stood very still.

And then: a flicker.

The mirror filled. She didn't see her reflection, but the mirror revealed the waiting room as it was a year ago. The chessboard stood empty. The mandolin was missing. Sam Zitting—full of noise and perfume—sat sprawled on the settee, laughing with one hand across Clara's thigh and the other around a bottle of his favorite wine.

His face turned.

He looked straight at Elizabeth through the mirror.

He winked.

And then: gone.

Her own reflection returned—flat, gray around the eyes, one hand still frozen mid-air. She moved, as though this were not an unusual experience for her, touched the chess table, and placed the white queen one square forward. She didn't know why. The game wasn't hers. But it felt like the right move. Then she crossed the room, lit the sconce near the hostess stand, and said the thing again.

"One day at a time."

Only this time, it sounded like a question.

She passed through each day like the gears of a pocket watch— checking candles, straightening the ledger, turning the open sign to open. She'd pause long enough to touch the banister of the stairs and say the same thing under her breath:

"One day at a time."

She never told anyone who she was saying it to.

Rosa called it the greeting room.

Mateo called it the room with no work.

Guests called it charming.

But the building didn't care what they called it.

It had been standing less than three years – built from adobe and salt pine by a Greek gypsy named George with a head full of angels and a Mexican chef named Mateo who knew the power of comfort.

They built it just off Johnson's Twist—the canyon road that curled like a lariat between the Hurricane Fault and the gates of Zion. The walls weren't red—they were blood-washed coral, the color of fever dream or a desert wound half-healed.

Two wrought-iron lanterns hung along the outer columns—ascending in size, as if marking time. They didn't flicker. They pulsed. And at night, they cast shadows like eyelashes down the stucco face of the building. And from light and shadow, a heart appears.

Below them, set in a perfect square of Talavera tiles, was the number: 770.

But the numbers weren't the part people remembered.

It was the border. The sunburst. The crescent stag. The repeating blue star that felt like something older than myth. The number was only an address. The tiles—something else. Warning. Prayer.7

Beside the number, a rose bush leaned inward, as if drawn to the heat between the lanterns. This was the time of year this rose loved blooming. And so it did—velvet red against the stucco, its thorns catching the wind like whispers. Visitors rarely noticed the bush. But Rosa watered it every Tuesday. Elizabeth once clipped a single bloom for the Zitting Room. It wilted in under an hour.

The land was scrub and red stone, the kind that burned your hands if you fell. Nothing but iron-rich dust, bone-dry sagebrush, and the silence of gullies carved too deep to echo. But the road—just widened by the state—cut a clean line past Virgin City, and someone said it would bring traffic. Pilgrims. Workers. Drinkers.

So they built the place.

Not the town. The town already existed, stitched together by clapboard houses, a one-room church, and the polygamist murmur that never quite left the canyon.

The place.

Balcony One.

They built it tall and wide, and it would rise from the desert like a living church. The building's skin was desert coral – thick adobe blushed with iron oxide and scorched wind. It bore the heat like memory. The columns were soft cornered towers that lifted toward Zion with no intention of reaching.

Bells hung from the hollows above – never rung, only watching. Beneath them, lanterns dangled like old sentinels, their glass panes crosshatched in black iron, glowing peach in the dusk. One always crooked. The other keeping watch.

The main entrance crouched beneath the shallow arch – timbered with a sun-bleached beam, hand carved and spined with desert thistle. Below that, a door: old wood, darker than it should be, carved with eight-pointed stars and circular knock-marks where pilgrims had once tested their luck. The path to that door was red rock, crushed fin and scattered like powdered rust. It dusted boots and ankles and skirt hems, coating the feet of those who came late or left early.

Adobe walls with Greek accent. Cyan-painted doors, hand-laid brickwork, a balcony that hung like an eyebrow over the sandstone slope. The rooflines didn't match. The shutters had ornamental carvings like Athenian lions. And George installed a water wheel that pulled from a hidden spring and spun all day long, turning turquoise stones beneath its wooden blades.

On the building's western flank, where the pink adobe caught the earliest light, a curve of arched windows watched the road in silence. Four toward the back of the building, shaped like cathedral eyes—those belonged to the sunroom. The remaining two belonged to the waiting room.

The arches weren't symmetrical. One sat higher than the others. Another had a cracked pane, sealed with resin and rumor. But they glinted just the same each morning—opal blue in the high sun, copper in the dusk, and blood-black when the storms rolled in. A bench waited beneath them, wrought-iron legs sunk deep in sandstone pavers. Someone had placed it there, but no one remembered who. It seemed too elegant for a building that made no effort to be. The planks were always cool. The iron always warm. A single guest once said sitting there felt like waiting for someone who'd already come and gone.

Beside the bench, a low wall of river stones curved like a shoulder. Mateo swore he hadn't stacked it. But it stood each season—never disturbed, never relaid, as if the stones themselves had agreed to stay.

Rose bushes flanked the windows, blooming too fiercely for the sand in the air. The blossoms pressed against the glass like eavesdroppers. And the scent—riotous, unapologetic—was strongest when the wind blew from the canyon.

The water wheel stood slightly off the path, not hidden, but never truly seen. Most guests passed it without pausing, mistaking it for decoration. But it turned—steadily, with an occasional squeak—as if moved by something older than plumbing.

Built from pine and cedar, the wood had darkened with age and varnish, splintered where fingers had once lingered. Each paddle bore the memory of a hand-carved edge, uneven as breath. Its axle was iron-bound, the bolts mismatched, as if the wheel had been salvaged from a mill long buried. Water did not pour. It trickled—from a hidden source beneath the stone—and spun the wheel not with force, but insistence. Beneath it, turquoise pebbles gleamed wet, surrounding a cluster of rough-cut glass crystals perched on black volcanic rock. They shimmered green in the sun, catching fire only at the edges. A shallow basin cradled it all—ringed in sandstone, layered in red grit, choked by the silence that came not from lack of sound, but the weight of watching. Rosa said the wheel ran backward once, on the morning of her mother's death. Mateo never mentioned it. Elizabeth swore the stones changed color in winter. No one ever found the pipe that fed it. Some said it pulled from an underground spring. Others whispered it ran from the same source as the mirror. An unseen channel beneath the foundation.

It wasn't marked on the blueprints.

But the building knew it was there.

And some nights, when the wind came low from the canyon, the wheel creaked. Not from movement.

The back of the building told a different story. Where the front stood like a chapel—bell towers, mosaic numbers, and solemn adobe curves—the rear unraveled into whimsy. A second story jutted up in sharp lines, modern and boxlike, trimmed with white windows that caught the sky in quadrants. The western end of the second story began as an open balcony—but one year when George was expecting special guests, a monsoon arrived suddenly. Elizabeth and another Greek, Aris the Artist, quickly wrapped the balcony with cloth and canvas to shield guests from rain and wind. After that—Aris decided to build walls and close in this part of the balcony, called it the upper banquet room. Below it, a long stretch of shade cloth sagged slightly with age, draped like a weary veil over the patio.

Behind that screen, music lived.

This was where the fiddlers played. Where Rosa once danced barefoot in the dirt. Where Sam Zitting held a gathering every Sunday afternoon with a mandolin in one hand and two wives bickering in the shade.

To the left, painted directly onto the adobe wall, was a false window. A mural—simple, uncanny. Two cobalt shutters flanked a pair of black railings, and in their midst, a planter box burst with painted sage. It looked real from a distance, this little balcony that led to nothing. Plaster and pigment. A trick of depth and light. But no one in the building remembered who painted it. Not Mateo. Not Magnus.

Not even Elizabeth.

"It's always been there," she'd once told Rosa.

"Even before the upstairs was built."

No one believed her. But no one painted over it.

Two blue pots sat beneath the mural, as if honoring the illusion. A gold bicycle leaned against the shade wall nearby, half-buried in red gravel, its tires long gone soft. It stayed clean. Unmoved, yet pristine. It probably belonged to Magnus with his little brown dachshund. And once, on the winter solstice, a guest swore the mural window opened.

From George's memory and soul, the building lived. Rosa said it felt like a temple. Elizabeth thought it looked more like a graveyard dressed for church. Most people who passed it didn't know what to call it. Some said the church had built it. Some thought it was a foreign consulate. Children whispered that the water ran uphill.

But those who stepped inside—and only a few did at first—never forgot the shift. The way the heat clung to the skin outside and disappeared completely once the door shut. The way the structure felt older than it looked. The way it watched.

Elizabeth still remembered her first time seeing it.

She had arrived on horseback from Washington City, boots scuffed from the twist, breath ragged from the slope. George had told her he was building the place and needed to staff up before opening. She hadn't expected to see something so strange standing past the edge of the fault line. A house with no clear era. A façade with no true face. A place that wasn't trying to fit in.

It simply was.

The heat of the canyon still clung to her sleeves as she crossed the threshold. She stopped inside the waiting room—struck dumb by the velvet furniture, the freestanding instruments, the air that smelled faintly of lemon and copper.

"Sit," said a voice.

It came from the dining room. A man standing—thick white hair, gleaming blue eyes, boots covered in dust. He held a hammer in one hand.

"I'm George," he said. "You're early."

Elizabeth stood without answering.

George crossed to the chessboard, picked up a black knight, studied it, and set it down exactly to a new position as if he were playing chess with a ghost. Then he turned back.

"You've waited tables before?"

"Yes."

"Tended bars?"

She again answered yes.

"Where do you come from?"

"My family was called to the Cotton Mission. We were too poor to leave when the floods came. So, I grew up in Washington City."

George sized her—not with judging eyes, but with discernment.

"Your hair is as short as a man's, reminds me of Sheriff Worthen."

She adjusted her broad-rimmed hat. A small six-pointed silver star hung from the left edge. Then she peered at George—knowingly,

"I'm as good a sharpshooter as the Sheriff. I was trained by Annie Oakley herself."

"You've worked with Greeks?"

She shook her head.

He smiled faintly.

"A woman sharpshooter might be exactly what we need around here. You're in charge of the bar."

The interview was over. He nodded once, pointed toward the end of the building where the bar was first imagined, and said,

"We want the bar built over there. You'll work with Aris; he is the Artist. When you leave, lead with the same foot you entered with. Where I'm from, you step in with the right, you leave with the right. Same foot, in and out. The building notices."

She wanted to ask what he meant.

But she didn't.

He turned and moved toward the boxcar he had converted into a construction hub, hammer in hand, boots kicking up silent red dust. She heard the sound of a towel hitting metal, followed by humming—not from a phonograph, but the chef in the kitchen. Mateo. A strange tune in a language she didn't recognize. They were the original crew.

Elizabeth looked at the chessboard again.

The black knight hadn't been moved at all.

But now the white king was missing.

In the southwest crook of the waiting room—where the walls caught late-morning light and the roses reached in like eavesdroppers—sat the chess table. It wasn't large. Carved walnut legs. A top polished down to a thumb-worn shine. The red-and-black inlay had been retouched once, long ago, but not perfectly—so that one square near the center bled a little too red, like it remembered something. One high-backed leather chair faced it. The other side was a booth, its cushion half-split and its tapestry clinging to a threadbare geometry that whispered of older origins—woven symbols that didn't belong to this desert or this century. The locals called it "the lost rug." No one could agree where it came from.

The light came through the arched window, fracturing into mosaic across the floorboards. Outside, red roses pressed against the glass. Their shadows swayed in time with the breeze, giving the illusion—if one stared long enough—that the flowers were inside the room. Elizabeth never moved the pieces—or she thought. Neither did Rosa. Or Mateo—or he thought. Or anyone else.

And yet somehow, they moved.

Sometimes the queen shifted one square forward. Sometimes a pawn vanished overnight. Once, Elizabeth was sure she'd seen the black bishop tilted at a crooked angle—as if in mid-thought.

No one spoke about it anymore.

Not since Sam Zitting had muttered something over his shoulder, three bourbons deep:

"Checkmate's a funny thing. You think you've won—till you realize who set the board."

No one laughed. He left early that night.

Elizabeth stopped dusting the chess table the day after Sam passed. The game, it seemed, would now clean itself.

Outside, the rose bush bloomed.

And in that little corner—between curtain and sunlight, woodgrain and whisper—the room remembered.

There was one wall in the waiting room that never quite looked the same twice.

It faced the outer edge of the canyon, catching whatever light the morning spared—and framed that light like a painting. Not a simple window. A recess. A hush in the adobe. Cut deep, with purpose. The alcove itself had been softened by years of warmth and candle smoke, its curves dulled to the texture of sun-warmed stone.

But it was the carving above the window that made people stop.

A single piece of dark mesquite—nearly black, veined with age— hand-carved into a crest of geometric feathers and spirals. Some guests said it was Greek. Others insisted it was Hopi. One man from Kanab swore it matched a keystone he saw in a monastery in Northern Cyprus.

Elizabeth had dusted it twice in three years.

The first time was when George asked her to.

The second was just after Sam Zitting died.

She never touched it again.

The stained glass inset beneath the carving wasn't bright, not in the way of cathedrals or saloons. It was dusky, subtle—ochre and ash-blue and a single shard of green, like a thorn in the light. When the sun hit at the correct angle, it sent a fractured beam across the waiting room floor, right to the leg of the settee.

The couch—too formal to be called a sofa—was upholstered in wine-red velvet that had aged into a brown bruise. The cushions had long since settled into the shape of old shoulders. There was a lace doily folded at the center. No one knew who put it there. But Elizabeth smoothed it nightly.

The floor beneath the couch was uneven—heart pine worn down to a groove by boots and apron shoes, the long walk of service. In that groove, the light from the stained glass sometimes flickered.

Sometimes it didn't flicker at all.

Just held.

Like it was waiting for something.

And in the moments when the room fell quiet—no guests, no Rosa, no clatter from the kitchen—Elizabeth sometimes stood there, one hand on the doily, and watched the light land in that groove. It always landed the same way. But the shape it made was never the same. The sun didn't simply shine into the waiting room.

It filtered.

Filtered through a wall of hand-carved wood—no one knew the name of the pattern, only that it was old. Too old for the building. Older, even, than George the Gypsy's designs. George claimed it had been a gift. Mateo hung it himself, panel by panel, over the west-facing windows. The screen never stayed flush to the wall. It tilted forward, like a head bowed in prayer. In the right season, the light would pass through its fretwork in a sprawl of shifting lace.

And it always landed on the velvet.

The couch—plum-drenched, button-tufted, legs curved like thoughts unspoken—caught the light as if it expected it. As if it had known for years that the screen would tilt forward, and the beams would pass through the gaps like keys through a cipher.

The shapes it left behind weren't random.

They patterned the velvet in soft dashes and petal-like ovals—pale ghosts of the carving above, mirrored in light. It looked, at times, like a language. A script from the old world. A hymn no longer sung. And if you stared long enough—you might think it was moving. One guest swore she saw a name spelled there. Another said it was scripture. A third, shaking, whispered that the light spelled the word *stay*.

Elizabeth dusted the settee twice a week.

She never brushed the light away. And she only sat there once. Before the guests arrived. Before the kitchen came alive with saffron and oil. She sat in the center of the couch, hands flat on the velvet, eyes closed. The light shifted across her skirt in slow dials, like a sundial with no hour to point to.

Instruments sat quietly in the corner where the yellow wall met the copper sconce that never quite flickered right. A trio of stringed bodies, each curved in its own way, leaned like friends who no longer spoke, but still waited for the same train.

The guitar was the largest.

Spanish. Well-made. The kind Mateo might have played when he was still young enough to believe in performances. The rosette around the sound hole was inlaid with pale blue tile—hand-painted, cracked at the top, like a mosaic brought from somewhere coastal. No one touched it anymore. Except Rosa, once, after hours. She plucked two notes and flinched when the second one stayed in the air too long.

Beside it: the Greek laouto.

Slim. Tall. Burnished. The tuning pegs curled like horns, and the fretboard had ghostlines from a thousand forgotten songs. George claimed it had belonged to his uncle—the one who stayed behind in Athens and sang to the cliffs. Whether that was true or not, the instrument kept a salt-worn smell.

The third was smaller still.

A child's bouzouki, carved from soft wood with vines etched in delicate whorls around the hollow. Rosa had asked once who it belonged to.

No one played the bouzouki now.

But sometimes—when the door to the kitchen opened too fast, or the lights near the mirror dimmed without cause—it hummed. A low hum, like breath caught in the hollow of something still trying to remember its purpose.

Rosa started calling that corner el rincón de las memorias. The memory nook. Elizabeth never corrected her. She polished the tuning keys once a month. And whispered "shhh" when no one was near.

The next morning, Rosa arrived late. The door *whumped*, catching on the dust at the threshold. Rosa always entered with her whole body— shoulder first, hair pinned in haste, cheeks pink from the walk, skirt dusted with flour from the trail that split behind the stable. Elizabeth was already at the host stand, setting out the blue glasses.

"Buenas," Rosa called.

Elizabeth didn't look up. "You're late."

"Only by a minute. The sky's still warming."

She crossed to the mirror, leaned in to fix a stray curl, but didn't quite look herself in the eye.

"Ay, por Dios—this cursed thing." she muttered. "One day she'll crack."

Elizabeth adjusted a glass so it caught the morning light.

"You're not paid to flirt with your reflection."

"I'm not paid enough, period," Rosa shot back, turning with a grin. "You want to hear what Tía Carmen says about that mirror?"

"No."

"She thinks it's a looking-glass to the other side," Rosa said, half-laughing.

Elizabeth raised an eyebrow.

"To where?"

"To whatever can't let go. Spirits, maybe. Regrets. Old things with names no one speaks anymore."

She picked up the chalkboard menu and wiped it clean with the corner of her apron, knocking off yesterday's specials with practiced swipes. Her nails were short, her knuckles still raw from washing crates.

Elizabeth turned away. The blue glasses were sweating already, though the air wasn't warm. From behind her, Rosa added, quieter,

"She says it only shows what doesn't want to go."

Elizabeth didn't answer. She walked to the door, flipped the sign to *OPEN,* and stood for a moment in the threshold. Outside, the canyon shimmered in pale morning heat. The wheel turned. A hawk circled. The road beyond twisted like a ribbon into nothing. Johnson's Twist. People would come. They always did. And the waiting room would watch. Outside, the clouds were gathering again.

These weren't Midwest storms—no black squall lines, no siren winds. Desert monsoons came differently. They coiled low. Crept in bone-first. Built from heat and hush and the kind of pressure that gathers behind your ribs before it ever touches the clouds.

The light shifted early. Shadows lengthened at odd angles across the waiting room floor, and the red dust beyond the front walk kicked up in fits, dancing like it didn't know whether to settle or fly.

Elizabeth watched the window. In the distance, the sky above the Virgin mesa had turned the color of dried wine. A low grumble uncoiled across the horizon—not thunder, only the promise of it. Like a warning from beneath the world.

It would rain tonight.

It always did this time of year—September's curse. And when it rained, the scent of the high desert changed: creosote and iron and something wild, like juniper waking from sleep.

But the waiting room never changed.

It stayed dry.

Warm.

And watching.

Some doors open memory.

Scroll

THE DINING ROOM

Balcony One – Dusk, the Day the Music Returned

The waiting room exhaled.

And the dining room received.

No door between them: space—widening, brightening. A threshold crossed by scent before footsteps. You didn't enter the dining room. You were welcomed into it. Ceilings rose. Voices embellished. Light from the high western windows spilled down like citrus, gathering on the wood floor in golden puddles.

It was the largest room in Balcony One.

The ceiling was tall but not distant. Rough-hewn beams crisscrossed above like an open ribcage—pine darkened by years of heat and song. If a guest paused beneath the center beam, they might hear it echo—softly, with the memory of them. Laughter lived there. So did long silences between courses, when someone considered whether to speak of grief and decided, finally, to simply eat. The beams held all of it. George called them the spine of the place. Said no good building stands long without one.

Two arches along the right wall opened toward what guests would later learn was the sunroom, but for now they were just passages—shadows and softness, not yet named.

The scent of yeast and citrus lingered in the walls. Butter browned in the kitchen. A fry pan hissed once, sharp and short, and someone near the back laughed at the right pitch. Aris had designed two large windows that allowed dining room guests to see inside the kitchen.

The staircase caught the eye. And beyond it was the hallway to the bar.

But if you turned just enough to see the far south wall—there was a painting.

A vertical canvas, tall and slim, framed in weathered gold. Beneath the gallery lights, a girl stands alone. Pale-haired, garlanded, robed in white that gathers at her feet like unfinished prayer. Her gown bears the soft suggestion of winged shadow, and her hands cradle a bouquet of long-stemmed lilies, petals folding inward like they've overheard something sacred. A small white animal—part rabbit, part memory—rests beside her hem.

The forest behind her is rendered in deep greens, almost black where the brush leans thickest. But the light around her face never dims. It's not painted, it's remembered. She doesn't smile. Doesn't pose. She looks. Directly outward. With a kind of ancient softness, like she's seen what comes after grief and decided to stay anyway.

Above her shoulder: three dark vertical markings. Crosses, perhaps. Or glyphs. Or trees stripped of their names. Cynthia called them "inspiration" once. Said they arrived like volunteers. Said she let them stay. Mateo calls the painting the Watcher. George calls it the girl from the grove. Cynthia never confirmed any of it. She only adjusts the light now and then, so the girl's face catches the dusk. She says the painting hangs best when it's near people who linger. And it does. Even the servers step slower beneath it. Not out of reverence. Out of recognition. But Rosa always made sure someone was there. She said the painting helped people say things they hadn't meant to. And that was good for the tip jar.

And like the painting, the interior stairs were created by Cynthia as well. Each riser was dressed in Santa Fe tile. Sun-warm reds. Desert ambers. Patterns like stars and flowers and echoes. A young guest once asked if they matched. Cynthia's reply:

"They match to me."

She moved through the room with shawl draped and voice like honey on linen. Her hair was soft and silver—cut blunt at the ends, resulting in a slow elegant curve. She wore lipstick the color of dusk, and earrings that glinted like old coin. When she stopped at a table, she didn't hover—she joined. And then, like always, she pointed to the walls.

"I painted that one the year we tiled the stairs," she'd say. "Used all leftover pigment. That's why the ochre's so stubborn—it remembers the grout."

Her husband—George—followed behind, slower but no less sure. White hair cropped close. Forearms like a smith. His voice carried without effort. He shook every hand. Told every story twice. But better the second time. He wore shirts with the sleeves always rolled and buttons never quite even. He smelled faintly of olive oil, smoke, and summer stone. He told a couple near the window how he came from Greece and started the ship's head on fire.

Across the room, Cynthia raised two fingers—subtle, as if tucking hair behind her ear. George caught it without looking. He adjusted his route, took the long way around a crowded table, and intercepted a server just before they dropped a plate. That was their signal. Two fingers meant reroute, one meant pause, and no fingers—everything's fine. They'd never said it aloud. They developed their language over time… after floods of guests and years of service.

Some couples fight.

Some freeze.

Cynthia and George rerouted.

Like two rivers bending around the same stone. Then he turned to another guest and said he built the chairs himself. Both were true. Both made people stay longer.

The guests were laughing near a painting, a low, rolling sound like riverwater over stone. Cynthia leaned slightly toward George, her hand grazing the edge of the staircase post as they passed each other in the middle of the room.

"You see that man with the cane?" she said, voice just under the noise. "He's sat at the same table for two years. Never once tried the pork chop."

George glanced, then smiled.

"He's waiting for the chop to convince him."

They paused by the entry where Rosa was seating a new party. Cynthia looked toward the tile work on the stairs—one of the turquoise ones had dulled.

"I think I'll replace that one," she said.

George shook his head, eyes on the same step. "You'll replace it ten times. That's how I'll know you're still here."

Cynthia's expression softened. She reached for his sleeve, straightened the button.

"Then promise me you'll tell them. When I'm not."

"I'll tell them," he said, quietly. "But I won't need to. This place says your name louder than I ever could."

They stood there for a second longer than they needed to.

Then Rosa cleared her throat—not impatiently, efficiently—and they stepped aside.

It was winter once, not long after they'd opened. A storm had closed the pass into Zion, and George was sure no one would come. But Sam showed up just after dusk—three brothers in tow, all loud with drink and dressed like men who'd never washed a dish. He clapped George on the back, said, "Tonight we fill this place. Just us."

Cynthia was furious. The kitchen wasn't prepped. The liquor shelf half-stocked. But Sam grinned like the devil with a secret, and by night's end, all five men were singing some half-Cretan, half-drunken ballad near the fire while Cynthia danced with a bottle in her hand and one boot off. George swore he didn't know the song. Swore he didn't dance. But he did. Once. That night.

Later, when Sam's youngest brother fell asleep on the cedar floor, George fetched a pillow, placed it gently beneath the man's head, and whispered,

"We built this for nights like this. For people who forget they're ghosts."

Every winter since, he lit the hearth a little earlier. Just in case.

She still kept the first olive pit he'd handed her—tucked inside a silver box in her dresser drawer. He'd offered it shyly, wrapped in a paper napkin, told her it was from his last jar before leaving Crete. She'd laughed, thinking it a joke. He smiled and said,

"So you'll know I'm real when I'm not here."

He didn't mean death.

He meant the vanishing that happens when men work too much and speak too little.

But now, years later, she understood. And every time he told the story slightly differently—more salt, less sorrow—she kept the pit close. It helped her believe in him twice.

The dining room wasn't quiet—but it wasn't loud either. It breathed. At the front, Rosa adjusted the seating chart like it was a chessboard. She didn't need to raise her voice. She raised an eyebrow. When she nodded toward a couple waiting near the hallway—guests who had come all the way from Logan—Cynthia was already moving.

And when the light from the west dipped low enough to touch the tiled stairs—just the corner—George looked up.

"It's time," he said.

And it was.

The long tables bore signs of living—ink stains, candle wax, nicks from belt buckles. Rosa, the hostess, stood near the center. Small frame, firm gaze. She ruled the floor with a tilt of her chin. Napkins were folded, menus squared, plates and flatware presented to specifications of the gypsy himself. She had inherited her father's precision and her mother's heat.

The chairs didn't match, but that seemed intentional. Some were salvaged. Others brought in by travelers who traded old wood for new meals. One chair near the fireplace still bore the scorch of a traveling potter's kiln. She'd arrived just after sunset, apron stained with slip and asked only for soup and a story. In return, she left her chair behind—cherry wood, three-legged, too low for comfort. But George kept it. He said it balanced the room. A woman from St. Thomas once offered her entire dining set for a bowl of cinnamon stew and a place to cry for the afternoon. George said yes.

The air was full of dinner—rosemary, clove, and the ghost of smoked corn. Someone in the kitchen sneezed, and a faint laugh followed. Silver scraped ceramic, low and steady.

George moved through the room like a river—greeting every guest, pausing to refill a water glass by hand, or nodding at a child who looked too shy to speak. His hair was snow-thick. His hands calloused but warm. He wore a vest with a hidden pocket, and inside it: a pack of smokes, a matchbook, and a silver cross from the old country.

He'd told that story more than once—how he left Crete with nothing but a belt and a jar of olives, how he crossed through Canada, slept on coal sacks, thought about marrying a girl who smelled like oranges and spoke with her hands. He never mentioned the ring, though he wore it always, tight on his pinky. The only thing his mother left him. He said the building was his memory box. But some memories don't stay in the box. They slip. They echo. Sometimes he'd pause near the stairwell and look at nothing for a beat too long, as if remembering the shape of a voice.

Cynthia followed not far behind, smiling at a young couple near the far window. Her hair had turned silver years ago, but she wore it like an heirloom—loose, long, curled at the ends. She pointed to one of her own paintings on the wall—orange cliffs, brushstroked sky—and told the table it was for sale. She always did that. Not because she needed to sell them. But because she needed them to know it mattered. And because it was her gift.

A boy spilled water. A woman whispered grace. Rosa glided past them all, correcting the napkins without looking down.

Somewhere near the kitchen, someone hummed a hymn—not loudly. Just enough to remember something.

And as the plates were cleared and the copper caught the dusk, no one noticed how still the far corner had become. As if it were listening. As if something old was just starting to arrive.

Rosa didn't like surprises. She especially didn't like them near the corner table. The one with the high-backed chairs and the small window that didn't quite close all the way. Tonight, someone had moved the salt and pepper. She remembered George had explained to her,

"Never pass salt hand to hand."

"Bad luck." She'd aligned them herself, left to right, pepper behind, angled at ten degrees like always.

Now they stood side by side. Centered. Balanced.

Rosa exhaled, then fixed them without fuss. But her eyes lingered a moment longer than usual. On the window. On the chair. Rosa's mother—Mateo's wife—used to say some corners keep memory the way others keep dust. You sweep and sweep and still it returns. She'd meant to tell her father once—about the salt. How it moved sometimes. How one night, after his wife had died, she found it tipped over with no one near. She watched it spill across the table like sand. He'd sat there the next morning. Ran his finger through the mess without flinching. He said, "Guess she's still seasoning the place." Then stood and walked to the kitchen without another word. Rosa never asked who he meant. But she started a new page in the ledger that day.

A section she called: Presences.

Behind her, Cynthia was explaining the stairs again. How she chose every tile. How the turquoise meant protection and the rust meant good health.

George was three tables away, laughing too loud at something no one else heard.

And Rosa—

Rosa stood still in the breath between table turns.

Felt the pulse of the room shift.

She thought of the ledger she kept beneath the podium. Each shift's names, seating, anomalies.

Rosa once noted: Table Five goblet fogged before it was touched. Another time: two shadows on the kitchen door but only one body passed through. And once, near closing, she'd heard a laugh from the empty dining room. She wrote: Sounded like Sam. Six months too late.

Once, she walked past the corner table and swore she smelled salt and roses, even though the kitchen hadn't plated either that night. Another time, a guest asked for *the widow's wine*, though no such drink had ever been printed on the menu. Rosa added everything to the ledger. No explanation. Just an underline. As if someone was learning to speak through arrangement.

The broom closet door moved slightly, though no one passed it.

Rosa blinked, then moved on.

By the time the next table sat, the room had smoothed itself again. No salt. No hum. No memory out of place. Only a warm glow, a low hush, and the feeling of someone watching—but not unkindly. A gaze more curious than cautious.

Sophia didn't press forward—not yet. Something in the room remembered her—before she remembered herself.

But she noticed the girl.

The way Rosa tucked her hair behind one ear before every seating.

The way she folded menu corners like small offerings.

The way her eyes tracked Cynthia—not for instruction, but alignment.

It reminded her of a courtyard in Sparta.

Not the stone of it, but the shade.

The way her own mother once watched her thread olives in the still hours before dusk.

Sophia missed women like this.

Neither loud nor meek. Just faithful—to the work, to the weight, to the watching.

She stayed by the chair near the small window.

And Rosa—without knowing why—lit another beside it.

Later, as wax puddled and guests thinned, Rosa passed by again.

She paused.

The window rattled once—not wind.

Like breath remembering itself.

Rosa rested a hand on the chair back.

It was familiar—not like memory, but like recognition.

The way sunbaked clay holds an echo.

She thought of her abuela's kitchen—the way the clay walls there held the day long after sunset, the way you could hear a song still humming in the rafters if you were quiet enough. She only adjusted the candle again, trimmed the wick, and left it lit—though she didn't know why.

Later that week, Mateo would find the salt crooked again. He wouldn't mention it. But he'd take the long way around the kitchen to pass the table. And Rosa—watching from the podium—would note how he paused. Like a man who believed the building listened. And maybe, tonight, had something to say back.

And as she walked back toward the front of the dining room, something brushed against her apron. Not air—but memory.

In the corner, the chair did not shift.

But the light beside it glowed steady—and a single blue glass, untouched all night, was now filled to the rim.

Still.

Waiting.

Watching.

And no one, not Cynthia, not George, not Rosa—would remember setting it there. But all of them would feel it the next time they passed that chair.

Like a hush.

Like a benediction.

Like a story no one quite told, but everyone somehow knew.

After the last chair was stacked and the lights dimmed low, Elizabeth returned once more.

She didn't return from habit. The rhythm brought her.

The sunroom had already surrendered its heat. Only the adobe held it now—tucked into corners like old breath. The copper inlays had dulled. The glasses were cleared. Only a faint ring of condensation remained on Table Six. Centered. Still fading. She left it untouched. Outside, the roses pressed against the glass—their petals leaving breathmarks. And on the far table—the blue glass had returned. Full again. No hand had touched it. She hadn't looked away. But there it was.

She sat in the rocker—not because she was tired. But because the room had asked. Across from her, the water caught the last copper light. It glowed. Something old stirred. A presence—braided from salt, cedar, and bread. She didn't try to hold it. Recognition was enough.

The room curved slightly inward.

Shadows moved with grace.

The rocker stilled.

And in that hush, the building exhaled.

Elizabeth rose. Left the glass untouched. And before turning, whispered something—not a word, just a sound shaped like thanks.

Behind her, the blue glass stayed full.

And the floor remembered the weight of her footfall.

Where there is salt, there has been weeping. Where there is butter, forgiveness.

Scroll

THE SUNROOM

Balcony One – The Sunroom, Dusk, Autumn 1918

The waiting room welcomed, the dining room flowed, and the sunroom drank the light.

You could move through Balcony One without opening a door. Each room gave way to the next—breath to breath.

She paused at the arch—where the floor warmed slightly from the sunroom's long breath. This part of the building always felt alert—aware. As if it were listening for someone worth remembering.

Elizabeth passed Rosa's hostess station—through the main dining room where the walls warmed toward golden saloon doors hung in an archway along the left wall – leading to the bathrooms. To the far back, the kitchen steamed behind carved pillars—Cynthia's arches. And there, beyond the curve of the Santa Fe staircase, the hallway to the bar began. But to the right, a different light pulled her:

The sunroom.

It was the western most room in the building—rectangular, golden, and so saturated with light it seemed to hum. The adobe in this room felt more sun-warmed than anywhere else—like the clay had been listening since morning and was now ready to speak.

If the dining room was the hum, the sunroom was the hush that followed—a hush that made you aware of your own breath.

Two arched thresholds held it like parentheses. Between them, on the red adobe wall, a copper sconce flickered low. Candlelight—steady and unsupervised. Elizabeth didn't remember lighting it.

The air here always felt slightly different. Bright. Alert.

Three tall windows arched along the west wall, their curved tops splitting the view like chapel glass. Outside, ash trees stood solemn in the gravel courtyard, their trunks catching the wind like metronomes, while a wild tangle of rose bushes leaned inward—bold, unsanctioned, half in love with the sun-warmed sill.

Some said the glass in the west windows came from the old courthouse in St. George, salvaged before it was torn down. They caught the light in a way no new window ever could.

Beyond them: the plateau. A sweep of red and ochre cliffs, softened at the edges by dust and distance. Sky like a story not yet told. Clouds with weight.

But it was the inside that held the heat.

The floors weren't laid so much as assembled—red cedar, salvaged from the fallen trunks of Cedar Mountain, each piece milled by callused hands and set like a jigsaw puzzle.

The polygamists brought the lumber down from the hills and stacked it at the back door like offerings. George refused to waste a single sliver. Every knot, warp, and edge found its place in the grain.

The Greeks don't waste wood, he'd said. Not when they're raised where marble is cheaper.

You could feel it in your feet, this floor. How it gave and held and kept its heat. A mosaic of memory. A floor laid in pieces, meant to be remembered whole. Thick-planked, knot-flecked, streaked with veins of turquoise distressing that caught the light like memory. Some boards were bowed. Others bitten at the edges by years of boots and bar stools. When the sun came low across the glass, it gilded the grain, and the whole room glowed from the ground up.

Above: a ceiling of raw pine slats, laid in a fishbone pattern that whispered of mountain cabins and quiet, learned hands. The warmth it held made the room glow, as though the ceiling itself was worshiping the sun.

The walls were adobe, peach-tinted and faintly warm to the touch, cracked in corners from months of heat. High on the southern wall, above the wooden door frame, hung a painting—crooked, but no one touched it. The figure in the center looked like a saint or a sister, cloaked in blue robes and half-swallowed by brushstroke. They never agreed—protector or trick of light. Others swore the face changed depending on the weather.

The tables were oak. Solid. Heavy. Each one inlaid with a copper leaf, hammered flat and polished until it caught the day like a coin. George once said that was a mistake—no one knew how it got there. He said some leaves don't fall from trees. They fall from memory. Guests would sometimes touch them, absentmindedly, then pull their fingers away and say nothing. The leaves were never in the same place twice.

Some tables were round, some oval, all smoothed by elbows and small gestures. They held stories in their lacquer. Tiny burn marks from careless candles. Scratches from wedding rings. One edge was charred slightly from a wine glass left too close to the flame.

As usual, the chairs didn't match. Some were ladder-back, others spindle-thin, and one near the end window had been sanded down by time until it leaned like it was listening. There was a red-cushioned rocker with a broken glide, and a wide-backed captain's chair with initials carved into the spine. *Y.R. 1911.* No one knew who that was.

And on each table: a cobalt blue glass.

Always blue.

Thick-stemmed, cool to the touch, and heavy at the base. The glass warped light, like a shallow lens. Candle flames flickered wider behind it.

People's eyes looked older through it. Some guests turned theirs upside down the moment they sat. Elizabeth never asked why.

The air smelled of rosemary and yeast.

Each morning, Mateo's daughters rolled the dough by hand—an old family recipe whispered in two languages, left to rise on one of the tables in the sunroom, where the light was strongest. By noon the rolls were braided, brushed with butter, and slid into the oven. By two, the scent filled the building. And by three, they'd begun to appear in baskets on tables throughout Balcony One, rosemary-infused, already steaming.

Tonight, the baskets had been cleared.

But the warmth lingered—low and sour and sweet. Elizabeth could still smell the pork shoulder that had been marinated for three days in cider brine, clove, and cracked garlic. The fat had crackled over the cast-iron before dusk, and the sound had echoed all the way to the waiting room.

Two plates still sat near Table Six—one bearing the leftover tentacle of a roasted octopus, caramelized and fork-bitten, the other an empty bone scraped clean. Beside them, a butter knife balanced on a folded napkin with a single red thumbprint in the fold. Raspberry tart.

Elizabeth collected the basket from the window seat. Two rosemary rolls remained, still warm in the cloth. She set them on the counter with quiet reverence and reached for the goblets.

Brooke was already sweeping under the table—quick, nervous in the hips. Her apron smelled of starch and citrus, napkin tucked into her waistband like a forgotten petition. The broom made soft rhythmic sounds against the floor, but Brooke's hands kept stopping as if waiting for something unseen to pass.

"Sit," Elizabeth said, wiping down the copper inlay on the tabletop. "You're wearin' through the floor."

Brooke hesitated, then perched on a mismatched ladder-back. Her fingers fidgeted with the cloth napkin. One of the blue glasses was still on the table beside her—untouched, half-full, sweating in the warm light.

"I ain't lost my mind," she said. "But I saw something strange."

Elizabeth polished the copper leaf. It caught the light and glowed. The inlay looking less like a leaf now, and more like a flame curling flat into the wood.

"I was settin' Table Six for supper," Brooke went on. "Three glasses like always. Turned to get the forks, and when I came back—one was gone."

Elizabeth moved to clear the dessert plates. The chocolate torte had been mostly devoured. The lemon tart was barely touched. She scraped the edge with the fork and sniffed it once before setting it aside.

Brooke kept going. "I looked everywhere—tray, floor, even under the cloth. Nothin'. Then I turn back again and there it is. Same glass. Same spot. But full of water."

Elizabeth paused. Then resumed stacking.

Brooke leaned forward. "Miss Elizabeth, that ain't right."

Brooke's voice wavered, but didn't fall. Elizabeth didn't look at her. Instead, she reached for the wet goblet, held it up to the fading light. The cobalt deepened, catching the sun at a slant that turned the glass nearly black. She studied the way it distorted her own fingers behind the bowl—how they seemed older, bent slightly inward, almost like her mother's had looked in the final months.

"Truth," Elizabeth said softly, "isn't always what sticks around. Sometimes it's the thing that echoes longest."

Brooke tilted her head, unsure if she was being agreed with or dismissed. But she didn't interrupt. Elizabeth set the goblet down, not hard, but with precision.

"You know how many times I've wiped down this table?" she said. "More than you've been alive."

Brooke flinched. Not at the sharpness of the words, but at their weight.

"Then maybe," she said, voice smaller now, "it's trying to show you too."

Elizabeth finally met her eyes. Brooke didn't blink. The air didn't sag—it thickened. Like the sky before a monsoon.

"You think the glass moved itself?" Elizabeth asked.

"I think," Brooke said slowly, "something needed it to be full."

Elizabeth nodded once. A quiet motion. Not agreement—just acknowledgment. The room had grown dimmer in their stillness. Elizabeth reached toward the copper inlay on the table again, ran her thumb along the vein that split it like a scar.

"This leaf," she murmured. "I remember the day George laid it in. Said the copper would call the light. Said every room needed something to anchor it."

Tucked behind the last painting on the south wall—an oil of the mesa drenched in rose light—was a clipped and yellowed article from the Washington County News, dated March 1916. The headline read:

"Motion Picture Man Visits Balcony One."

Below it, a photograph—grainy and ghosted at the edges—showed George, smiling beside none other than Charlie Chaplin. The caption noted Chaplin had been traveling from Las Vegas to Salt Lake City and had stopped to visit Zion National Park. He noticed *Balcony One* in Virgin and took a rest *"for fresh bread and finer company."*

According to the piece, Chaplin dined twice that week, asking for the same table both times: the west-facing seat at the corner of the sunroom. He left a gold coin and a sketch of his bowler hat on the back of the menu, which George laminated and hung in the office until the ink faded to whispers.

Brooke looked at the glass.

"Is that what the blue ones do?" she asked. "Anchor something?"

Elizabeth exhaled. Not tired. Aware.

"No," she said. "They magnify it."

Silence again. Outside, a breeze stirred the roses. One petal fell against the glass with the sound of a sigh. Inside, the warmth from the roll basket reached Brooke's hands. She hadn't meant to stay this long. But she hadn't meant to see the glass move either.

"Do you believe in ghosts?" she asked suddenly.

Elizabeth's eyes didn't flinch.

"I believe in memory," she said. "And memory's got hands."

She passed her the roll—still warm, still fragrant. Brooke took it like a benediction.

"Don't eat too fast," Elizabeth said. "You'll miss what comes next."

And Brooke, for the first time that shift, smiled like she might stay a little longer.

Elizabeth finally turned.

"You know what ain't right? Livin' on bread and strong coffee since noon." She tilted her head toward the basket. "Last roll's yours."

Brooke didn't reach for the bread. Instead, she looked at Elizabeth—really looked.

"You ever believe something before you understand it?" she asked.

Elizabeth's hand paused mid-wipe on the copper leaf.

"I was raised to understand first," she replied.

Brooke nodded slowly, eyes tracing the rim of the blue goblet. "I think I was raised to hush."

Elizabeth's gaze softened. She set the cloth down. "And here you are. Talkin' anyway."

"I don't mean to pry," Brooke said quickly. "It's just… this place. It's like it knows who I am before I do."

"Places like this tend to know what we carry," Elizabeth murmured. "And they ain't shy about holdin' it up to the light."

Brooke hesitated, then pressed further.

"Have you ever lost time in this room?"

Elizabeth lifted her glass again but didn't drink.

"I've misplaced time. Misremembered it. Once watched a shadow cross the wall—one that didn't belong to anyone in the room."

Brooke straightened. "So it's not just me."

"I didn't say that." Elizabeth drank, slow and steady. "I'm sayin' this land is old. And old lands remember things we haven't lived yet."

Brooke's brow furrowed. "You think it's—memory? Not ghosts?"

"Maybe both," Elizabeth said. "Maybe neither. Maybe we're the ghosts sometimes."

The glass in front of Brooke pulsed faintly in the candlelight—just a trick of condensation, or the way light bent behind water.

But it felt like breath.

"I wasn't gonna stay," Brooke said. "After my first week here. I had three plates crack in my hands. A bottle fall off the shelf. Thought I was cursed."

"And now?"

"I think I'm— chosen," she whispered. "Not in a holy way. Just—like I've been invited."

Elizabeth tilted her head.

"That scares you?"

"A little."

"That's good," Elizabeth said, standing again.

"Means you ain't foolish."

Brooke's shoulders dropped—enough to loosen her.

"I keep waiting for someone else to notice," she said. "To confirm I'm not losing my mind."

Elizabeth met her eyes, full and direct.

"If you're gonna work here, learn this early: not all truths are polite. Some will sit with you. And some make you sit with yourself."

The light through the window dimmed. The roses outside had pushed further against the glass—almost pressed now, like they too were listening. Elizabeth glanced toward the crooked painting on the wall.

"She's never fallen," she said.

Brooke turned. "The painting?"

"She's never once fallen, tilted, or been bumped. Even in wind. Even in the earthquake last spring. But every few days, someone new will swear she was weeping."

"Was she?"

Elizabeth shrugged. "Doesn't matter. They saw it. And now it's part of the room."

The broom Brooke had set aside slipped—its handle tipping off the wall, tapping once against the cedar floor. Both women turned. Silence followed. Then Elizabeth moved to retrieve it, resting the handle back in place as if nothing had happened. Her expression had shifted—ever so slightly. As if acknowledging something that couldn't be named, only nodded toward.

Brooke flushed.

"I'm tellin' the truth."

"I didn't say you weren't." Elizabeth poured herself a finger of rye. "I think it's better not to chase ghosts that ain't left breadcrumbs."

Brooke watched her in the dim light, the glint of something silver catching at Elizabeth's collarbone. A chain. Not ornate—but strange. At the end of it, tucked beneath the collar of her blouse, hung a flat disk etched with faint lines. Geometric. Maybe astrological. Brooke didn't ask. But she noticed.

Elizabeth caught her glance, and for a moment, didn't blink.

"You see somethin'?"

"No. Just—" Brooke hesitated. "I thought I recognized your necklace."

Elizabeth smiled enough to stop the question from growing.

"Reckon you might. Some things follow folks."

Brooke folded her hands in her lap.

"You ever seen it?" she asked.

Elizabeth didn't answer right away. She set the rye glass down next to the blue goblet and looked out the arched windows. The roses were leaning hard into the glass now. Their shadows danced across the copper inlays, flickering like hands pressed to the other side.

"You ever watch a candle burn through blue glass?" Elizabeth asked.

Brooke blinked.

"No, ma'am."

"Makes the flame look like it's moving when it don't. This room's full of corners. Full of stories. And folks like stories more than silence."

"So you think I imagined it?"

"I think you saw what the room wanted you to see."

Brooke was quiet. Outside, a single ash leaf floated down onto the dirt. Inside, the light caught the pine ceiling and made it blush. Elizabeth stood.

"If a glass moves again, just nod to me. I'll nod back. We'll call it even."

Brooke cracked a smile.

"You're strange."

Elizabeth didn't answer. She turned her gaze to the windows, where the light was thinning into gold's final breath. The roses outside were no longer leaning—they were pressed, nearly trembling, against the glass. Inside, the blue goblet caught the last beam of day and split it—two slivers of light arching across the tabletop like open wings.

"You know," Elizabeth said finally, "these glasses weren't always blue."

Brooke paused, surprised.

"They used to be clear," Elizabeth continued, her voice low, reflective. "Plain. No weight to them. You could lose one and not notice."

"What happened?"

Elizabeth touched the stem of the goblet gently, almost reverently.

"A customer's daughter," she said. "She saw something. A woman sitting here. Middle of the afternoon. Said she was humming. Wearing blue."

Brooke waited.

"The woman wasn't on the ledger," Elizabeth said. "Wasn't served. No one else saw her. But the child—she swore the water in her glass was the clearest thing in the room. Like it held light even in the shade."

She leaned in.

"Two days later, all the glasses turned up changed."

Brooke blinked. "How?"

"Same shape. Same shelf. But blue. Like they'd been dyed from within."

Brooke's fingers curled slightly on the edge of the table.

"No one admitted to switching them?" she asked.

"No one could have," Elizabeth said. "We didn't have the money. Or the time."

She looked back at the glass, eyes narrowing.

"They just—became."

Brooke stared at hers—The water inside was still, but deep. The kind of still that isn't calm.

"Is that when Sophia started appearing?"

Elizabeth didn't answer. The room, somehow, had hushed further. Brooke looked up. The candle on the wall had burned lower—but its light was longer.

"I think this room likes you," Elizabeth said, tone lighter now. "That's why it showed you."

"Showed me what?"

"That you can see."

Elizabeth stood, collecting the dishes with practiced quiet. Brooke stood too, but her eyes lingered on the glass. It looked fuller now. Or maybe older. And when she picked it up—just to clear it—she could swear it pulsed. Like it remembered every hand that had held it. And maybe hers was the latest one willing to feel that weight. Brooke rose, gathered the linen, and tied her apron tight.

She passed through the archway without another word. Elizabeth stayed. She always did. Not because the room needed tending. But because she needed the room. When she was younger—long before the rye, the routines, the brittle humor—she'd walk through empty places just to see which ones held breath.

Balcony One was the first that exhaled back. She didn't talk about it. Not to Brooke. Not to Mateo. Not even to George, who'd offered her the job with a nod and a bottle of something too strong for daylight. But the building knew. And the building trusted her. It didn't ask her to believe in ghosts. Only to believe in presence.

And she did.

The kind that folds chairs after hours.

That refills glasses no one touched.

That warms a cushion when no one's been seated.

She moved now to the edge of the room, fingers brushing the table nearest the west window. It had a hairline crack in the inlay, copper splitting, catching the light sideways. She crouched to retrieve a stray fork beneath a rocker and paused.

The air under the table was warmer. Not from the sun, but from something held there – an echo, a pulse, the shimmer of memory. Like dust rising in silence that never fully settles.

She stood slowly.

Looked back at the table where Brooke had sat. The blue glass was gone now—cleared with the rest. But the light on the table still curved around its absence. Like a halo for something unnamed.

Elizabeth rubbed her fingers together absently. They smelled of copper and rosemary. And something sweeter. The room was golden now—truly golden. The sun had dropped just enough to slant through the window glass and turn everything to amber: the forks, the walls, the curl of butter left behind on the white plate.

She brushed out the lamps.

Passed Table Six.

Paused.

Later, after the copper had cooled and the crumbs were cleared, Elizabeth sat alone. Her feet had stopped walking before her thoughts had caught up.

The Sunroom didn't feel empty.

It never did.

Even now, with the broom propped silent by the door and the cloths folded smooth on the counter, the room held its posture. Like someone waiting to be spoken to. Elizabeth rested one hand on the table's edge.

The blue glass was still there.

Still full.

She left the glass untouched.

Still, it watched her back.

She thought about Brooke—how her hands hovered. There were things Elizabeth knew without needing to ask. Things the building whispered before the girl did. Loneliness had a shape. A scent. So did belief. And something in Brooke believed—in what she saw, or what she hoped, Elizabeth wasn't sure. But either way, it was enough to matter.

Elizabeth stood slowly. Crossed to the windows. The roses now seemed to have infused into the glass somehow—petals wide, as if displaying themselves toward something just out of reach. She stood there, quietly.

And for one breath, one small moment,

she let herself wonder—

not whether the glass had moved,

but whether it had been placed.

And if so—

by whom.

Some said you could see the past in those glasses—if you stared long enough, and quiet enough, and wanted something badly enough to return. They warped time like heat waves—soft, shimmering echoes of things not quite gone.

Rooms remember. Glasses wait. And some truths? You only glimpse them when the silence leans in.

*
**

Some rooms remember better than people do.
Some glasses are never empty.
Some truths appear only in the corner of your eye—
where the light bends, and silence listens back.

THE STAGE

Balcony One – The Stage, Evening, Late Winter 1919

It came to life as a stage. A raised platform in the back corner of the dining room, three steps high, framed by a curtain that rarely closed all the way.

People felt the shift – how the room leaned in, listening. The shift in air. Even the staff hushed their steps, like the wood had ears. Some places amplify the voice. Others quiet it.

This one? It refined.

Trimmed away pretense. Burnished the outline of whoever sat there, until only the essence remained.

People said food tasted different up there—sharper, somehow. As if salt and story rose more freely in the air. Elizabeth once muttered that sorrow sat easier up there too. Not heavier. Just less alone.

It was a place for watching—but not always for performance. A place where attention shifted inward. Or upward. And every so often, when the light hit right and the room went quiet mid-song, you could swear the stage watched back. Seven could sit there comfortably. Eight, if one was small.

There was one large table—with chairs too close together, set with the same blue glasses and weighted flatware as everywhere else—but it all looked brighter up there. Reflected. Like the light hit different.

And above it:

A carved wood valance crowned the curtain—too ornate for the space, too distinct not to forget.

It had once been a desk. George found it somewhere, half-disassembled, drawer faces still attached like sealed mouths. Defaced with paint and clutter. George looked at the desk and said—

"You deserve better." As if it were alive.

He sanded the surface, stained the grain, and mounted it as if it had always meant to look down. If you stood close and squinted at the trim, you could see where the knobs had been removed—still faintly indented like eyes that never quite shut.

The stage had its own gravity. Even when empty, it pulled the eye. Pulled memory. Pulled unease. Once, during a private event, a child crawled up the steps unnoticed. She sat in the center chair, silent, wide-eyed. When her parents finally found her, she whispered, "I was listening." They asked to what. She only pointed downward and said, "the floor."

From that night on, Elizabeth would light sage smoke after any private rental. She'd light it slowly, draw the smoke along the curtain's hem, and murmur words no one else quite caught.

Cynthia never interrupted. She adjusted the lights until they fell soft again—no shadows on the brick, no harsh angles on the glassware.

"That stage doesn't want control," she once told Rosa. "It wants reverence."

The burgundy curtains drooped slightly at the base, thick velvet that pooled like wine. They muffled sound but not memory. When the dining room was quiet enough, they seemed to breathe with the walls.

Behind the stage: a wall of red brick.

Not the soft kind from city buildings, but kiln-fired, deep-colored, rough-edged. The sort that drank echoes and gave nothing back.

Centered on it hung a painting—tonight, a longhorn, half-shadowed and mid-turn, rendered in hues of bone and flame.

The artist was Cynthia, as always. She painted what she dreamed.

Sometimes the staff claimed the horns in her paintings were never quite the same length when they passed twice.

Elizabeth cleaned the stage last. Every night. Without fail. She didn't rush. She wiped each place setting like it belonged to someone who might arrive late. She straightened the chairs, even if they hadn't been touched. She always checked under the cloth—just once—for the trapdoor that wasn't there. It wasn't superstition. Not entirely.

Elizabeth never said what she was looking for. Only that the cloth sometimes felt warmer than it should. And once—years ago, before the brick wall, before the curtain—she swore she heard the wood beneath the table creak in a rhythm too steady for settling. She told Mateo it sounded like breathing. He told her it was the pine adjusting to the temperature.

"Desert wood always tries to remember its tree," he'd said, half-joking.

But she started cleaning the stage last after that. Always last. And always with that single pause—hand pressed to the cloth, as if it might rise or respond.

Brooke caught her once. Paused in the kitchen doorway with a tray of figs and soft cheese, she saw Elizabeth crouched low, one hand on the edge of the stage, the other tracing a line no one else could see. Later, when they were alone, Brooke asked about it.

"Was there ever a trapdoor?"

Elizabeth didn't look up from the silver she was polishing.

"No."

"But you keep checking."

"That doesn't mean it's not there."

Brooke blinked, confused.

"I don't follow."

Elizabeth held up a spoon, catching her own reflection in its bowl.

"Not everything you check for has to be real to be true."

That ended the conversation. But it didn't stop Brooke from glancing at that corner every time she crossed the dining room. Especially when the light shifted. Especially when it was quiet. The door opened just past the hour. A family stepped inside. Two adults, five children. Not hurried, not hesitant. As if they belonged here, though no one had seen them before.

The father was tall—clean lines, olive skin deepened by sun. His jaw was strong, but his gaze was soft with crystal blue eyes. He wore a dark linen suit, unbuttoned at the collar, and his glasses caught the light like the edge of polished silver. His wife walked slightly behind him, her posture regal but not rigid. Skin like sunlit sandstone, hair deep black and straight to the waist, eyes the warm brown of brewed oolong. She wore a simple ivory dress and no jewelry—except a gold bangle that caught the light with every turn of her wrist.

The children followed, in order of age, like a procession.

The eldest boy was seventeen, with a build just shy of imposing, softened by youth and grace. Dark curls, square shoulders, and eyes so vividly blue they caught Rosa mid-step. He wore dark-framed glasses and a blue cotton shirt rolled at the sleeves.

Beside him, the fifteen-year-old girl moved like a ribbon—quiet, alert, long black hair falling like water over one shoulder. Her eyes matched her mother's—brown, steady, absorbing. She held her youngest sister's hand without being asked.

The thirteen-year-old boy looked younger than his years until you saw his eyes—amber gold, wide and unblinking. His curls were a tangle, barely tamed. His smile, when it came, was immediate and devastating.

The twelve-year-old brother had the deepest skin of the five, eyes nearly black, hair straight and thick. He didn't fidget. He simply walked and waited, as if he had already memorized the room.

And then the youngest—ten, looked around with wonder that wasn't childish. Her hair fell in tight, spiraled curls around her face, and her eyes were a blue-green hazel that didn't seem possible. Cynthia would later joke,

"No way those curls are natural," but she'd say it with admiration, not disbelief.

Rosa greeted them with her usual composure, but even she hesitated before leading them toward the stage.

Brooke caught the motion from the far side of the dining room. She frowned—no one got seated up there without discussion. It was always reserved for anniversaries, ceremonies, George's old friends. Brooke didn't recognize them. She scanned the floor, unsure.

"Do you know who they are?" she asked, voice low.

Elizabeth, folding napkins with quiet precision, didn't look up.

"Don't worry about it."

"They're on the stage."

"I noticed." Elizabeth curtly replied.

Brooke leaned closer.

"But—who—"

"They're guests," Elizabeth said, a note in her tone that didn't invite follow-up.

"Of George's."

By the time Brooke turned back, Cynthia was already ascending the stage steps. She moved quickly, but not rushed—like something had pulled her forward. She touched the mother's hand gently, smiled, said something Brooke couldn't hear. The mother nodded once, and Cynthia laughed, surprised and delighted.

George appeared from the office shortly after. He stopped the moment he saw them. His posture straightened. His eyes softened. He wiped his hands slowly on his apron, then crossed the room with the same gravity he used when inspecting new wine.

He greeted the father with a grip to the shoulder—too familiar for a stranger, too respectful for a friend.

"Petros."

Then George turned to Elizabeth.

"You'll take their table," he said.

Elizabeth nodded. She didn't ask why. Brooke noticed George didn't return to the kitchen right away. He stood at the foot of the stage, arms crossed, gaze slightly lowered—not at the family, but at the floor. As if remembering something. Or someone. She'd seen that look once before— months ago, when Sam Zitting's widow came to settle the bill no one expected her to pay. The same stillness. The same soft, involuntary blink— like he'd just been handed a memory.

George didn't speak. Just turned and walked the long way around the dining room, fingers trailing once along the edge of Table Twelve, where the varnish had cracked.

When Elizabeth brought down the first cleared plate—lightly smudged with whipped butter and fig compote—Brooke dared to speak again.

"They seem… familiar."

"They are."

Elizabeth didn't elaborate.

Brooke tried a different tack.

"Have they been here before?"

Elizabeth met her eyes then.

"Not like this."

She let that hang a moment, then added,

"Some arrivals aren't about coming back. They're about being recognized."

The words hung heavy, like they meant something Brooke didn't yet know how to carry.

She turned to watch the youngest girl press her cheek to the curved back of the stage chair. Her curls framed her face like ivy. She wasn't restless, just—listening.

The stage, Brooke realized, wasn't performing tonight. It was receiving—like a hand outstretched, to give, and to hold. Across the room, a mirror waited. Thick-framed, square-shouldered, and slightly angled from the wall, it held itself like a thing aware of being looked at. The crown molding above it bore a carved diamond motif—three raised cuts repeating like a code. Below the glass, a row of seven coat hooks jutted from the base like teeth.

It didn't reflect so much as interrogate.

The wood was a dark reddish-brown, warm but severe, and the hooks were dull metal, worn at the tips. Someone had once painted the wall behind it a golden yellow—too cheerful, too domestic—and the combination made the mirror seem more like a portal than a furnishing. When the light from the sconces hit at the wrong angle, the carved trim above cast diagonal shadows like crossed spears.

Brooke looked at it now.

It reflected the family on the stage.

Mostly.

But something was off. The angle wasn't quite right. The youngest girl's curls froze. The father's hand lacked its ring. The eldest son's chair— just for a moment—appeared empty.

Brooke blinked.

The image corrected itself.

Elizabeth stepped beside her, gaze fixed forward.

"Don't try to see everything in it," she said, barely above a whisper.

Brooke swallowed.

"Why not?"

Elizabeth didn't answer. She adjusted a napkin on the bar, smoothed it flat, and turned away. The longhorn hung still on the brick, but it was never still for long. Cynthia had painted it in a single night. No sketches, no models, no studies.

She'd come into the dining room after closing, hair wet from a late shower, and stared at the wall until George brought her a chair and a thermos of hibiscus tea. Then she stood and began to paint. What emerged looked less like a composition and more like a vision burned into canvas.

The longhorn knelt in a half-turn, one shoulder angled forward, its hooves pressing into a wash of lapis so vivid it stung the eyes. The horns arched outward, asymmetrical, yet perfect—one longer than the other, the curve of each alive with tension. The left horn grazed the upper edge of the frame, as if reaching beyond what could be contained.

The animal's face was pale—bone white, mottled with russet and grey—and its eyes, barely visible under the heavy brow, were flecked with amber and black. Behind the primary figure loomed two more—ghosted outlines in golden ochre and smoke-grey, their horns echoing and diverging like variations on a theme. One curved upward in a nearly perfect spiral. The other jagged slightly, as if broken once and re-healed. Together they formed a spectral triad, less herd than echo.

The background was layered with dry brushwork—yellows, creams, faint suggestions of desert heat. But beneath it all, barely visible unless you squinted, ran a sublayer of lavender and coral. The kind of underpainting you only notice when the sun hits at an angle. Or when you're crying.

Cynthia had said nothing the next day when the staff complimented it.

She only told Elizabeth, softly,

"It's not a longhorn."

Elizabeth had paused.

"What is it then?"

Cynthia shrugged.

"A visitation. It came as that shape because I needed to see it."

From the floor of the dining room, the image held weight.

But from the stage—from inside the space it watched—it radiated.

Guests seated beneath it often leaned back at some point mid-meal, unknowingly mirroring the creature's posture. Hands folded. Eyes turned. As if taking on the same contemplative readiness.

Children stared too long. One old man muttered a prayer. A soprano from Albuquerque once refused to sit with her back to it—said the horns were pointing at her thoughts.

That night, in the hush after close, Elizabeth glanced up at the painting again. The blue beneath the longhorn gleamed—duller than lapis, but thick with depth. And for a breath—no longer—she thought it raised its head. Looked straight at her.

Then the sound returned: a fork fell, a chair scraped, and the creature went still again.

But something had shifted.

That night, long after the family had left, after the tables had been cleared and the kitchen had gone quiet, Elizabeth ascended the stage one last time.

The velvet curtain held the room like a womb—still, weightless, gently breathing.

She moved from chair to chair, straightening them without thought. Her hands knew the rhythm. Fork, napkin, glass. Sweep, fold, align.

When she reached the farthest place setting—the one where the eldest boy had sat—she paused. The blue glass lay on its side, resting as if someone had set it down carefully. Deliberately. Like a whisper laid beside a plate. Elizabeth didn't touch it at first. She looked to the painting. Then to the mirror.

Its surface reflected only darkness now, but the hooks beneath it glinted faintly, like a row of watchful teeth. She reached out, lifted the glass upright with two fingers, and exhaled. Behind her, the curtain shifted. As if gravity had tilted. Elizabeth stepped back from the table. She smoothed the cloth once, gently, then descended the steps.

Three quiet steps.

From the floor, it still looked harmless. But she'd been up there. Felt the hush that holds shape. She didn't need the room to agree.

The stage had held many kinds of silence. Sam's was the kind that lingered after a story. Heavy with afterthought. This family brought a different silence.

Not emptiness. Not tension.

Presence.

As they sat, the space around them seemed to smooth. The air settled. The blue glasses stopped sweating. Even the curtains—usually prone to the faintest movement—lay still against the walls. Brooke watched from the kitchen, unsure why she'd stopped moving.

They weren't loud. They weren't particularly demonstrative. But the rhythm of the room changed. Conversations softened. Forks paused mid-air. A child near Table Nine set down her napkin.

Elizabeth moved among them without hesitation. She refilled their water glasses before they were empty. Set the silverware with quiet exactness. Listened—truly listened—when the youngest asked for extra butter.

When she descended the stage steps, Brooke caught her eye.

Elizabeth shook her head, half-smiling.

"Don't name it."

"Name what?"

"The hush."

It was the same hush that used to follow Sam's laugh—the one that crested too loud, too wild, before falling into that sudden stillness. But this hush came first. Unasked for. Undisturbed. And somehow, more complete. It didn't erase Sam—it balanced him.

Like the stage was remembering more than one kind of weight. By dessert, the eldest boy had removed his glasses and was cleaning them with a folded cloth. He paused once, eyes distant, then looked directly toward the far mirror.

Not into it—toward it.

And for one long second, the glass did not reflect him. Just the stage.

Empty.

Then the reflection blinked, and everything was as it should be. Except Brooke's heart, which had begun to beat faster. Elizabeth returned to the bar to pour a glass of elderflower soda.

"Did you see that?" Brooke whispered.

Elizabeth didn't answer.

She placed the glass on a silver tray, and said quietly, "The room doesn't forget."

She took the tray and walked back to the stage, where the boy was already waiting, hands folded, as if he knew it was coming.

She placed the glass before him without a word. He didn't thank her. He just nodded, like they both understood something wasn't meant to be spoken aloud.

Above it all, the ceiling was plank-laid pine, golden and warm, with knots like coins embedded in sand.

One square near the speaker had been replaced—lighter wood, unfinished. It sat flush but wrong. Elizabeth noticed it every time. She said it looked like a hatch, though there was no latch. Mateo once joked it was a panel to nowhere. No one laughed.

Sam loved the stage.

He'd sit at the back chair, boots crossed, grinning like he already knew the end of the story. He liked the view. Said it made the food taste better.

Said it was like "sittin' above the world without the bother of God."

The mariachi band played here once. One night only.

The violin cracked on the last note and the fiddler said it wasn't the string—it was the air. Too dry, or maybe too full. Elizabeth believed him.

After Sam died, no one sat there for weeks. Guests avoided it. Staff stopped suggesting it. A platform for the memory of someone not entirely gone.

Then one night, a couple asked to be seated there. Brooke said sure. Halfway through the meal, the woman stood up. Said she was cold. But there was no breeze.

Later, when Elizabeth cleared the table, she found another glass misaligned. Another hush left behind.

As if someone had reached across the table and set it down deliberately. The curtain fluttered without wind. She reset the table, placed the glass upright, and stepped down. From the floor, the stage looked harmless. But she could still feel the warmth of the place setting where the boy had sat.

On the wall across the room, the mirror waited—same carved top, same row of watchful hooks. Guests saw themselves in it—and sometimes didn't.

The kind of mirror that didn't reflect so much as verify.

The angles it caught weren't natural. And sometimes the reflections didn't leave when the people did.

Mateo swore he saw it: a hand setting down a wine glass—in the mirror only. The table was still.

Elizabeth had stopped looking into it.

This room wanted an audience.

But not always for what you planned to show.

And beyond the edge of the curtain, unseen, Sophia lingered.

Not watching the family.

Watching the stage.

As if waiting to be called forward.

The stage does not ask for your story.
It waits to return your outline.

Scroll

THE UPSTAIRS BANQUET ROOM

Virgin, Utah – Nightfall, Late Winter 1919

The kitchen had already emptied. The last of the dishes had been stacked, wiped, and silenced. Only the tick of the hanging clock remained—too slow, too loud, like it was remembering time instead of keeping it.

Elizabeth crossed the back hall with quiet purpose. The floor beneath her boots creaked with a long, dry sound, not quite protest—more like recognition.

She passed the kitchen, the old spice cabinet, the wall with the warped frame where the air always turned colder. Coal and pepper still lingered in the air. But there was something sweeter beneath it tonight—like old violets crushed under salt.

The staircase curved gently from the main dining room, each step dressed in painted tile—a quiet climb toward something unseen.

Some staircases demand attention. This one offered permission.

It didn't insist she ascend. It simply opened, like a held breath, inviting a kind of reverence without requiring it. There was something old in the way the curve lifted—not architectural age, but memory. As if each step knew its name, and hers too, and the names of others who had passed this way carrying trays, grief, offerings, rumors.

She ascended the staircase and reached the landing. To her left, the balcony. And to her right—a narrow passage that led to the banquet room angularly, unnaturally, as if the building itself didn't want it remembered. There was a locked door leading to the passageway. It was the kind of door no one ever painted. The kind no one ever noticed missing. The kind that didn't look locked until you tried to open it.

She reached into her apron pocket and drew out the key. The key slid into the lock without resistance. The latch gave with a weary click. And the building, ancient and watchful, seemed to exhale in reply. The door was plain. The latch warped with age. The passageway itself was filled with Cynthia's art and George's photographs, lit by two wall sconces that flickered like it knew more than it let on.

Halfway down, something hung askew on the wall. Not a painting. Not quite a tapestry. A framed textile—hand-stitched, sun-faded, edges curled like it had crossed the ocean more than once.

The threadwork was precise. A massive blue parrot, stitched in broad cheerful loops, loomed at center. A tiny man rode astride its back—one fist raised in triumph, the other clutching a wine glass.

Beneath it, the words "The Blue Parrot – Elounda" were stitched in English script, loose and looping like it had been copied from a tavern sign or cargo stamp. The date was smudged.

Elizabeth paused. She'd never known George to speak of Elounda. But once, years ago, he'd mentioned a bay where the shadows moved backward across the water. Where the locals drank raki and told jokes to their dead.

She didn't touch the frame.

Some objects carried more than dust.

But the upstairs banquet room belonged to no one now.

And Elizabeth, though she never said it aloud, had always felt it belonged most of all to her.

She paused at the threshold. The banquet room held its hush. Not silence—hush. As if a voice had just left, and something was listening. Elizabeth blinked. Across the far wall, the mural caught her eye again. Not for its color—but for its fracture. Blue stretched across the panel in veined ripples, too fluid to be sky, too clean to be sea. A surface that wasn't surface—memory, rendered as water. And through it—piercing down like architecture, like judgment—copper lines radiated from one upper corner. Not sunbeams. Not quite. More like light remembered from underneath.

And then she saw the girl.

Walking. Not on the floor, but on the lake. On the copper-lit blue.

Small. Dark-haired. Barefoot. Her white dress clung to her legs like she'd been moving through dew. Elizabeth didn't startle. Didn't move. She simply watched. The girl turned slightly, like she might look back. But didn't. And just like that, she was gone.

Elizabeth didn't breathe. Not yet.

Her knees prickled. Her spine cooled. The vision, if that's what it was, had slipped through some trapdoor in the room's light.

It was Bear Lake again. That long summer night on the Utah border. She'd been just a girl herself, sitting on the sand, watching the dark water hold its glass.

She'd seen the child then, too. The same dress. The same walk. As if time wasn't real in places like that. As if memory lived outside her body.

And later, when she told her mother what she'd seen, her mother had cried. Said that was exactly how she imagined her lost daughter, Elizabeth's sister, might've looked if she'd lived past six months.

She never spoke of it again.

Until now.

She stepped up into the hush.

Stained glass on the west wall sliced the dusk into ribbons—gold, garnet, and smoke. The windows weren't decorative; they were devotional. George and Cynthia had chosen them together, matching the glass colors not to any creed, but to how it would fall at that exact hour. They called it "angled grace."

The room was never used.

But it was always ready.

That was the unnerving thing about it.

Elizabeth paused inside the threshold. The air was still. Not stale—preserved. As if the walls held their breath only when someone who understood entered. She let the silence press against her skin, and the room responded. The tables had only been used twice in the past year. Once for a baptismal lunch hosted by the church. And once—just once—by Sam Zitting.

He reserved the room without asking.

George said yes before Sam even finished the sentence.

No one knew the occasion, not precisely. A family gathering, they thought. But Sam invited everyone—family, yes, but also ranch hands, distant cousins, traveling preachers, a railroad widow he'd met once outside of Kanab.

"Every table should stretch," he said, laughing, "or it's not worth sittin' at."

The night had been warm. Late spring, with the windows open to let in the scent of pine and faraway rain.

Sam stood at the center of the room and said grace like he was telling a joke only God might get. Then he toasted each table, one by one. To the children who'd never been scolded. To the old who remembered how to lie. To the women who said no and the men who let them. And last—to those not present, but surely watching.

The staff served roast squash and sweet pepper hash. The drinks were never empty. Cynthia wore a soft blue dress and poured tea like it was a blessing. George played an old German record on a portable phonograph he'd brought from the cellar.

Elizabeth had watched from the edge of the room, linen in her arms, unsure whether she belonged.

Sam had caught her eye.

Nodded once.

Poured a glass of sparkling water and placed it at the corner of the table.

"To you," he said, voice low enough that only she heard it.

She hadn't touched the glass then. Just nodded back.

It was the same corner she stood near now.

No tablecloth.

No glasses.

No Sam.

But the space still hummed, like the walls were holding onto sound. She could almost hear the scrape of chairs, the echo of that toast, the softness in Cynthia's laughter.

She moved slowly along the table's edge, fingertips brushing the wood. Even untouched, it felt warm.

The light from the stained glass shifted across the floor—gold on her boots, garnet across her hand, smoke pooling near the far chair.

The same chair Sam had pulled out for the woman who arrived late, breathless, cheeks red with apology. He'd stood, greeted her with a bow, and said, "We saved you the end. It's where the best stories start."

That chair was empty now.

But it was still pulled out.

Elizabeth moved to the head of the table. She didn't mean to remember. The memory came anyway. This room had held Sam Zitting once.

All of him.

The coat, the laugh, the presence that softened a room without lessening its strength. He'd reserved the banquet space. George said yes before Sam finished the request.

That was Sam.

No invitations. And somehow, everyone knew to show up.

She moved along the table's edge, fingers grazing the backs of the chairs, and remembered exactly where they sat.

Clara and Bethsheba—his wives—had taken the middle seats along the right-hand table, side by side like they'd been born twin-hearted.

Elizabeth had been confused by them at first.

It wasn't the polygamy. She had gotten used to that.

Clara and Bethsheba Hammon.

Sisters by birth, and still called the Hammon girls even after they'd been Zittings for decades. It sounded more like a story than a marriage. More like a hymn.

Clara, steadier. Bethsheba, quicker to smile. They both wore dark green dresses and brought their own linens, just in case. Sam teased them gently for it—then used the napkins for toasts.

The children had come in like a wave—Ingrid, with her thick braid and sharpened eyes. Thaddeus, ever formal, standing before he sat. Boone and Signe, always bickering, always finishing each other's complaints. Ezra and Halvor, identical in name tags but not in energy—one quiet, one restless. Marta, the quiet fire. Heber, Linnea, Calder, Ruthen, the youngest, still unsure where to place his hands at a table that long.

Elizabeth hadn't expected to remember all the names. But she did. Each one echoed as her hand passed their chair. And she remembered Jens, the baby grandchild, passed from lap to lap like a blessing.

Sam had stood at the head, flanked by nothing but air and grace. He wore the same wool coat he always did—the one with the stitched seam and one thread always out of place. He didn't give a speech. But he held up his glass and looked around the room like it was a congregation and a promise all at once.

Then he toasted his family.

Not just the ones with blood in their mouths—but the ones who had shown up, who had held sorrow for someone else, who had offered silence when it was needed.

"To all of you," he said. "To what holds, even when we don't."

The room didn't cheer. It breathed.

Cynthia had leaned in the doorway that night, her apron half-off, her eyes full. George brought out honeycake, unannounced. George adjusted the music three times to get it just right.

Elizabeth hadn't stayed long. She'd just passed through, carrying empty glasses, when Sam caught her eye.

"Eat something," he said, nodding to a plate near the end.

She hadn't touched it then. She wasn't sure she was allowed.

Now, years later, the same plate shape sat at the far end of the table, alone.

The room was empty.

But she could still hear the movement of a chair, the laughter from the corner, the hush that followed Sam's blessing.

She placed her hand flat on the back of Bethsheba's old chair.

And whispered, "Thank you."

Not because she was sure anyone heard.

But because the room still felt full enough to deserve it.

The quiet returned—not the kind that empties a room, but the kind that presses into the chest. Elizabeth stayed standing, her hand still resting on the chair's back. She didn't want to move. There was something in the air again, settling into the grain.

She glanced toward the windows. The stained glass had lost its brilliance—gold dulled to amber, garnet faded to rust. Only the smoke color held. The color of breath before a name. She stepped once toward the far end of the table.

Then again.

The table was long, but it felt longer now. Like the room had stretched in some invisible direction. She passed the spot where Ruthen had sat, then Linnea, then Calder—each place a hollow. Each one oddly preserved.

She reached the last chair—the one Sam had pulled out for the latecomer that night. The chair was still pulled out. But the cushion had a slight depression in it. Like someone had just risen.

Elizabeth didn't sit.

She reached for the plate instead—plain white, same as ever, and found herself holding her breath. Her eyes moved to the glass beside it. It hadn't been there a moment ago. But it was there now. Clear, tall, and full.

Not with water.

Something paler.

Something still.

She didn't touch it.

Behind her, the mirror above the sideboard caught a flicker of movement. A shoulder. A breath. The beginning of a profile, disappearing before it was fully formed. She turned slowly. The room was unchanged. But something behind her ribs had clenched.

She stepped sideways, her boots silent against the pine. The air had grown heavier—not in weight, but in detail. Every grain of wood, every shadow, every brush of fabric against her skin had sharpened.

The mirror above the sideboard watched.

Its frame, darker than walnut and thick around the edges, absorbed the light without offering any back. Elizabeth had avoided that mirror for years—not out of fear, but because it remembered too clearly.

Now it shimmered.

Not with color, but with movement. Subtle. Repeating.

Her own reflection, still and quiet, faced her with one difference:

The glass in the reflection was already in her hand.

She looked down.

Her fingers were empty.

She looked back.

Still in her hand.

Still raised.

Still full.

She stood back from the table, breath short. The mirror didn't blink. But the scent did – rising like forgotten hymns.

Behind her, a whisper of scent lifted—faint lavender, old wool, something scorched. The same scent she'd noticed once when clearing out the closet near the bar. The closet that had belonged to no one.

She turned.

The room was still empty.

Except now, the chair was pushed in. She hadn't touched it. The plate was clean. The napkin folded. The name card gone. But beneath the plate, just visible at the edge of the charger, the wood bore a faint new mark— curved, deliberate, unmistakably handwritten.

Elizabeth leaned in.

It was a name.

Not hers.

Not one she used often.

But known.

Sophia.

Again.

Only this time, it wasn't her handwriting.

It was spikier. Slanted. Old.

Like it had been written with a hand remembering how to hold a pen. She stepped away. The mirror caught her movement and refracted it— slightly delayed, just a little wrong.

She saw herself stop.

Then turn.

Then a second later, her body did the same.

The delay wasn't constant. It pulsed. Syncopated, like a breath taken at the wrong time.

Then a shape behind her.

Only in the mirror.

Only for an instant.

Long hair. A shoulder. A hand resting lightly on the back of Elizabeth's own chair.

She turned again.

Empty.

But the room did not feel returned to her.

It felt reoccupied.

And in the place where the glass had been—now gone—there was only a ring of condensation on the wood. Elizabeth stood in silence, heart ticking like a wound clock, and did not dare look in the mirror again.

The scent hadn't left. It hovered above the sideboard now—lavender, yes, but old. The kind of lavender pressed into a letter no one ever opened. Elizabeth inhaled and felt a tickle in her chest, like a memory that belonged to someone else. She turned toward the mirror again, but stopped halfway.

Her eyes fell on the artwork.

Cynthia's.

It had always unsettled her. Thirteen doors in a narrow hall, each ajar enough to suggest something within. The ceiling made of feathers—soft, mottled, drifting downward. And those symbols: the lamb, the broken lyre, the turquoise dot in the corner, the faint scratched cross.

The artwork had darkened over the years, or maybe the varnish had simply stopped pretending. One of the doors, near the center, had something written on it. She hadn't noticed it before. The line curved upward, then down. A loop, then a line through it. Almost like the beginning of a cursive S.

She turned back to the table.

The place setting was still empty. No glass. No name card. But the wood looked different now—darker at the edges, as if someone had leaned there too long.

A strange thought came to her then:

Maybe Sophia didn't know she was dead.

Or maybe she did.

But she wasn't done.

Not with this room.

Not with Elizabeth.

Elizabeth's chest tightened.

She remembered when she was first hired—how the manager at the time had said,

"Don't clean it unless someone asks."

No one ever had. And yet it was always clean. The dust never landed. The linens never yellowed. The room held itself in readiness, not because of events—but because of someone. Someone who remembered how a place should feel. How a table should be set. How names should be written carefully, in ink that didn't fade. And maybe—how to wait.

Elizabeth didn't speak. She walked back to the chair. Sat, for the first time. And folded her hands on the linen as if summoned. Nothing happened. Not for a breath. Then the mirror brightened—slightly. Enough to show two place settings now.

Hers.

And another.

Opposite.

Empty.

But not unclaimed.

Two long tables stretched the length of the room—long, narrow, heavy with wood grain and intention.

Draped in white linen with maroon toppers folded sharp as altar cloths. The clear glasses gleamed differently here—thinner, taller, catching the light without holding it. Unlike the cobalt glasses downstairs, these felt bare. Witnessing.

The floors were white pine, smoothed by time but still soft at the knots. You could hear a person's mood in their footsteps up here.

The walls were painted a shade of Santa Fe terracotta, the kind that held both warmth and hush. At the far wall, across from the entrance, hung a handcrafted wooden sculpture—a house, three stories tall, with windows lit from within. A miniature scene carved in walnut and cedar, every plank etched with care. Tiny people sat at balconies, gathered at a porch. One leaned out a second-story window with her hand raised mid-wave. A staircase wrapped along one side, impossibly thin, leading to a front door no larger than a coin. To its right: a tree of twisted copper wire, delicate and leafless, as if caught between seasons.

Above the house hung a radiant panel of art glass—midnight blue as a canyon sky, slashed through by copper rays fanning from a burnished sun. The copper had tarnished unevenly, catching flecks of green, gold, and something like stormlight. Cynthia called it *Morning Through Sleep*. She had found the copper in a mining yard west of Hurricane and sketched the design in a notebook she never let anyone read.

Overhead, thick beams framed square coffers with tin inlays—punched and patterned with a design George said was inspired by Italian ceilings. The tin had dulled over time but still caught whispers of light, refracting tiny suns that danced faintly when the wind shifted the drapes.

The window trim was knotted wood, raw at the joints, as if it had never fully decided to be furniture. It held the curtains in a kind of embrace, and even closed, the window glowed faintly from the fading day outside.

No one ever dusted the artwork.

No one ever needed to.

The room resisted time, but it welcomed memory.

On the south wall, two panoramic windows framed the world like an offering.

They were taller than a man and wide enough to hold three seasons in a glance. Trimmed in knotted wood—pale and twisted, like driftwood with a memory—they faced the mouth of Zion Canyon, where the land inhaled light and held it longer than it should.

In the morning, the sky turned a blue so clear it seemed backlit—less a color, more a breath. Hawks sometimes traced the edges of mesas in slow loops, and the first light kissed the snowcaps like a priest with oiled fingers.

By noon, the southern exposure turned bolder—especially in winter, when the sun hung lower in the sky and slanted in with a golden geometry.

The light stretched across the banquet floor like a second ceiling, warming the tin-coffered roof and brightening the pine until it glowed.

And then night.

Nightfall in the banquet room was a quiet baptism.

The windows framed a sky so dark it looked painted—black velvet stretched to the corners of heaven, punched with pinholes of light so numerous they seemed to sing together. The stars weren't scattered; they were placed. A composition in white fire and fathomless silence.

But the windows were at their most holy during storm season.

When the monsoons rose in July and August, the room became a chapel to weather.

The air would shift first—warm and wide, smelling of minerals and red mulberry sap. Then the clouds: low, dark-bellied, trailing their fingers across the cliffs like dancers searching for lost music.

The thunder didn't crack.

It rolled.

It surged through the canyon in low frequencies that made the glasses shiver on their shelves. The kind of thunder you didn't hear so much as inhabit. Lightning came in pulses—forked, jagged, sometimes so wide it lit the whole room in a single blue gasp. Once, Elizabeth saw a bolt trace the shape of a tree upside-down, branching from the sky toward the floor of the desert. The rain came in sheets, then in slanted strands, and finally in silver mist—shrouding the cliffs like the land was remembering something too ancient to say aloud.

Elizabeth had watched one of those storms alone, years ago. Just her, leaning against the frame, listening to the sky break and mend itself in rhythm. She never prayed in that room. The storms did it for her.

Set for no one.

Or almost no one.

At the far end, one place was set.

A blue water glass.

A gold-handled knife and fork.

A folded napkin.

A white plate.

And a name card.

Sophia.

She didn't want to look at it.

But she did.

Her own handwriting. A curl at the end of the S—the kind she hadn't used in years. The same half-slant script she once used on a birthday card. She hadn't written that name, or at least she didn't remember.

And yet—here it was.

Her breath caught.

Like a tide rising behind her ribs.

She didn't move.

Didn't touch the card.

Didn't touch the glass.

The air in the banquet room was different. Denser. It held its quiet like a secret. Dust floated in columns of colored light, but none settled on the table. The chair at the place setting was pulled out slightly. The exact amount Sam used to leave it. As if waiting for someone else to sit first.

Behind her, across the room—hung a broad, framed mirror.

Heavy, beveled, dark around the edges.

One of George's salvaged pieces, placed too high for vanity.

In it: the table. The name card. The blue glass.

And a figure.

Brief.

The impression of someone standing where no one stood.

A shoulder.

A tilt of the head.

Long hair, catching the stained-glass light.

Elizabeth turned.

The space was empty.

She looked back at the glass.

It was gone.

Then—there again.

Same position.

Same shape.

Filled.

Her hand reached toward it.

She brushed the rim.

The chill startled her.

Her hand trembled.

She drew it back. Slowly.

Then—bootsteps on the stairs. A whistle. Faint. The door creaked. Mateo. He paused.

"Didn't mean to—oh. You're up here."

He looked around like it was any other room. She didn't answer. His eyes landed on the painting above the sideboard—another by Cynthia. A hallway of thirteen doors. Each door slightly ajar. Colors wrong. Ceiling made of feathers. One door bore a lamb, another a broken lyre. In the lower corner: a turquoise dot. And, barely visible, a scratched-in cross.

"Frightening," he said, smiling. "Is this new?"

"No," she said.

"It's always been here."

He nodded toward the table.

"That your glass?"

"No."

He blinked.

The blue glass was gone again.

He didn't seem to notice.

"George needs something from storage," he said. "I'll come back."

He left.

The silence returned. Not as absence, but as pressure.

Elizabeth stepped to the place setting.

Lifted the name card.

Underneath it, faint and etched into the wood:

Sophia.

The same name.

A different hand.

She did not turn the card over.

She tucked it beneath the napkin.

Walked slowly out of the room.

Locked the door behind her.

And folded the key into her apron.

The corridor felt longer this time, or thinner. Like something had narrowed behind her and wouldn't quite let go.

At the base of the stairs, she paused.

Looked once over her shoulder.

The door didn't creak. It didn't whisper.

It just stood there—shut, as if it had never opened at all.

She touched the key through the cloth of her apron.

Not to check for it. To remember that she had, in fact, returned.

Down the hall, the kitchen ticked again. The same slow clock.

But it didn't sound so loud anymore.

Just present.

She set the table for silence.
But it remembered her name.

Scroll

THE BALCONY

Virgin, Utah – Evening, Early Spring 1919

Behind the building, where few guests ever ventured, two wooden staircases rose at angles. They flanked the building—open, unfinished, framing the balcony above. George had built them with his own hands, long after the plaster had dried and the guests had found their rhythm. The stairs weren't treated lumber or modern composite. Raw wood. Pale. Splintered in places. Warped slightly by seasons of sun and desert air.

Each stair groaned when stepped on, but not in protest. In acknowledgment.

The left staircase curved with a subtle lean—as if compensating for something the blueprint never caught. Its railing, worn smooth where George's hand had traced it again and again, bowed slightly outward at the midpoint, like an old man's spine. The right staircase was straighter but less sure—missing a cap rail at the top where George once stopped mid-construction and never finished. He never said why. Some things in the building stayed incomplete on purpose.

No one used the stairs but George.

But they belonged. Weathered guardians of a quiet threshold. They led to the balcony where George sometimes sat alone, sandpaper in one hand, oil cloth in the other, mending chairs no one asked him to fix.

To the rest of the world, they were nothing.

To George, they were the way back up.

His workspace was behind the building. Sometimes he paused at the base. Let his hand rest briefly against the carved newel post, its shape smooth from decades of human oil, etched with a curl that might once have meant something—a symbol, a flourish, or a forgotten initial. The wood felt warm from having held intention.

The light on the staircase changed in the evenings.

Illumination gave way to language. An hourless dialect of shadow and warmth. The kind of light that knew where not to go. It settled along the ridges of wood like old stories returning to their favorite corners. It wasn't dramatic. Not like sunset over the cliffs. But it was particular.

George stepped carefully, one hand on the rail. The building seemed to breathe slower at this hour. It wasn't metaphor. Not to him. He knew, over time, how structures exhaled—through cracks, through joints, through heat easing out of the walls. Some buildings sighed with age. Others with sorrow. Balcony One did neither. It breathed like something listening.

He could feel it on the stairway most of all. The way the temperature shifted between landings. The way sound softened before reaching the next step. As if the building was giving him space to arrive, soulfully.

When guests commented on the architecture—the curves, the light, the tile: he nodded politely. But inside, he always thought: *You're not wrong. You're just not listening long enough.*

The building didn't try to impress.

It tried to remember.

From this angle, as he reached the midpoint of the staircase, the east-facing landing offered a slice of eastern sky.

He had once lived in a place where the sky arrived in wide, feral bands—windswept and salt-kissed, always arriving from somewhere wilder.

Crete.

And just like that, it came back.

The hotel. The joke. The sun-worn platform where the old royalist used to hold meetings with his espresso and his thin-lipped nods. George could still feel the wind off the bay, the way the ocean bit back even in spring. Mirabello. The name came back clear.

He hadn't meant to remember it. But memories, he'd learned, didn't need invitations. They arrived when the architecture allowed it.

He grinned—quiet, to himself. That joke about the king and the soup. The way the old man didn't flinch, didn't laugh. He held the tension like it was gold. And George, ever the fool, ever the hopeful, walked right into it, letting humor try to do what blood and language never could: earn him a place.

But place had been the problem, hadn't it?

He'd opened The Blue Parrot after leaving Mirabello. Named it after the bar in Casablanca. White stucco. Marble floor. Clean lines, clean plates. His mother had helped. She'd seen it—stone walls thick enough to outlive grudges. But Greece hadn't welcomed him back the way he'd hoped. Not fully. Not honestly.

He was still the outsider.

Rodinos, yes. Greek by blood. But not Greek enough for the island. Not Greek enough for the neighbors. The accent had betrayed him every time. When business was bad, they pitied him. When it was good, they tried to ruin it.

He rubbed the railing with his thumb. Felt the splinter there. Didn't pull it.

It had been a different kind of exile. One born not of war, but of belonging denied.

And still—he'd built it.

Just like this place.

Not from approval.

From persistence.

He reached the top stair. Looked out toward the canyon. Zion held its line in the distance. Quiet. Undemanding. But present.

The restaurant below was settling into its own breath. Chairs stacked. Oil lanterns flickering. Somewhere, Mateo was still humming. And Cynthia was probably counting receipts she'd already memorized.

George took his stool on the landing. Same one he always dragged out when the light turned ochre. Sandpaper in one hand. Oil in the other.

He looked toward the ridgeline. The wind hadn't shifted yet. But it would.

The stairs had already heard everything.

No one in Virgin knew this part of him. That there were mornings the canyon light seemed too mannered. That the silence here felt different—less oceanic, more subterranean. As if the hush came not from distance, but from something watching.

Still, he did not compare them. Each place had its claim on him. One had loosened his bones. The other had kept them.

The clay of the balcony half walls held warmth from the day. The memory of wind across coastal ridges was there in his shoulders, his calves, his gait.

And in the hush that met his, there was no longing.

Only recognition.

Only return.

George paused, not because the view was remarkable, but because it never tried to be. The light that entered here didn't dazzle. It anointed. Pale and peripheral, like something holy arriving without sound.

There had been a morning, years ago, when he stood there after waking from a dream he didn't understand. But that day, it had been storm-dark, vibrating with silent thunder. And as he reached the landing, the rain started. A single drop traced the outside of the glass like a finger.

He had whispered, then, without knowing why: "Thank you."

Some memories don't belong to stories.

They belong to staircases.

Just a sliver of the full expanse. Enough to see how the light moved in the canyon this time of year.

Early spring.

The eastern sky didn't blaze in color like Greece. It quieted. Softened. Became a palette of subtle gradients—ice blue melting into lavender, edged by a brush of rose. The cliffs across the Virgin River glowed in reverse: their western faces catching gold, while their eastern spines dipped into indigo. Shadows deepened not from darkness, but from distance.

Below the cliffs, the lamb pasture shimmered faintly. Not from moisture. From life—dozens of tiny puffs rising from newborn mouths. The fence held a lacework of grapevine, not yet full, but already clutching toward the coming season. Each leaf seemed inked in dusk.

The cypress trees swayed gently, their needles hushing the breeze. In the half-light, they looked less like trees and more like watchmen—blurred at the edges, but tall with purpose.

From his place on the stairs, George breathed.

The breath wasn't with hesitation.

It was something older. A kind of reverence. Like the breath one takes before crossing into a room where someone has just died—or just been born.

He had learned to trust these pauses.

The building offered them like sacraments. Tiny hushes. Spaces between knowing and deciding. They never lasted long. But when he honored them, things aligned. Candles burned longer. Doors didn't stick. Glasses didn't crack.

There had been a morning, not long after Sam passed, when he'd stepped too quickly at this same place. Distracted, thinking of the floorboard he'd forgotten to repair. His boot had caught the lip of the riser, and he'd pitched forward hard. The only thing that stopped his fall was the smooth press of the wall beside him.

But when he caught his breath, he'd felt it: warmth on his palm. As though a living hand had caught him. Since then, he paused.

Every time.

Not out of fear.

But because some things deserve to be noticed more than once.

A scent met him—cedar warmed by fading sun, soil newly turned, and something sweeter: the first blossoms of spring.

He recognized the ground vine first—not by name, but by the way it caught in his memory before it reached his lungs. It was the same vine that had threaded the hem of his mother's skirt in an old photo of her.

She never mentioned it. But George had noticed. The way the scent clung after she passed. A green-sweet trace, like wild honey steeped in stone. It wasn't perfume. It was placement. The way his mother moved through the world: without forcing, but always leaving something behind.

He didn't move for a moment. Just continued to sit quietly on his stool.

Above the vine's sweetness, the cedar offered its grounding note: resinous, resolute. That scent belonged to the bones of the building. George had carried it in on his clothes when he first began the dining room.

And the soil… the soil had just been turned. He could smell the work in it. The work he had done earlier that day. The scent was a chord. Memory. Wood. Work. And something waiting. It was the scent of patience. Of waiting things.

He stood up from the stool and stood at the threshold of the staircase.

The upper steps felt different.

Not in texture (they were laid with the same wood, kissed by the same sunlight) but in tempo. As if the air itself thickened slightly here, not to slow him, but to calibrate his attention.

He didn't rush.

There was no performance in his time on the Balcony. Only breath and weight and the sound of his own footfall aligning with something older than footsteps.

He had climbed this staircase hundreds of times. Before dawn, after storms, between service. Once in silence the day after Sam died, when the whole house felt like it had swallowed a flame and didn't know what to do with the smoke.

He had carried tea up these stairs for Cynthia. But not tonight.

Tonight he carried only himself.

That was enough.

As he stood atop the landing, he resisted the urge to descend. Not because he was afraid—but because the past was always in front of him. And this moment wasn't for it.

It was for what waited ahead.

The Balcony made him feel closer to the sky—not overhead, but ahead. As if the upstairs rooms weren't just above the kitchen but aligned with some quieter threshold.

The staircase bent gently at the top. The landing held its breath. To his right: the eastern balcony. Sky, air, and the hush of a land not yet night.

The lambs called to each other below.

New— alive.

The balcony was narrow but deep, carved into the south side of the building like a secret porch. He stepped along the balcony as one steps into a chamber long closed—not with fear, but with the understanding that silence lives differently here. The boards gave slightly beneath his weight, not creaking, yielding. They remembered him. And more than him. Others had stood here. Some still did, in the way certain moments refuse to end. He designed the shape of the balcony as improbable—too tucked, too deliberate. His own psychic architectural flourish—an intention. It faced south, then east, not for light, but for recall. He felt it each time: this was not a place for looking forward. It was for looking again.

Wind moved through the cypress columns with the hush of a confession. The stone beneath the wood still held the warmth of day, and the air carried a thin thread of mineral—like the river was exhaling into the canyon before sleep. The scent of grapevine reached him now—earthy, rising. Not from bloom, but from the tangle along the fence, where roots had gripped tight through seasons of drought and rot. The vines weren't ornamental. They were survivors.

And tonight, they were listening.

Columns trimmed in cedar. Floorboards laid in a herringbone pattern, pale from sun and time.

He crouched for a moment—fingertips brushing one of the herringbone seams where the boards met in a weathered chevron. The grain here told a different story than the rest of the building. This wood had been salvaged, he suspected—older than the floor it served, repurposed with care.

He had once found a shipment from Santa Fe. Left forgotten at a depot for months, then found and brought back in haste. Some of it warped. Some of it perfect. This balcony had been born of what remained.

He could feel that. In the way the boards welcomed his weight. Not with luxury, but with resilience.

Above him, the juniper columns weren't ornamental. Their trimming was simple, hand-carved, a language of gestures rather than flourishes. George intended the markings—not symbols exactly, but choices. Each notch an act of human hand and intention. George had never signed his work, but this—this was his fingerprint.

He let his palm rest against the base of the nearest column. It was cool.

But not indifferent.

A half-circle of chairs faced outward, framing the view.

As usual, the chairs were not matched.

One had a curved back with iron filigree, another straight pine slats softened by sun, the third—woven leather, aged to a deep umber. Each had been added, and they belonged.

He knew which ones rocked slightly, which one caught at the leg, which absorbed more moonlight than it reflected. There was one, third from the right, that still held the faint impression of Cynthia's shawl. He knew the weight of it, the way it must have draped. Some evenings, the chair tilted subtly to one side, as if remembering.

No one rearranged them. Not out of laziness, but out of respect. There was an order to their disorder. A memory in their angle. George stepped lightly among them—choosing where not to disturb. The chairs were not waiting to be used. They were bearing witness.

And tonight, they were watching him.

And what a view it was.

But it wasn't the kind of view people wrote about in travel journals.

It wasn't the drama of cliffs at midday, or the aching blaze of red rock beneath a July sun. It was quieter than that. More faithful. The kind of view that stayed.

The cypress framed the edges— guardians. Their dark arms rose like liturgy, each needle humming faintly in the breeze. He couldn't remember when he began to think of them as sentinels. Perhaps it was Cynthia who said it first. Or maybe himself, half-laughing, arms full of wood, whispering,

"They're keeping secrets, those trees."

Beyond them, the grapevine fence caught the last edge of light. The vines twisted like old questions—unanswered, unsent. They had survived frost, hail, pruning, silence. And still, they reached. Upward, outward, toward something they didn't need to name.

George breathed in the entire field: the lambs, the dusk, the continuance of it all. The unspooling of a place that didn't need to change to be alive.

This wasn't a view.

It was a vow.

The cypress trees stood like sentinels, their tops flicking silver under moonlight. There was a particular way the moon touched those trees. Not like the sun did—but selectively, like it was remembering them in fragments. One flicked top. One slow-gleamed trunk. One branch barely outlined, as if the light wasn't shining but returning.

George had long felt the cypress were not growing, but listening. Their presence didn't expand. It deepened. He sometimes caught himself apologizing aloud when he passed between them. Not from fear. From acknowledgment.

He knew they weren't ancient by age. But they were ancient by wisdom.

And tonight, they shimmered in pieces. Fully visible—enough to know they still stood. Still kept.

One leaned more than it used to. He'd noticed it last week. Cynthia had mentioned it too, gently, with that particular tone she used when reading signs in root shifts and bark cracks. George hadn't responded. Not because he disagreed, but because he agreed too much.

Some leanings you don't name.

You just prepare for.

Beyond them, a slat-wood fence twisted with grapevine—overgrown, unruly, alive. And past that: the lamb pasture.

The pasture breathed differently at night.

In the day, it flickered with movement—hooves, wings, the shifting weight of clouds. But now, under the early spring moon, it exhaled slowly, like something tired but tender.

He could just make out the lambs, their outlines more suggestion than form—small, wool-bound shadows flickering in and out of focus. They didn't move much. Just enough to affirm life. Enough to remind her that arrival is often quiet.

George had learned not to anthropomorphize them. They weren't symbols. They were beings. New ones. Full of hunger and beginning. But even so, there were nights like this, when their presence felt like a reply— to the earth herself.

The fence held firm. The grapevine threaded through it without asking. That relationship—thorn and timber—was older than the lambs, and likely to outlast them.

He took that comfort into his body without needing to call it such.

Some evenings, the land held the kind of stillness that didn't require explanation.

Only attention.

It was early spring.

The lambs had begun their songs.

Not quite bleats—softer. The trembling hums of creatures new to sound, calling without urgency. A lullaby in reverse.

He listened like someone who had once lost their hearing—not entirely, but enough to know how precious quiet could be.

Not silence. Quiet. The difference mattered.

Silence was what came after shouting. Or grief. Or gunfire. Quiet was what lived before sound. Around it. Beneath it. It was a condition of the soul, not the air.

And this quiet was layered.

It held the breath of lambs. The friction of moonlight on tile. The trace-memory of someone once laughing here—Sam, perhaps, in the way he always did, with enough volume to make you wonder if it was joy or defiance. It held Cynthia's footsteps, slow and certain. It held Rosa's hum, never full, never absent.

And it held George.

Not as a sound.

As a rhythm—soul.

A spacing between the notes.

He let his body adjust to it, the way one does when entering water that is colder than it should be.

There would be time for speaking later.

But not now.

Not here.

The sky was open above him. The sun setting.

It was not a dramatic sunset. Not the kind that made guests rush to the west balcony with glasses half full and opinions they mistook for poetry.

This one was nearly invisible. The kind of sunset you had to earn.

George tilted his head slightly, tracing the gradient—deepening lavender folding into bruised blue. The line of the cliffs across the river no longer shone; they absorbed. They drank the last light slowly, like something sacred.

He had watched many skies in his life. Cretan skies—wild, slanting, sky that made no apology for its vastness. The sky here was quieter. Less majestic. More exacting.

He liked that.

It asked him to look closer. To see not the spectacle, but the shifts: one hue folding into the next, the softness of dusk arriving not in colors, but in temperature. In tone.

And there, right at the margin—where light met rock, where rock met memory—was the same pause he had felt on the staircase.

Threshold within threshold.

This was no longer a moment.

It was a listening.

The air carried cedar, mineral, and the memory of rain not yet fallen.

That last part—the rain not yet fallen—was what he trusted most.

It was spiritual. It was a presence. The way the air thickened with expectation, the way the leaves stopped whispering and began to listen. It was the kind of rain that had not yet chosen its moment, but had already arrived in scent.

He closed his eyes letting the air press against his skin.

It smelled of slate and salt, even though they were miles from the sea.

He thought of his mother—not as a person, but as a sensation. His mother had carried weather with her. That same anticipation. That same soft inevitability. You didn't know what she would say, but you knew it would change the room.

George let the thought move through him, without clutching.

Some memories were not to be summoned. Only received.

Like the rain.

Like the quiet before it.

He stepped further onto the balcony. His boots barely scuffed the boards.

The boards remembered more than footsteps.

They held the weight of Sam's two springs ago—the way he leaned too far back in the leather chair, boots crossed, smirk just soft enough to disarm. He'd brought cigars that evening. Not for smoking. For showing. Dominican, rolled tight and arrogant.

There was something about the way he sat—shoulders loose, eyes too direct—that reminded him of before. Not his own before. Someone else's. George's Father, Evangelos. Or a version of his father from when he still had hands that healed more than they held.

Sam hadn't lasted.

But parts of him did.

The oil from his fingers had darkened the railing's edge. The way he drummed the toe of his boot on the same spot, over and over—that mark was still there, a crescent faintly worn into the floor.

The memory was not tender. But it was true.

And the balcony kept truth, even when it wasn't kind.

To the right, at shoulder height, was the carved eagle.

He turned toward it slowly, as if acknowledging a host rather than an object.

The eagle had never seemed decorative to him. Its placement was too exact. Like it had chosen that post, not been placed there.

He had tried, once, to trace its origin. He couldn't remember. He should have known, but by the time he'd begun to care, he was already vanishing in the corners of rooms. Cynthia had simply said, "It was here before me. That's enough."

Tonight, though, it felt closer.

The carving's edges held dust, yes, but also memory. The feathering on the wings, so precise it seemed soft at dusk. The talons, curled with enough tension to suggest holding, not grasping.

He stepped beside it, shoulder nearly touching the beam. The beak was half-open, caught in the moment before a cry—or just after.

It jutted from the wall beam like it had always been there—a talon clutched around the post, wings partially unfurled, beak slightly open as if mid-warning.

He had once dreamed it moved. A shift—the smallest turn of the head, as though it had heard something he could not.

The dream had stayed with him for days.

What would it mean for a carving to listen?

What would it mean for him to be listened to, by something made of wood and will?

He had stood before it that morning, coffee untouched in his hand, and whispered—I see you.

And for a moment, he thought the grain shimmered. Like heat on stone. Like breath held a second too long.

Now, months later, the carving looked the same. But the space around it had thickened. As if more than time had passed. As if something had been invited.

He didn't reach for it.

Not yet.

But his shoulder brushed the beam, deliberately.

That was enough.

The eyes had no gemstone, but they caught light in strange ways.

He may have been the one to carve it. Or maybe he chose to forget. But it was always there.

This evening, it seemed different.

The kind of different that lives in the skin. In the fraction of a moment between breath and knowing. Like someone had spoken his name in a room he thought was empty. His body had already adjusted, like a compass tipping toward a pull it couldn't name.

There were times, rare and not to be summoned, when the balcony folded in on itself. Not physically, but metaphysically. The edges softened. The air grew denser, but quieter. As if the space had curled inward, making room for something just arriving.

Tonight was such a time.

The eagle hadn't changed. But it was no longer alone. George's hands stilled at his sides. He felt something. As if the veil between movement and memory had thinned, and what stood with him now wasn't a ghost, but a totem. An event happening. Inside the silence.

As he turned to look past it, his eyes caught something behind the eagle.

A shape. A lean.

The lean was unmistakable. Shadow and light. It had depth. The way a memory does when it surprises you with its weight. Like the scent of a person you haven't named in years suddenly wafting from someone else's coat.

This wasn't Sophia.

And it wasn't Sam.

But it was presence.

As if the building itself was exhaling in a direction. As if the grain of the wood had formed around something that once leaned there often, with purpose. He thought of his father, Evangelos.

His breath slowed. He had learned long ago that such experiences required equal stillness. Like water in a bowl left undisturbed all night, reflecting only what dares to draw near. Like someone had rested their weight just behind its wing—a shoulder's worth of absence. A presence marked not by form, but by interruption.

The lambs fell silent all at once.

The silence held.

It was the kind of silence he used to fear.

When he was younger, silence meant absence. Neglect. The rooms that swallowed his voice, the spaces where no one turned to look, even when he entered. He had filled those silences with noise—traveling like a gypsy.

But here, now, this was different.

This was listening silence—passive, present. It was not waiting for him to speak. It was honoring that he might not. The balcony breathed with it. The grain of the beam seemed to hum with it. Even the lambs, silent below, were part of it. It felt like the kind of silence that follows an answer you didn't know you asked for. And George, standing in the soft hollow of that awareness, felt no urge to break it.

Only to remain.

George touched the edge of the eagle's wing. His fingers didn't tremble. They simply arrived. Contact wasn't the goal. It was the echo. The way warmth lingered not on the surface, but beneath it—bone-deep, old, familiar in a way that required no origin story. Like resting your hand on someone sleeping—feeling the pulse of their unguardedness. The wood was smoother than he remembered. Not polished, but worn. The way tools wear down in the palms of those who use them with care. This wing—this carved and silent wing—had known other hands.

The warmth wasn't metaphor. It was memory made tactile. It was the hush before song.

His breath stayed low in his chest—quiet, real.

He turned slowly, taking in the balcony's edges. The wind shifted. One of the grapevines rustled against the fence like a memory brushing past.

Then the bleating resumed.

Not all at once.

Just one—soft, reedy, a sound that might have been mistaken for wind if he hadn't known better. Then another. And another. The way stars appear—not in a burst, but in permission. One light allows the next.

It reminded him of the first words after grief. Not profound ones. Just ordinary speech. Asking for salt. Naming a task. The moment when the world resumes its language without needing to explain its silence.

He kept his hand on the eagle's wing a moment longer. The lambs were alive. Not just in the biological sense. In the song sense. They had returned to their rhythm, to the pulse of being. And in that return, the spell broke—not as a loss, but as a blessing ending.

Not all moments are meant to last.

Some arrive only to remind you that you're part of a pattern too wide to see.

And then, gently, they move on.

Soft.

Innocent.

The world righted itself.

He did not linger.

The decision to leave was not dismissal. It was the completion of a circuit. The way a candle extinguishes not from wind, but from having fully burned what it needed to.

He stepped backward, not to retreat, but to seal the space. The kind of backward that holds reverence. The kind that dancers use when bowing out of sacred terrain.

His final glance wasn't searching. It was acknowledgment.

Of the eagle.

Of the lean.

Of the hush that hadn't vanished, but folded itself back into the beams.

This was not an ending.

It was a pulse returning to source.

And he, a part of it.

He stepped through the threshold, not back down the outdoor stairs, but through the narrow corridor toward the indoor staircase.

Back into the building that never forgot his shape.

With a final glance at the eagle, he stepped backward into the corridor.

It received him like a vessel already shaped to his presence.

The shift from balcony to corridor was small in distance, vast in density. The air grew warmer, edged with kitchen spice and the faint wax of old floors. But he didn't walk yet. Not right away.

Behind him, the air settled.

He let the memory of the balcony remain at his back—pulsing, as if the space had been folded into his spine. He could still feel the texture of the eagle's wing against his palm, not as temperature, but as impression. The way skin remembers certain touches long after the nerves have stopped speaking. He inhaled slowly through his nose. The building responded in its usual way—a soft creak from somewhere far off, a loosened scent from the plaster. The kind of response that said: You were seen.

He touched the wall as he passed, out of ritual.

Some places are not left. Only parted from—

briefly.

Down the tiled stair.

Back into the spine of a building that remembered everything.

What you think is silence may only be something listening with its whole body.

Scroll

THE RAFTER ROOM

A room that doesn't exist—except to the one who built it

It wasn't on the blueprints. Not in the ledger. Not on the tour. But if you asked George—on a quiet day, before the cognac kicked in—he might lean forward and nod toward the upper staircase. Beyond the hallway. Beyond the door with the frosted glass. Past that. Up near the rafter beam where the light bends sharpest at dusk. He'd say,

"That's Elizabeth's room," and then go back to polishing a glass he'd already polished twice.

It wasn't really a room, not in the way people meant. But enough space above the banquet hall and dining room to kneel or crouch, to press your back against a beam and listen. A place that held breath and waited. Like a held note. Like a finger on a trigger, not pulling—just ready.

Elizabeth never spoke of it. It wasn't for her to hide in. It was for her to see from.

She never rushed the stairs. Not even when George called her name too sharp, or when Cynthia dropped a glass and the air went still.

She moved like a soldier between wars—every step certain, but never loud. Wood under boot, shoulder to rail. You wouldn't call it a ritual. But she never missed a step.

She kept the key on a leather cord around her neck—though calling it a key was generous. It was a sliver of forged steel, planed flat and notched by her own hand, slipped clean into a groove behind the third rafter panel. No one else knew it was there. And even if they did, they wouldn't know how to turn it without making the latch complain.

She never let it complain.

Inside, the crawlspace opened just wide enough to sit back against the beam and watch the whole of the banquet hall through a seam in the upper molding. One glass pane above the buffet line had been swapped years ago for thinner lead, clearer edge. She could see shapes, motion, riders through the dusted window before anyone downstairs noticed the rhythm of hooves.

She knew that sound.

There was no lighting—just what the sunset gave. No furnishings— just an oilcloth, a bolt-action rifle wrapped in flannel, and a leather-bound field log that no one had ever seen her write in. When the air shifted— when it moved like it remembered something coming—Elizabeth didn't tense. She just reached for the cloth and unwrapped the rifle. No hesitation.

She crouched near the corner vent, where the draft from the eaves brought scent before sound. Today it carried dust. And something else.

Horse sweat.

The horses stopped before the steps. No gallop. No dismount. Just that long silence lawmen use when they want to be seen before they speak. Two of them. Hats low. Dust on their sleeves. The kind of dust that didn't come from town. George stepped out first. He didn't say anything. Just wiped his hands on a towel and stood straight enough to remind them he wasn't afraid—but not so straight he'd provoke.

"We're looking for a man," the taller one said. "Zitting."

George squinted into the sun.

"Don't know that name."

The second one shifted in his saddle. Young. Eager. The kind of deputy who practiced speeches in the mirror.

"This is about harboring polygamists, they're fugitives you know," he said, like it meant something here.

Elizabeth didn't move. Not yet.

She had the rifle barrel half-swiveled, angled just past the ventilation slot.

Not aimed.

Tracking.

They weren't here for blood. She could tell by the way the taller one's boot hung limp in the stirrup—worn leather, cracked sole, not the kind you chase a man through the desert in. But they were here for theater. And that could be worse. Below, Cynthia appeared in the doorway. No apron, just ledger in hand, the way she always held it when she didn't want her hands free. The deputy noticed. Shifted again. George gave them water. Didn't ask them in. The taller one drank without thanking him. The younger one tried to peer past the staircase like it might offer testimony. Elizabeth's breath stayed low in her chest.

Measured.

Ready.

She had no intention of firing. She never did. But her presence filled the loft the way tension fills a string—held between two fixed points. If they crossed a line, it would snap. Not out of anger. Out of design.

They left without a name. No threats. No questions worth remembering. Just the sound of reins tightening, hooves turning, and dust settling back into its old rhythm. Elizabeth waited until she could no longer hear them. Then another minute. Just to be sure. Then one more—for her own measure.

She rewrapped the rifle. Slow. Careful. Not reverent—just exact. Her fingers moved like memory. She leaned her weight back against the beam. Let her head rest. Let the quiet return.

And that's when she felt it—presence. The kind that waits until you're still to be noticed. It hadn't been there before. She was sure of it. Tucked into the upper corner of the rafter's apex—just where the shadow kissed the wood grain. Small. Oval. Barely the size of a face.

A mirror.

Framed in dark metal gone soft with age. Not hanging. Embedded. As if the wood had made space for it. It reflected only the crawlspace. But not quite. The angle was wrong—too low, too deep. She should have seen her own knees, the bolt cloth, the rifle bag. Instead, she saw her shoulders. And just behind them—something like breath pressed into glass.

Not Sophia's face.

Not yet.

Just the shimmer of someone learning how to follow.

Elizabeth didn't flinch. But she didn't look away either. The presence didn't speak. It never had. But something in the stillness answered her. She was being tracked. By someone who had chosen her. The mirror began to hum and flicker. The air around it grew denser—like altitude shifting, like reverence. As if the rafter room had just been made real by being seen.

She nodded once, to no one in particular.

Then reached out and pressed her palm, open, to the beam beside it.

And at that moment, she saw herself. But not really herself.

Hair parted short, tucked beneath a felt hat two sizes too large. Brows darkened with ash and lye soap. Jawline shaded just enough to catch the morning light wrong.

She wore the coat loose across the shoulders, but weighted the hem with stitching—so it wouldn't flap when she walked.

The tie was the key.

Plain. Crooked on purpose.

Not arrogance—just inattention. The kind that made men look real.

She learned to square her feet when she stood still. Hands behind her back—not folded, but locked. The way he did.

And when she spoke, it was always one sentence fewer than expected. Men listened to brevity. Especially when it came from someone who looked like they'd never had to shout.

She wasn't pretending to be a man.

She was pretending to be the kind of man no one questioned.

In Utah, women regained the right to vote in 1896. So Elizabeth decided she had every right to run for Washington County Sheriff in 1907. But they said she was unfit for duty and laughed out of the process. So she invented Charles R. Worthen—and Charles returned to run for County Sheriff in 1909. Charles won—and *she* became Sheriff Worthen, the best sharp-shooter west of the Mississippi.

She leaned closer to the mirror, and the angle shifts—revealing not just her reflection, but her past self. The face in the glass was hers. And not hers. The weight was the same. The quiet resolve. But the lines around the mouth told stories no one had ever asked to hear.

She was Sheriff Worthen elected in 1909, then again in 1911, then again in 1913, and so on until she didn't run for re-election after 1917. No one questioned the credentials. They were just impressed with her, *or his*, perfect aim. And the fact that she never missed. She didn't wear the name like a disguise. She wore it like a key. To doors that had been bolted shut to women since birth.

As sheriff, she never raised her voice.

But when she walked into a room, even the guilty sat straighter.

She could look a man in the eyes and see how many lies he'd already told himself.

She didn't break suspects down.

She just gave them the silence to confess.

Even the crooked judges asked her advice before passing sentence.

And maybe some folks new Sheriff Worthen was really Elizabeth, they didn't care. Because they trusted her. And trust, in a place like this, was as close as love got."

She laid Charles to rest without a funeral. Sherriff Worthen would retire, or disappear, or whatever. She folded the hat, and kept the badge. She didn't miss being him. Because at Balcony One she could be herself.

She lowered herself through the rafter slot. Just eased the panel back into place with the side of her palm, careful not to catch the latch too hard. The rifle stayed behind. Wrapped. Ready. She never brought it down unless she needed it. The light in the banquet room had changed. Less gold now. More blue. The hour where shadows soften but don't vanish—where memory lingers in corners too tired to argue. She walked the perimeter once, slow. Ran her hand along the back of the buffet, adjusting a stray glass. No one was watching, but she straightened the silver anyway. At the base of the stairs, she paused.

Listened.

Not for the lawmen.

Not for ghosts.

For breath.

The building didn't answer. It never did directly. But it held something. It trusted Elizabeth. It trusted her to love it, to keep it safe, to keep its secrets. She stood still, knowingly. In stillness that wasn't empty. The kind that made space.

For presence. For remembering. For return.

She exhaled once.

Low. Even.

Then turned toward the bar.

Somewhere upstairs, a mirror waited.

Not watching.

But following.

A woman didn't need a badge to keep the peace.
Just a place to watch from—and the will to wait.

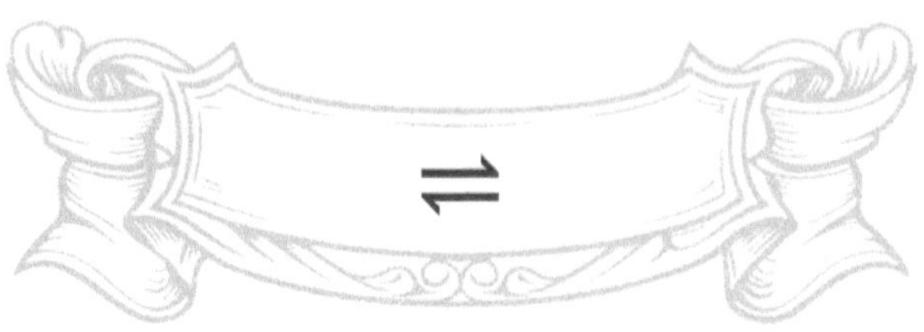

Scroll

THE STAIRS

Balcony One

The stairs creaked beneath his weight—not from age, but from memory.

George paused halfway down the interior steps, one hand on the curved wooden rail, the other resting against the wall where the ochre paint had faded into amber. Light from the side window streaked across the Santa Fe tile, catching one of the turquoise squares just enough to make it shimmer. It always caught there, on the fifth riser, just where the wall turned in slightly. Cynthia had called it the sunstroke tile.

"When it gleams, we see spirit," she used to say. George didn't know what she meant, but he never questioned it. He just made sure the light still found it.

He adjusted his stance, letting the quiet of the house settle around him. These weren't his stairs. The outdoor staircase was his: bare pine, no polish, straight utility. This one—this curve of light and pigment—

104

belonged to her. Every tile had a story. Every grout line was a sentence she never finished.

He hadn't meant to stop here. He was just walking, coming down from the balcony like he always did when the air got too thick. But the fifth tile caught the light, and now he was standing like a fool, halfway down the stairs, waiting for something he couldn't name.

A long breath. Then another.

He remembered the way she knelt here, back when the place was still just frame and dust. Cynthia had worn a band around her head, sleeves rolled, a bucket of water beside her and a towel tucked into the waist of her pants. She wiped each tile before setting it, even the underside. Said the dirt had to come clean before it held shape. Said it mattered what touched the wood first. He'd laughed at her then, from the top of the stairs, hammer in hand.

"You're baptizing the steps," he said. She didn't look up. Just said,

"Someone has to."

They met in Virgin. Not in one of the usual ways. George had been fed up: with Vegas, with the endless noise of it, the racket of other people's appetites. Before that, it was Miami. Before that, Cleveland. He'd lived cold. He'd lived humidity. He'd lived heat with no horizon. By the time he arrived in Virgin, he was done. Fifty-seven. Busted up inside in ways he didn't yet understand. He told himself he'd just shoot photos, help with the horses at Jacob's Ranch, stay out of trouble. Keep life simple.

Then came Cynthia.

She entered Red Coyote one morning—sunburned, sure of herself. There was a flicker. A moment. He thought: she's cute. She thought—well, he never did ask what she thought.

A few weeks passed. Then the call.

"This is Cindy," she said. "Here's the deal. You're not coming to my house. I'm not going to yours. No hanky-panky. We'll go on a picnic. What do you think?"

George said, "All right."

They packed sandwiches, a bottle of wine, and his camera. Drove up Smith's Mesa. Spent the whole day on red rock, watching shadows slide across the canyon wall. She asked questions. Listened. Didn't try to fill his silences. At one point, he snapped her photo mid-laugh—head tilted, one hand shading her eyes—and something clicked in him louder than the shutter.

They married—in Santa Fe.

Later, Cynthia insisted they go to Greece. He resisted. She ignored him. Booked the tickets, packed light, said they'd be back before the paint dried. His mother was still alive then. A mountain village near Delphi, they walked through the village hand in hand. Cynthia knelt to smell the fig leaves. His mother looked at her once, then looked at him and said, "About damn time."

They didn't speak the same language, but Cynthia held her hand on the bench outside the old house for hours. No translation needed.

That night, Cynthia said,

"Your country is beautiful."

They would go back to Greece eight or nine times before his mother died.

They opened the Stagecoach Grill in Hurricane. Cynthia ran the front. George handled the kitchen and menus. The place had a rhythm almost immediately. Locals, travelers, truckers, even a few LA types with cameras. They worked side by side, every day, every hour.

And it was there, one night just after closing, a letter came. His mother was gone. George didn't say much that night. After that, they decided to retire. But that didn't last very long. Cynthia had an inspiration. And together, they conceived Balcony One.

That was her gift. She didn't repair. She revealed. She found the thing worth keeping and made space around it. That's how she looked at him, too. Not as a man to manage. A man to meet.

She chose the tiles in Santa Fe. Cynthia had this way of walking into a store and seeing the one thing no one else noticed. The turquoise tile had been wedged behind a stack of faded terracotta, chipped on one corner.

"That one," she said. "That's our entry tile."

She'd wrapped it in a linen napkin and kept it in her lap like a relic. Now it gleamed faintly under morning light, and George stood still as if waiting for her voice to come around the corner. They bought paint. She said that was more permanent.

George crouched low, knees popping, fingers trailing the grout.

The fifth riser still held. The turquoise tile gleamed at its edge, slightly cracked—hairline, but visible. He didn't dare fix it. Cynthia had sealed that one herself, pressing it into place with the heel of her hand and a muttered curse when the grout bled over. She'd said,

"This one's stubborn. Like you."

The stairs curved just enough to catch the afternoon light through the sunroom arches. Cynthia had designed that, too. Said the light had to "greet the tile before it touched the glass." He'd laughed then. Now he just watched. The sun landed right where she said it would. It always did.

George moved one tile down.

He didn't sweep this part of the building anymore. Rosa had taken over, ever since Cynthia's knees started giving out and George started forgetting where he put the broom. But he still checked the tiles. He called it maintenance. Cynthia called it tending.

There was a rhythm to it:

Left hand on rail.

Right hand on riser.

Press. Pause. Shift.

Each tile had a name in his head: moments, or memories.

The blue square on the third step? That was the stew night—when the kitchen flooded and Cynthia danced barefoot with Rosa while the pipes screamed. The ochre one near the baseboard? That was the pork chop tile. It still smelled faintly like rosemary. No one believed him. He didn't care.

He reached the sixth step and felt it: a slight give. Just enough to register under his palm. Not loose, but different.

He pressed harder.

Nothing shifted.

But the air changed.

It was subtle—like the faint shift before a monsoon. The wood inhaled. The walls leaned in.

George stayed there, crouched, hand on the sixth step, eyes fixed on the base of the curve. A memory wanted to rise—something about a box of pigments, a letter from Crete, a fight they never finished—but it stayed low, under the ribcage. Not ready.

He stood slowly, knees trembling, spine straightening in clicks.

From the top of the stairs, the dining room was filled with golden light. The lanterns hadn't been lit. The mirrors were still dull. But the stairs—these stairs—carried the only warmth for the building.

Cynthia had said the building's heart was in its slope. That people trust a place if the stairs curve just enough to feel like they're being welcomed.

He hadn't believed her then.

Now he checked the curve more carefully than anything else.

There was a time he couldn't keep his hands to himself.

Not in the way most people meant it—not lust, not cruelty. Just- need. A twitch in the wrist. A compulsion in the bone. Anything not nailed down felt like it belonged in his pocket. Not out of greed. Out of hunger. Out of shame.

He started with apples. Then pencils. Then coins from drawers he wasn't supposed to open. By the time he was seven, George had a dozen ways to lift a wallet without getting caught. He'd once taken a priest's crucifix during the Feast of the Falling Asleep of the Theotokos. Slipped it off the robe mid-blessing. Didn't even feel bad. Not then.

He told himself it was about survival. His mother scraping together breakfast from stale bread and boiled cabbage. The long silence after his mother slammed the door. The way people looked at her dress, at her limp, at him.

He learned to disappear into corners. Learned the soft hinges of drawers. Learned how to avoid mirrors.

The orphanage didn't help. Kalamata was gray and bitter and full of boys who stole for worse reasons. He kept his head down and his hands busy. By the time he made it to Cleveland—shipped like cargo, letter in hand, cheeks hollow—he was already good at pretending to be good.

That habit—of reaching, of hiding, of never fully settling—never left.

And the stairs? These stairs? One of the places in the building that were hers. Every tile was hers. Every color chosen. Every curve blessed. George had built the frame. But Cynthia had made the rise.

And that crack in the fifth riser?

It was him.

The part of him that still believed beauty had to be stolen to be deserved.

He sat now, on the fourth step, palms on the tile, eyes closed. He whispered something—in Greek. Just a sound, low and soft, shaped like regret. The tile beneath him stayed warm.

The light shifted again, softer now.

George stood slowly, bones reluctant but steady. The sun had settled fully into the house—quiet and golden, the kind of light Cynthia used to call "bread dough light." Soft enough to rise into.

He reached the bottom of the stairs and paused at the post she painted last. A little turquoise triangle, hidden just behind the base molding. It wasn't part of the pattern. Just something she'd done while laughing with a brush in her teeth. Said it would keep the spirits from falling back down too fast.

He ran his thumb over it now.

There was a ritual he followed when he missed her, though she wasn't gone. Just running errands. Resting more. Talking less.

He checked the fifth tile. Pressed it once.

Then walked to the broom closet and pulled out the rag she used for grout work—still stiff, still streaked with rust-red lines.

He didn't wipe the tile.

He just folded the rag, placed it on the second step, and sat beside it.

Rosa would be here soon, banging the door open with her hip, talking to the floor like it owed her a story. But for now, there was just the stair curve, and the light, and the sound of the tile settling into silence.

George closed his eyes.

One hand on the rail.

One hand open.

Waiting—not for memory this time, but for whatever came next.

Every blade of grass has an angel that bends over it and whispers, 'Grow.

Scroll

THE STAGE COACH GRILLE

George's memory – 1906
After Hours, La Verkin, UT

George hadn't planned to build again.

He was done with kitchens, done with the rush and racket of service. The camera had become his instrument now—silent, patient, private. He spent his days wandering the desert near the ranch, chasing light, avoiding questions.

But Cynthia changed that.

She never asked for more. Never pressed. She had already survived enough—forty years in a marriage that strangled her quiet, her faith the only thing keeping her tethered. When she finally left, it wasn't in anger. Just clarity. She didn't want drama. She wanted dignity.

George saw that. And he knew—if he loved her, he couldn't let her spend the rest of her life in someone else's shadow.

So he called an old friend.

His name was Aris. He was a restaurateur from the islands, a man George had known since his days back in Greece. They weren't family. They were something closer. Aris had helped with the Blue Parrot, back when George was still living half in grief, half in exile. He was the one who understood kitchens not just as business, but as rhythm. As expression.

Together, they laid plans.

The building was small—barely 2,000 square feet—but they wanted it to feel expansive. Aris suggested the trick: raise the ceilings, slope the roof. From the road, the place would look twice its size. Like it had ambition. Like it had breath.

Cynthia handled the design. George curated the menu. Aris handled the bones. A local La Verkin woman would say, "You're building a restaurant in La Verkin? Restaurants never survive in La Verkin."

And George would say,

"Were any of them Greek?

They called it the Stage Coach Grill.

They opened, the first year was rough. Just a chalkboard menu, Cynthia's smile at the host stand, and George, back in the kitchen, carving lamb with a steadier hand than he'd used in years. He told himself it was a gesture—for her. For their new life. But the truth was, he missed it. Missed the heat. The pressure. The exactness of it. He just didn't know how much—until the first ticket came in.

Construction moved fast.

George thought it would take months. Delays, busted timelines, contractors running behind—he'd seen it all. But Aris had flown in from Athens with a notebook full of sketches, a leather bag of tools, and the confidence of a man who'd built five restaurants and buried three.

"This place has good bones," Aris said, standing in the dust of the lot. "We just have to wake them up."

They framed the space with cedar and steel. The ceiling rose to fourteen feet at the front, then sloped higher in the back, pulling the eye upward, elongating the space. From the road, it looked massive. Locals slowed as they drove past, squinting at the facade like it had grown overnight.

George smiled the first time he saw it lit up at dusk. It didn't feel like a restaurant. It felt like an offering. Cynthia had chosen every detail inside: wrought-iron sconces, copper tile, stained concrete that mimicked the blush of southern Utah rock. She brought in her own art for the walls, hand-picked silverware from a supplier in Santa Fe, and rejected four chairs before she found ones that "could hold a secret without complaining."

The menu was small, tight. George wrote it in pencil the first time, then again in pen once the ratios felt right. Lamb chops with rosemary jus. Ribeye seared hard. Greek-style potatoes, thick with lemon and oregano. Cynthia insisted on adding a cheeseburger—called it "non-negotiable Americana"—and George didn't argue.

On soft openings, friends packed the booths. Cynthia greeted every guest like family. Aris wandered table to table, never sitting, just touching backs and laughing in Greek. George stayed in the kitchen, wiping down his station after each plate. He didn't say it aloud, but he felt it: this was his best work.

One night, he caught Aris watching him from the pass.

"What?" George asked, wiping a hand on his apron.

Aris shrugged.

"You're cooking like your father never lived."

George looked down at the cutting board.

"I'm cooking like he never followed me here."

He cleaned the grill himself.

Didn't matter how late it was or how tired his knees felt—Cynthia would stack the chairs, wipe down the tables, count the drawer. George stayed with the steel. One hand on the scraper. One eye on the grease trap. He said it was about quality control, but it was more than that. It was ritual.

Stage Coach closed at nine, but they never left before eleven.

The place had a hum at night. Not the noise of day—no clink of silverware or fryers or someone chirping, "Drive safe!"—just the soft thud of bar mats being rolled, the faint pop of the cooler compressor. And the smell. Always a ghost of lamb, lemon, smoke. That was Cynthia's signature. She called it "the afters." Said a good restaurant doesn't just feed you. It lingers.

George moved the brush in even strokes across the hot plate, watching the remnants curl and crisp into nothing. He could tell what was popular by the stains—the burger streaks always deepest, seared in like tire tracks. Sea bass left a shimmer. Potatoes never left anything. Just scent.

He paused a moment, looked around. Greek statues in the corners. A rusted horseshoe mounted above the bar. A painting of a bull and a lyre hung side by side, slightly crooked. Cynthia had designed it that way—said it shouldn't be tidy. Said people liked a place that didn't try too hard to match.

She was probably in the back by now, counting out the register. She always whispered the numbers. Said she could feel if the drawer was right by the sound of the tens.

The rhythm came quickly.

Mornings were prep—George in the back, radio low, Cynthia at the front table with coffee and invoices. Manolis arrived like clockwork an hour after sunrise, wearing the same leather apron and a grin that said he didn't care how small the town was. A kitchen was a kitchen.

They fell into pattern.

Aris tuned the wine list. George tuned the grill. Cynthia tuned the experience—floors clean, light right, napkins folded once, not twice. "Too crisp feels like theater," she said. "I want warmth." George marinated meat like it was meditation. He stopped talking when he cooked, stopped thinking. Only taste, fire, speed.

Locals returned. Tourists made detours. Truckers parked across the street and called ahead. One day, George looked out through the pass and saw the line out the door. Cynthia stood near the host stand, calm as ever, clipboard in hand. She caught his eye. Winked. Just once.

He never forgot that wink.

But even in the rhythm, shadows curled at the edges. George's hands ached more at night. He took breaks he never used to need. He found himself looking east in the morning, toward the red ridges and farther still—toward something else.

Aris noticed.

"You're quieter," he said one night, finishing a bottle of retsina after close.

George didn't answer.

Instead, he asked:

"Have you heard anything from home?"

Aris paused.

"Not in months. But I'll call tomorrow."

The next day, a letter arrived.

It was Aris.

George wasn't able to read it until late into the evening after all the guests were gone.

"She's gone," It was Aris wrote. "Your mother."

George stared at the dumpsters, at the grease trail under his boots.

He told Cynthia.

They cried together.

They prayed together.

Then they sat together on the prep table in the dark kitchen and held each other's hands.

Outside, the cicada buzzed softly.

Inside, the knives gleamed like untouched grief.

When they got home, she went straight to bed. Left the door cracked. A gesture, not an invitation. George stayed in the dark of the kitchen, holding the tea towel in his lap like something sacred. He didn't cry by himself. Not because he didn't want to. Because he didn't know where to start. His mother sent him across the ocean give him a better life. And now she'd died an ocean away from the only child who ever lived.

In the silence, the restaurant felt far away.

He remembered the cracked tile by the prep line.

He remembered the smell of avgolemono in February.

He remembered his mother's voice in Kalamata, when he was nine, leaving him at the orphanage for boys.

He thought he could remember what she sounded like.

Now he wasn't sure.

He didn't sleep that night.

Cynthia did. Or at least pretended to. George sat on the edge of the bed for hours, elbows on knees, hands locked like a prayer he couldn't finish. The house was quiet—too quiet for the kind of noise inside him.

The thing was, he'd lied.

Not to her. Not out loud. But to himself. For years.

He told himself the grill was enough. That the rhythm of the kitchen, the clatter and sizzle, the slow erosion of days into something repeatable— that it meant he'd made peace with it all. With Greece. With his mother. With the part of him that never really came clean.

But the letter—it didn't just tell him she was gone.

It told him he wasn't able to be there when she died.

And now all he could think about was: remembering who he used to be.

A thief. A liar. A boy who took what wasn't his because it was easier than asking.

He remembered the crucifix.

He remembered the coin purse.

He remembered the day he walked out of the orphanage with nothing but a camera strap and a smile that didn't reach his eyes.

George had built a life around forgetting.

And now it was catching up.

Cynthia stirred beside him, murmured something he didn't catch, then stilled again. He looked at her hand on the blanket. The same hand that held the ledger, the same hand that poured wine over lamb shanks on Saturdays, the same hand that once gripped his across a canyon and said,

"Don't jump to conclusions. Jump to me."

He hadn't told her about the dream.

The dream of a staircase that led down into the ocean. His mother stood at the top, arms folded, eyes sharp. Just watched him descend, step by step, until the water covered his mouth.

George woke up gasping.

He hadn't told anyone that either.

He reached for the lamp but stopped halfway.

Instead, he slipped out of bed, walked to the front door, and stood under the porch light. The grill was five minutes away. He thought about going. About turning the burners on, letting the sizzle of meat drown the noise in his chest.

But he stayed.

He stayed because something had cracked, and he needed to feel it.

Not fix it. Just… feel it.

By the fourth year, George began counting spoons.

Not because they were missing—because they weren't. Because everything was in place. Because the rhythm had gone from music to metronome. They were good. The restaurant was full. The margins made sense. Even the critics came. Cynthia was radiant in the role—welcoming guests by name, remembering birthdays, offering wine pairings like she'd been doing it for decades.

And George…?

He was still behind the line. One night, after close, he watched Cynthia wipe down the bar with her usual care, each motion exact.

"You ever get tired of the repetition?" George asked.

Cynthia laughed. "The repetition is the point."

George nodded.

But he felt it—that itch.

Like the building itself had completed its sentence.

They didn't decide to sell in a rush. Buyers came fast. A local couple. Clean money. No egos. Cynthia was unsure.

"This was ours," she said.

George touched her hand.

"It is. That's why we can let it go."

The final night, they didn't tell anyone. Just closed early. Cooked for the staff. Sat in the back with leftover wine and old stories.

George told one about the Blue Parrot.

Cynthia told one about a goat that wandered into a beach kitchen in Greece and wouldn't leave. She laughed, deep and real. And for a moment, George felt something he hadn't ever felt before.

Completion.

They locked the doors together.

No speeches.

No goodbye.

Just the click of the bolt and a long silence on the sidewalk. Cynthia looked at George.

"Now what?"

George didn't answer.

But later that week, he walked the old road through Virgin and saw it.

An empty patch of land.

Flat. Quiet. Unclaimed.

He stood there a long time.

The shape of the future had already started to rise.

They called it retirement. George didn't believe the word. They slept in. Took slow drives. Cooked at home and left the dishes in the sink. Cynthia bought new reading glasses. George fixed a broken camera lens. Aris remained in Greece, promising to stay in touch.

The house was peaceful.

But George felt restless.

He didn't tell Cynthia right away. He waited, let the silence stretch. Watched the land behind their property shift in light. Shadows moved differently now, like they were trying to show him something. Then, one morning over coffee, he said,

"There's one more thing."

Cynthia didn't flinch.

She looked at him, nodded once, and said,

"Tell me."

He described the land in Virgin. The idea. The name he hadn't said out loud until that moment: Balcony One.

She said,

"If it's what we're meant to do, then let's do it."

They drove out that afternoon. Walked the property line. George pointed where the kitchen would go. Where the windows would frame the cliffs. Where people would sit, and eat, and watch the light change. Cynthia stood near a patch of wild sage and whispered, "It already feels like memory."

The wind lifted.

George looked at the horizon and saw it all—clearly, fully, the way a man sometimes glimpses his life only once it's almost behind him. This time, he wouldn't build with old ghosts in mind. He'd build for what was still living. What could still speak.

And eventually, Aris came back.

Helped pour the bar foundation. Built the stage. Expanded the patio when the band nights got too loud for the dining room. Sketched blueprints for the upstairs banquet hall between shots of ouzo and half-eaten lamb ribs.

But the first vision?

The bones of the place?

That belonged to George and Cynthia alone.

And this time, they didn't build for business.

They built for legacy.

Some homes you build once. Others you build again—just to see if your hands remember.

Scroll

THE BLUE PARROT

Then – Crete, 1890. Remembered from – Virgin, Utah, 1911–1915

The beam line was off.

George could see it by shadow—just enough sag near the western footers to pull the floor askew. No one else would notice. But George didn't build for other people's eyes. He built for alignment. For rhythm. He stepped over the half-cured foundation, boots thick with dust. The sun sat high and brutal. Dry air. No sea breeze here. He missed it more than he'd admit.

Cynthia was in St. George—picking colors for the dining room walls. She liked options. George liked silence. The job site gave him plenty of it.

He bent to check the elevation marker, thumb running the chalk groove.

And there it was again. Not this site. Another.

Delphi.

Not the version tourists knew, but the one George carried inside—the worn alleys, the salted wood, the way plaster cracked beneath heat.

He'd gone back after John died. Not to grieve—he'd already done that, or told himself he had. He went to steady his mother. To put his hands to something. After a while, wanted to build something. An old friend, Katerina Trifili, helped him get a job on the island of Crete at the hotel Mirabello. The tourists wanted seafood and sea views. He gave them both. Painted the chairs blue, because that's what sold.

He was thirty-nine. Alone. Not grieving—done grieving. That's what he told himself.

John had died unexpectedly, leaving his mother alone in Delphi. He sent flowers and stayed drunk for six days in Miami, then traveled straight to Heraklion with nothing but a duffel, a pair of worn chef's shoes, and a journal full of menu sketches.

After spending time in Crete—at the Hotel Mirabello, George started to feel that itch again. The urge to build.

The Blue Parrot went up fast.

He found a stretch of beachfront in Elounda—cheap rent, half-ruined walls, a kitchen with a rusted-out hood vent and a tiled floor slick with old oil. He paid cash. Worked with locals who didn't ask questions. He called up his friend, Aris, and together they knew exactly how they wanted the bar to bend—*not perfectly, but on purpose.* They repainted the ceiling four times before George said it felt right.

He bought chairs from a restaurant in Istro that had failed the summer before. Tables came from a widow who said one of them had belonged to a bishop. The kitchen pans were old, but heavy. Cast iron—he liked that. Made things feel anchored.

By May, he was serving twenty covers a night. By June, fifty. Mostly Germans and Brits. Sometimes a honeymooning American. They ordered souvlaki and sea bass and laughed at his accent, not knowing it was their own.

At night, he walked the back alleys behind the restaurant with a cigarette in hand, sometimes barefoot. He liked the feel of the stone on his soles. Said it helped him think. Mostly he listened—for scooters, for laughter, for anything that might break the silence inside him.

Nothing did.

The Parrot became known for its lighting—low amber sconces, handmade lanterns swinging from driftwood beams. He said it was for mood. Really, it was to make people look better than they felt. He understood that impulse. He lived by it.

The back room, just past the kitchen, was where he slept. No windows. He kept a bottle of retsina beside the mattress. A shelf of paperbacks. A photo of Evangelos and another—just one—of John. Tucked behind a pipe where no one could see it.

One night, a man from London asked why the name.

George said, "Have you ever heard of Casa Blanca? Humphry Bogart?"

The man laughed. Thought it was a joke.

He didn't explain it.

Instead, he built. Fed people. Walked barefoot in the alley after close, listening to the city breathe.

The Parrot never had ghosts.

But George had started dreaming in floorplans.

Now, in Virgin, with sweat down his back and cement on his hands, the dreams returned.

He hadn't sketched a straight line in weeks. Cynthia teased him about it—said he was building a "drunken chapel."

He let her.

What she didn't know: the angles made sense to him. He'd drawn them before.

In Crete.

He stood. Looked at the half-framed bones of Balcony One.

The beam line was off.

He'd leave it.

Some buildings needed to remember where they came from.

* * *

By the first spring, the Parrot ran on instinct.

No real menu. Just George's hand, his eye, his stubbornness. He'd wake to salt air and stone, roll from the mattress in the back and step barefoot onto cold tile. Fry pan, oil, knife. Olives in brine. Fresh mint chopped and slapped into the air for aroma. A rhythm. That's what he remembered now—standing on the red earth in Virgin, blueprint clamped beneath his elbow, debating whether the dining room ceiling should curve like a wave or bow like a chapel.

He closed his eyes. Let his body remember the bend of the bar in Elounda.

He hadn't planned to stay in Greece that long. When John died, he thought: two months. Close the affairs. Take care of his mother. Then back to Miami. But something held.

Or someone.

And then came Aris, his old friend from Athens who'd made a name for himself running seaside tavernas on the Cyclades. No relation, but brother in every way that counted. It was Aris who said, "Don't just drink. Build." And it was Aris who scouted the space with him—those ruined walls above the beach, half a chimney, no roof.

"Give them light," Aris said.

"And fish. And a name that sells."

George said,

"Parrot?"

Aris laughed.

"Blue."

The walls went up fast. Cheap stone, scavenged shutters. They laid tile from a bankrupt hotel in Iraklion—patterned sea foam and copper. Giorgos handled permits and neighbors. George handled everything else.

He painted the beams himself. He carved initials under the counter lip. He pulled chairs from wrecked beach cafés and refinished them one by one on the patio while stray cats watched from the eaves.

It wasn't grief. It was movement.

The Blue Parrot opened quietly, just down the road from Mirabello. Fifteen covers. Local wine. Whole snapper grilled with lemon and salt. He'd never forget the first night—amber lanterns swinging in the wind, plates clinking, a couple from Manchester dancing to a string trio down the block. He hadn't hired them. They just came.

By July, they served fifty a night.

By September, the French press ran a piece:

"Hidden Gem in Elounda—An American-Greek Affair."

Now, in Virgin, with his hands full of lumber and timelines and a half-deaf contractor insisting concrete was superior to sand-mix mortar, George tried to remember the smell of retsina in warm clay cups. He tried to remember the moment he'd first called himself a restaurateur.

He wasn't young anymore. But he still knew how to build something holy with his hands.

The Parrot was his first church.

Balcony One would be his last.

By the first summer, The Blue Parrot was self-sustaining.

Not profitable—George wouldn't call it that—but steady. He had a rhythm: lunch prep by ten, front-of-house check by noon, doors open by one. Dinner service started before the sun began to slide. By twilight, the patio filled with sweat-backed tourists in sundresses and linen shirts, already pink from the day. They drank white wine and ate olives like it was ritual.

George liked the rhythm. It kept things from sneaking up on him.

Most days, he never had to leave the property. He slept in the back room. Showers were taken at the beach—he kept soap in a Tupperware. Once a week he walked up to the old chapel and lit a candle for Evangelos, though he never stayed for the service. He said it was for respect. It was really about keeping the dead where they belonged.

Sometimes, the staff asked him if he ever got lonely.

He said, "How can I be lonely? I've got fifteen chairs that squeak and a walk-in that hums like it's singing lullabies."

They laughed. Let it go.

But some nights, after closing, George sat alone on the west terrace—legs crossed, a drink in hand—and listened for footsteps that never came.

That's when the details started shifting.

First it was the smell—rosewater, faint and sudden. Not in the kitchen. In the bedroom. On the edge of sleep.

Then it was the floor tiles. The second row past the prep line—he could've sworn he'd replaced one, but now it was chipped again, cracked clean down the middle, same as when he first moved in.

Later: the spoon.

It was one of the brass dessert spoons. Thin, decorative. Always kept in the locked side drawer. One morning, it was out—set perfectly beside the register.

No one admitted to moving it. George didn't press.

Another night, a woman came in alone. American. Mid-thirties. Photographer.

She asked to sit on the west terrace.

He froze. Then lied. Said the tables were reserved.

She gave him a look.

"You're not used to people eating alone, are you?"

He didn't answer.

She smiled. "You should try it sometime."

That night, he couldn't sleep. Got up. Walked the dining room in the dark.

Halfway through, the overhead light flickered. Just once.

But in the flash, he saw something: a man, leaning back in a chair. Laughing.

Gone by the time the light steadied.

George sat down at the bar.

And in the mirror behind the bar—blurry, faded—he saw his own face. But younger. And not alone.

The Parrot was the first place George made without compromise.

Not in theory. In stone.

There was no landlord with opinions. No budget committee. No codes except the sea's. The beams didn't align perfectly because he didn't want them to. Symmetry was a lie, he said. Beauty had drift. He built it so the sun would fall just right across the table in the southwest corner by 6:30 p.m. in late summer. It was the seat he'd reserve for John, even though John never came.

At night, after service, he and Aris would sit on the backstep and smoke. Drink a little. Sketch ideas in grease-pencil on the tiles. Archways. Storage shelves. A wine rack that was also a map of Crete. Aris once drew a spiral staircase just for the hell of it.

They laughed like men who'd won something they didn't expect to win.

When the rains came in October, George tiled the kitchen roof himself. He learned the pitch by error, ruined two buckets of grout before getting the ratio right. But when he saw the water run clean off the eaves, no puddles, no drips—he felt it: mastery. Not of food, not of people, but of place.

It was the Parrot that taught him how to shape space to hold feeling.

He stopped using the back bedroom that August. It wasn't one thing. It was everything, all at once. The mattress never dried out, no matter how long he left the windows open. The sink tap clicked every five minutes like it was turning itself. The overhead bulb blew three times in a week, and when he replaced it, it blew again within hours. A spiderweb appeared overnight from the baseboard to the doorknob—too large, too tight, like someone had measured it. So he moved into the pantry. Said it was more efficient, cooler in summer. Rolled out a mat between the olive oil drums and the crate of preserved lemons. It smelled sharp and honest in there.

Brine and earth and garlic. The back room smelled like breath—and not his.

The building was whispering.

He began hearing music. Low at first. Faint and distant, like a radio two rooms over. Never Greek. Never familiar. Just strings, soft percussion, and that minor tone that made his teeth itch. He tried to trace it. Once, he even unplugged the stereo system completely. Still, the music came. Late. Faint. A melody that circled but never resolved. He didn't tell the staff. Didn't want rumors. Just changed the playlist—switched to jazz, heavy rhythm sections, anything to displace whatever was playing in the walls.

The customers didn't notice. They raved about the tzatziki, the grilled octopus, the amber lighting. One reviewer in a British travel magazine called it "the most intimate dining experience east of Mykonos." George read the line four times, unsure whether to be proud or terrified.

One night he went to close the windows and found them already shut.

He hadn't done that.

He never shut them during service—the breeze was part of the draw. But there they were. Latched.

No one else had keys to the latches.

He didn't mention it.

Instead, he started sleeping with the door propped open and a knife within reach.

Now, in Virgin, he translated that forward. Cynthia envisioned the stairwell having Santa Fe tile and how the wood trim on the exterior balcony needed to curve in just the right way.

He just built.

And when he hesitated, he'd take out an old napkin he'd kept folded in his wallet—one of Aris sketches, drawn in wine and ash and remembered from memory.

The Parrot was gone.

But George still carried its bones. Now, at the empty plot of Balcony One, he hears that sound sometimes.

It happened just before Christmas—Crete.

A windstorm had rolled through the previous night—fierce enough to shake tiles loose and knock out power for three hours. When George opened the kitchen door that morning, he found no sand on the floor.

He didn't open that part of the restaurant that night.

Instead, he cleaned the back storage. Deep clean. Took everything out—jars, cans, crates—and re-shelved it from scratch. Like if he could make the space perfect, he could control whatever else had slipped in.

But as he worked, he noticed something strange. The space was bigger than he remembered. Not dramatically. Just enough to make him measure it. He took out the tape. Checked the floor plan from the old contract. The pantry was one meter too long. One meter of space that shouldn't exist. He slammed the shelf into place and left without closing the door.

The next morning, the shelf had moved.

By three inches. Angled toward the back wall.

That was the day George stopped pretending.

He didn't tell anyone. But he started locking the bar at night. Lighting candles in the corners. Not for ambiance—for perimeter. Light as boundary.

Then the dreams began.

Not nightmares. Not visions. Just *rooms that shouldn't be.*

A second kitchen, behind the first. A bedroom with two shadows and no bodies. A bathroom where the faucet wept seawater and whispered in a voice he knew but couldn't place.

He started sketching the layouts. On napkins. On backs of receipts. Rooms he'd never built but could see. Patterns that didn't match the restaurant's design but felt familiar.

One morning he woke with sand in his hair.

He hadn't left the building.

Hadn't opened the windows.

That night, he walked out to the water. Stood knee-deep in the surf. The sea pulled back. Sharp. Sudden.

As if inhaling.

He stepped forward once, twice. Deeper. Closed his eyes. And listened. The wind didn't carry music. It carried breath. Right at his ear.

Close.

Present.

He finally left the restaurant. He stopped sleeping there. After the sand. After the rosé. After the dreams and the phantom wineglass and the spoon that kept showing up next to the register—he rented a room above a bookstore two streets over. Paid cash. No questions.

He told the staff he needed more space.

What he needed was less memory.

But The Blue Parrot didn't let go.

He crossed the ocean, arrived in Miami.

Started working at a new restaurant there.

But on quiet nights—when the terrace was empty, and the wind moved just right—he'd set a glass at Table Two. Not to be clever. Not as ritual.

As acknowledgment.

The chair stayed empty.

But the glass was never full in the morning.

He never caught the refill.

Never tried.

* * *

It was a single nail that broke.

No hammer in sight. Still, it let go—dropped from the rafters of Balcony One and landed point-first in the dirt. George found it as he walked the foundation, one hand brushing the fresh framing, the other resting on his hip like it used to when he cooked eight burners at once. He bent to pick it up. Turned it in his palm. Bent. But not broken.

He thought of the Parrot. Of the smell of brine and rosemary and wet stone. Of Giorgos's last laugh before they sold the place and parted ways—one to the islands, one to the States. He never saw him again. But he felt him, sometimes, in the moment before a match caught flame.

He walked the half-framed outline of the dining room. Stopped where the back window would be. Looked west.

The Blue Parrot had been a house of heat and driftwood. Balcony One would be stone and shadow and slow winter light. But there was something from the old place—some curve of memory—that still lived in his spine.

He pocketed the nail.

And went back to work.

Some friendships don't leave a shadow. They leave a stance, a scent, the shape of your hands after you build something.

Scroll

THE ZITTING ROOM

Zitting Room – Between Shifts

The copper inlay glowed warm beneath Elizabeth's palm. It had been added after his funeral.

Sam loved copper—said it carried not just heat, but truth. The only metal, he claimed, that didn't lie as it aged. Elizabeth never asked where he'd learned that, or if it was even true. It didn't matter.

He always sat at the same table, fingers drumming just shy of rhythm—like he was keeping time with a song only he could hear. After the service, she asked Mateo for the scrap of copper left over from the bar retrofit. Asked him to cut it thin and inlay it there—into the wood where Sam's hand had always rested.

Mateo didn't speak. Just nodded. Then carved it in before the next moon.

No one mentioned it aloud.

But from then on, whenever anyone sat there, they set their hand down gently, like it was over someone's pulse.

Now, years later, it still held warmth.

Even before she touched it.

As if grief, when given shape, could hold temperature.

Not heat or chill—something else.

Warm—like breath. Or memory. Or something remembering her back.

She'd already wiped that spot three times. Still, her hand circled back—absently, like polishing a thought.

The Zitting Room was still in the way that wasn't quiet but compressed.

The air carried something floral—sweet but not named.

Bougainvillea, maybe. But it was too early in the season.

Too early for blooms.

Too late for imagining them.

A blue glass sweated quietly at the head of the table.

No one had touched it in hours.

She straightened the napkins without reason.

Spine stiff.

Jaw set.

Movements too precise to be casual.

Outside the doorway, the bar murmured with late afternoon rhythms:

The clink of cutlery.

The muffled laugh of Brooke teasing Mateo.

The long sigh of the building settling into its bones.

But here—

Here it felt like a held breath.

It had always been like this in the Zitting Room.

Even before it had a name.

It wasn't meant to be a room.

Just a hollow—an architectural accident between the bar and the back pantry.

Thick adobe walls.

A sunken floor.

A window too high to see through unless you meant to.

But Sam had claimed it.

Not by declaration.

By rhythm.

By repetition.

He came often, never alone.

Brothers. Clients. Cousins. Wives—all of them his.

Elizabeth learned the sound of his boots before she saw him.

When he walked in, the staff simply knew—

The room would be needed.

It wasn't a reservation.

It was gravity.

He brought stories.

And laughter.

And wine when it was forbidden.

He paid for strangers' meals without telling them.

Tipped cooks more than waiters because he said, "Service starts with fire."

Every Christmas Eve, he booked the whole place—

Not officially, not on paper.

But by presence.

He'd walk in with a wrapped box in his arms and leave it behind the bar—no name on the tag.

He told Mateo once, "It's for the building. She's older than all of us."

They toasted in this room.

They cried here too.

Sometimes weddings were whispered into being in these booths.

Other times, things dissolved just as quietly.

Elizabeth remembered the year he brought six pies and no explanation.

Or the day he sang mariachi verses in fractured Spanish to make a grieving man smile.

The staff didn't call it the private dining room anymore.

They called it the Zitting Room.

Not because he'd bought it.

Because he'd filled it.

And when he died—

the room emptied.

Not literally.

Not even all at once.

But something core went quiet.

People still used it—at first.

But quieter.

Smaller groups.

Shorter visits.

The laughter never returned at the same pitch.

The chairs never quite faced the right way.

And that copper inlay—

the one under Elizabeth's palm now—

had begun to warm differently.

Before, it hummed like music.

Now, it pulsed like warning.

She didn't tell anyone that.

Didn't tell Mateo or Brooke or even George when he asked if the floor needed resealing.

It wasn't the floor.

It was the memory.

The walls here weren't painted—they were remembered.

Rust-colored plaster layered like weather.

She'd once asked Cynthia why she painted it that way.

Cynthia just said, "Because pigment is easier to layer than pain."

The booths weren't comfortable. They weren't meant to be. They invited confession, not ease.

You could sit in them and feel safe.

But never hidden.

They were designed—maybe unintentionally—for selective vulnerability.

Elizabeth still didn't know if Sam realized that.

But he'd made use of it, all the same.

She looked at the blue glass again. Sweating—still full.

There were six glasses, always six.

Tonight, there were five.

She did a count.

Then did it again.

Still five.

No overturned chairs.

No broken stems.

No sound of departure.

Just absence.

She straightened the napkins.

Twice.

Then sat at the corner of the table where Sam used to take his second drink.

Never the first—he gave that to someone else.

She poured a small shot of cognac from the decanter Mateo never touched.

Held it in the light.

Swirled it once.

Then drank.

Not to honor.

Not to forget.

But to calibrate.

The copper inlay beneath her elbow warmed again.

Like acknowledgment.

Like breath.

She turned toward the mirror above the sideboard.

It caught her shape.

But not her weight.

Her movement.

But not her timing.

It was off.

Just enough to suggest that someone else might appear at any moment.

A faint vibration hummed beneath the table legs.

She felt it in her boots.

A string being plucked without sound.

Her hand moved back to the copper.

Pressed flat.

From somewhere behind the mirror, a smell emerged.

Cologne.

Not strong.

Just… specific.

Warm and pine-edged.

Clean.

Her throat tightened.

She didn't say his name.

Not yet.

 She stood.

Crossed to the corner booth.

Pressed her palm to the back seam in the leather—

the place where the stitching never quite held.

It had split the year Sam died.

No one repaired it.

Maybe no one could.

There were things in the building that resisted repair. Some wounds weren't meant to close.

They stayed open like breath—like the mirror, like the seam in the booth, like the space Sam used to fill with stories and heat and that crooked smile that turned confessions into invitations.

She'd pressed her hand to that split in the leather so many times, she could trace it now with her eyes closed. It had grown softer over the years, not frayed, just… resigned.

The seam no longer looked broken.

It looked honest.

As if the building itself had chosen to carry its own grief visibly—like a scar you don't cover because it means someone mattered.

George once offered to patch it. Said he had the right thread, the right tools.

She shook her head.

Told him, "It's not the leather that needs mending."

And he had nodded, once. Then never brought it up again. The chandelier above her dimmed, then steadied.

Outside the Zitting Room, the restaurant moved on. Dishes clinked. A chair scraped. A door creaked. Here—nothing moved. But everything waited. Sophia did too. She watched from the shadow behind the mirror. Not out of malice. Not even protection.

Curiosity.

Recognition.

Some blend of watching and wanting.

Elizabeth didn't feel her exactly. She felt toward her. Like a draft toward a window she hadn't noticed was open. She poured another drink.

"Some ghosts wear cologne," she whispered.

"And leave through the front door."

Then she laughed once—sharp, soft, unbeckoned.

She didn't choose Sophia. Sophia had already chosen her. Not out of favor—out of recognition. Something in Elizabeth let Sophia stay. Balcony One had already renamed her—Sophia. She couldn't remember why or where she came from. But she remembered the way Elizabeth stood. The way her silence made space. So she stayed and she would follow.

The blue glass shimmered.

Six again.

No sound.

No splash.

Just six.

Each one sweating now.

She shut her eyes.

Hard.

When she opened her eyes,

the copper inlay glowed slightly beneath her palm.

Not metaphorically.

Actually.

The glow didn't pulse or flicker. It just held—steady, warm, faintly golden like the sun caught in copper pennies long forgotten in a jar. It was quiet light. Meant for proximity, not spectacle.

Elizabeth's fingers hovered.

She wasn't testing it. She wasn't doubting herself.

She was remembering—not a moment, but a pattern.

The way Sam used to lean in just before delivering a secret. The way the room seemed to tighten its edges, drawing the walls closer, whenever he told a truth too strange for surface conversation.

This was that feeling.

The copper wasn't illuminated by physics.

It was participating.

She glanced toward the mirror.

Still blank.

Still booth.

Still invitation.

But this time, the reflection trembled—not like water disturbed, but like breath held a fraction too long.

Something was waking up.

Not returning.

Not haunting.

Just waking.

Elizabeth set her palm back on the inlay.

And whispered—half to herself, half to the room—

"I know."

And the mirror no longer showed the room at all.

It showed the booth.

But not as it was now.

It showed it brighter. Warmer. Lit by afternoon sun that couldn't possibly reach that far. Someone had just left. The glass was half-full. The napkin unfolded, not used. There was no Elizabeth in the reflection. No present tense at all.

Only atmosphere.

Only a moment caught in repetition.

The mirror was not malfunctioning.

It was remembering.

Or asking her to.

The kind of memory that didn't play in sequence. The kind that waited behind smell, or touch, or an unfinished sentence. She didn't move her eyes from the glass.

Not because she feared what would return.

But because she didn't want to miss what might.

And for a moment, just a fraction, her own reflection caught up to her. And then the booth disappeared again. It had always obeyed the room before.

Mirrors do that—reflect what's given. Keep to their assignment. But now, it resisted. Or perhaps it had simply chosen something else to reflect.

The booth it showed was untouched. No body. No motion. Just the quiet arrangement of what could happen.

The chair was already pulling out—deliberate. Like a gesture too long delayed.

She didn't cry. Not this time. Her grief had long ago calcified into a finer mineral—something ceremonial, mineral-bound, nearly sacred. This wasn't a pang. It was a rite.

Elizabeth watched the movement with stillness.

Let it finish.

Let it settle.

The wood dragged softly across the tile. That familiar hush. That pressure change. That micro-lift of air.

The chair didn't face her.

It faced the copper.

Like it remembered where he used to sit.

And wasn't quite ready to leave.

Just the booth where Sam used to sit.

There were days she thought the booth might split open.

Not in a violent way. Not with splinters or sound. But with a slow, deliberate cleaving—like wood remembering it had once been tree, and the tree remembering storm.

She felt the edges of it now, the seams of a secret pressing outward, soft and constant, like steam behind stone.

Sam wasn't in that booth.

But something of him was.

Not a ghost. Not a residue. A pattern.

It pulsed beneath the cushion. Curled in the armrest. Folded itself into the grain. It was how he stayed—not through memory, but through mechanism. He had left behind a rhythm.

And Elizabeth, for all her silence, was still keeping time.

She stepped closer.

Her hand hovered just above the backrest. Not touching.

She didn't want to invoke.

She wanted to align.

And the booth, impossibly, leaned.

It hadn't changed.

The wood held its grain. The backrest, its angle. The cushion still sagged where his weight used to settle. She'd expected wear. A slump, a seam. But the booth held—like it had chosen not to change.

No one had preserved it. It had just—remembered.

It was the only booth no one sat in anymore—not by rule, but by rhythm. Guests overlooked it. Servers forgot it. Even Brooke, precise as ever, skipped over it when assigning placements. As if the air around it whispered not yet.

Elizabeth felt the draw.

But didn't move.

She understood thresholds. Knew that some rooms require an offering before entry. And this—this was not just about Sam.

It was about the building. The naming. The ache that lived inside adobe and plaster, inside furniture and ceremony.

The Zitting Room had accepted its name.

But it had not yet finished its echo.

And echoes, she'd learned, are not repetitions.

They are responses.

And a chair pulling itself out,

slowly.

She knew the sound it would make before it did.

That soft scrape—not abrasive, but weighted. Like a memory dragging its feet toward her. A sound she could trace in her body before it reached her ears.

It wasn't loud.

It didn't need to be.

The room had already stilled for it, made space for its arrival the way lungs make space for a held breath. The Zitting Room wasn't reacting—it was participating. It had always been good at that. Containing without compressing. Receiving without needing to define.

The chair stopped.

A half-turn.

An angle of welcome, not command.

The kind of gesture Sam would make when inviting someone into a story—when the plot was about to pivot, but the tone hadn't yet warned you. The kind of angle that suggested: This will matter, but not yet. Sit anyway.

Elizabeth stepped forward—not into the booth, not toward the chair.

Just one step closer.

To confirm it.

To accept it.

And with that step, the chandelier above her flickered—once, then steadied.

A witness.

A yes.

Like an invitation.

Or a warning.

She'd learned not to dismiss those two as opposites.

Invitations came cloaked in danger all the time. And warnings—true ones—always bore a trace of tenderness. This felt like both. Not because she feared what was coming, but because she knew it had already begun.

The air was denser now.

Not heavy—consecrated. The way air changes just before a storm, or after a prayer.

Some rooms only activate when the right person enters with the right kind of silence.

She stood still enough to let the room breathe her in. Let it decide.

And it did.

The light shifted—barely. Just enough to tilt the shadows away from the booth, pulling them into the corners like skirts being gathered. She saw the glint again on the copper inlay. Not glowing now. Reflecting. Holding something not yet visible.

The cognac on the floor hadn't dried.

Her bootprint sat clean inside it.

A single step.

The mirror pulsed once—an irregular shimmer, like a fish under water.

And the air, impossibly, carried a second scent.

Not bougainvillea.

Not cologne.

Something almost mineral.

Like stone touched by fire.

She moved away from the table.

One boot landed in a small puddle.

Cognac.

Not hers.

Not spilled.

Just… present.

She knelt.

Touched the wood.

It was wet.

But there was no glass nearby.

It was not the presence of a drink.

It was the presence of a moment.

That cognac had no source, no trail, no logical arrival. It had simply become real, the way certain dreams linger in the body longer than they should.

Elizabeth crouched again, slowly.

She traced her finger across the ring of dampness—not searching for meaning, but for confirmation. It wasn't a spill. It was a marking. An echo condensed into liquid. A communion poured by memory itself.

And she could taste it before it reached her lips.

Char. Citrus. Something old and green.

Something Sam never drank but always ordered.

For someone else.

This wasn't a haunting.

It was a hosting.

And she—still kneeling, still unsure—had been invited to witness.

Nothing broken.

No trail.

She pressed two fingers into it.

Then brought them to her lips.

Bitter.

Not from the bottle.

Not from now.

The chandelier flickered again.

The scent of bougainvillea returned—thicker now.

Too strong to ignore.

But not artificial.

Like bloom pressed into wood.

Like a gift too long wrapped.

Sophia was closer now.

Still behind the mirror.

Still unseen.

But more willing.

Willing—but not summoned.

Sophia didn't arrive like the others. She didn't press through thresholds or leave trails of temperature. Her presence came like the suggestion of movement in a still frame—subtle, peripheral, almost mistaken. Almost.

Elizabeth never said her name aloud. Not because she was afraid—because she knew it would interrupt something.

There was a thread between them. Not language. Not lineage. Something quieter. A sympathy that lived under the visible. Panagiota, Sophia, the name didn't matter. What mattered was the hush.

It wasn't haunting.

It was hospitality.

The kind that only old houses learn how to offer—rooms within rooms, grief within grace, and mirrors that listen more than they reflect.

The scent of bougainvillea grew sharper, not artificial now, not even floral. It was becoming earthy, root-bound, as though the bloom had turned backward into seed.

Sophia was listening.

Not to be remembered.

But to remember.

Elizabeth's fingers hovered over the copper inlay.

Still warm.

Still pulsing.

Then it went cold.

Just like that.

The kind of cold that meant something had moved.

She turned back toward the door.

But the handle looked farther away.

She blinked.

Still six glasses.

Still one empty booth.

Still the split in the seam.

That seam had never widened.

Not once.

Despite weather, pressure, time—despite hands pressing into it night after night, grief rubbing itself into the edges like oil into stone. It had split the year Sam died, and then stopped. As if the room itself had gasped, and then held its breath for the next four years.

Elizabeth ran her hand along it now.

She didn't expect revelation. Just the texture of ache. The quiet proof that memory still lived in the seam.

And it did.

It offered no new clues. No symbols. No ghosts reaching out of shadows. Just that same, exact gap.

But something in the air had changed.

There was a soft magnetism to it now. A tug beneath her ribs. Like something gently asking *Are you sure?* before opening a deeper drawer.

She didn't answer aloud.

But she kept her hand there.

That was enough.

But the room felt taller.

Thinner.

She said his name softly. Not to bring him back. Just to name the place where he still touched the room. Names didn't work like that here. They weren't summons. They were surrender. Acknowledging what already hovered near, shaping the air, warming the copper, pressing bougainvillea into the seams.

His name didn't echo.

It rested.

Like it belonged there. Like it had never left. It fell into the architecture—absorbed rather than bounced. That was the Zitting Room's gift: nothing spoken in it ever truly ended. It just folded inward.

Elizabeth felt something unfold in return.

Not dramatic. Not ghostly.

Just a loosening in her chest, like a ribbon coming undone.

No wind.

No shimmer.

Only the silence of being heard.

"Sam."

The chandelier went dark.

Elizabeth wasn't concerned.

She had long since stopped fearing the dark in this building. The dark here was not void. It was velvet. It held shape. Sometimes scent. Sometimes memory. Tonight, it held Sam.

And something else.

The laughter beneath the floor was not echo. It had roundness. Depth. A voice memory. Not a hallucination, not a haunting. A presence felt so physically she could trace its contour in her jaw.

She didn't call out.

Calling out was for disbelief.

This—this was belief in stillness. Belief that the floorboards remembered where he last stood. Belief that some part of him had not left, just sunk—quietly—into the adobe and the wine-stained wood.

The chandelier remained dark. But she could still see—not with her eyes, but with that other sense.

The one that comes when memory and presence blur.

And from the floor beneath her feet—the faint sound of laughter.

She had forgotten how laughter could thrum like that—how it could arrive not from joy, but from return. That sound didn't belong to a person anymore. It belonged to the place. To the Zitting Room. To whatever dimension it bent open each time someone remembered just right.

She listened, long enough to feel her spine adjust, as if aligning to the same harmonic.

And the floor?

It sang.

Low, like the beginning of a chant. A gathering. A chord waiting for its second note.

She placed both palms on the copper inlay now, grounding herself—not to stay, but to stay connected.

Laughter isn't always joy. Sometimes it's the sound your chest makes when something inside finally hears itself.

And Elizabeth had found hers.

Low.

Rounded.

Beloved.

Then gone.

She didn't follow it.

Didn't chase the sound or ask it to return. Some things—when they go—leave a door open behind them, and that's enough. The room felt taller now. Wiser. The air no longer pressed against her. It held her—steady, without weight.

Elizabeth stood slowly.

The copper beneath her hands had cooled again, not with absence, but with rest. The kind of cool that comes after a fever breaks.

Balance, not withdrawal.

She glanced toward the mirror.

It no longer shimmered.

It reflected.

Truly, fully.

No warping of time. No delay. Just her. Boots damp at the heel. Cognac drying on the floor. Six glasses, still. And the booth—still turned ever so slightly, as if waiting for one last guest.

The room had heard her.

The house had answered.

And for now—that was enough.

But it left something behind.

Nothing she could smell or hear. Just a shift—small, insistent, like the room had blinked. Like the molecules in the room had rearranged themselves to make space for the memory that had just passed through. The silence wasn't emptiness. It was occupied.

She scanned the room—not with suspicion, but with permission. Each object had taken on a kind of posture. The glasses stood straighter. The table seemed heavier. The air thickened, not with fear, but with form.

It was a form she knew.

Not by sight.

By resonance.

It wasn't Sam's form exactly—but it was born of him. As if the room had taken the shape of his absence and kept it like a mold. Not to trap him. To trace him.

She whispered again.

Not his name this time.

Just one word:

"Still."

And the copper beneath her hand pulsed—once.

Not heat.

Not light.

Just acknowledgment.

Some rooms remember how to listen even after the voices are gone.

Scroll

THE OUTDOOR PATIO

Outdoor Patio – The Ritual Begins

Out back, the building softened.

It didn't vanish.

It recalibrated.

The adobe didn't bow out of view—it inhaled. As if the building itself knew the value of exhale. After the kitchens, the corridors, the rooms of remembered ache—this was where the structure let itself loosen.

The walls curved not as shelter but as offering.

You could feel it in your ribs—the way tension dropped one vertebra at a time, the way the gravel gave slightly under your heel, not enough to trip, just enough to remind you that the ground could shift.

And it had, once.

More than once.

This was the only part of Balcony One never designed on blueprints. It had been drawn by memory and made permanent by mistake. Sam had called it "the spillover," like it wasn't a patio but an aftermath. A place where the building couldn't help but keep speaking, even after the meal had ended.

It was where the inside exhaled into open air.

And where Elizabeth could finally hear herself again.

The adobe curved toward the canyon in a half-embrace, forming a courtyard ringed in raw timber, blooming sage, and strings of lights strung like constellations on fishing wire.

It didn't matter how many times she saw it.

This curve—the way the building cupped the canyon like a promise half-kept—always took her breath away.

The sage didn't bloom for spectacle. It bloomed because it was time. Because the canyon whispered warm enough and the roots obeyed.

And the new electric lights—strung by George in a reckless hour, hung with Brooke's laughter in the background—caught the dusk as though they were constellations slowly appearing in a sunset sky.

Elizabeth never rearranged them.

Not once.

Even when one sagged, even when a storm rewired a corner, she left them crooked. Beauty, she'd learned, wasn't in balance—it was in continuity.

And here, even the asymmetry had memory.

The patio stones, warm from the day, held their heat into the night—heat, and the sound of heels, forks, fiddles, and stories too loud for the inside rooms.

Elizabeth had always loved it best out here.

Not because it was beautiful.

Because it was true.

This was the one place the building didn't edit itself. It didn't correct posture. It didn't modulate volume. It let the wind interrupt stories. Let the birds crosstalk at twilight. Let grief walk through the tables wearing joy's face.

Out here, people stopped performing being fine.

They leaned. They listened. They unbuttoned their second thoughts and let them breathe.

It was where she could see who people were when they thought no one was watching.

And where she could stop watching herself.

There were no ceilings to press down. No chandeliers to scold. Just the open sky—vast and violet—and the hum of things both present and not. A plank stage stood in the far corner, built by Sam and his brothers on a weekend fueled by whiskey and bravado. It leaned slightly, and she never had it fixed.

It wasn't made for symmetry or code. It was made for sweat and daring and the kind of laughter that only came when something almost fell apart. That stage leaned slightly—leftward, as if listening to its own weight—but it had never collapsed.

Elizabeth remembered the hammer swings between jokes, the way Sam balanced on the edge and shouted for someone to bring him lemonade, then cognac, then both.

And afterward, when the sun went down and the wood still smelled like skin and dust and beginnings, she had stood on it barefoot, arms loose at her sides, and felt something align.

Not with the men.

With the canyon.

The stage never needed fixing.

It was honest.

Tonight was Tuesday.

It always arrived differently.

Sometimes with wind. Sometimes with stillness. But Tuesday had a spine.

Even when the week blurred—when grief ran over from Monday or joy tried to spill into Wednesday—Tuesday kept its shape. It didn't ask for attention. It asked for return.

And people came.

Not just locals.

Not just loyalists.

People who didn't know why they came back until the music started and something in their chest fell into alignment—like vertebrae adjusting in the presence of truth.

Tuesday wasn't on the calendar.

It was in the body.

And Elizabeth had learned to follow it like a tide.

Which meant ritual.

Not in the ceremonial sense—no bells, no blessings, no scripts.

But still: a rhythm. A knowing. The kind of unspoken consensus that drew the same people to the same tables week after week, as if the building itself kept a guest list.

Mariachis tuned under the mesquite. The guitarrón let out a test note that trembled like a second heart.

Elizabeth moved through the tables, half-watching, half-waiting. Her hands knew the ritual: adjust the chair, straighten the napkin, sweep the corner with her boot. She wasn't sure when Tuesday became sacred. Only that it had.

At first, it had just been convenience.

A night when the kitchen wasn't overrun, when the deliveries had been sorted, when the staff was loose enough to improvise. But it didn't stay that way.

Rituals rarely announce themselves.

They accrue.

A violinist showed up once without asking, then came again the next week. A pair of widows began sharing dessert and silence at the same table. Someone started bringing bougainvillea wrapped in newsprint, always left near the edge of the stage. No name. No note.

Elizabeth didn't orchestrate it.

She allowed it.

That was the difference.

To force rhythm was to kill it. To notice it—and make space—that was something else. That was devotion.

So when Mateo asked why they never ran a formal event on Tuesdays, she simply said, "Because it already is one."

And Brooke, years later, would call it "the hush between story and song."

But tonight—

tonight felt older than any of that.

As if the ritual had remembered something even she hadn't.

The way the air moved. The way the canyon light took longer to leave. The way the blue glasses looked darker before they were filled. There was a kind of lean to the night, a tilt in the spine of the hour that felt… ancestral.

She glanced toward the sage in the far corner.

It was blooming again.

Early.

Again.

Brooke brought out the candles—blue glass holders set one per table, like offerings. The flames caught the wire of the overhead bulbs and made halos.

"Table Seven says the air smells different," Brooke said, brushing past.

It always started with the air.

Before the first note, before the glasses clinked, even before the candles were lit. The air on Tuesday nights thickened—not with moisture, but with attention.

Brooke was the first to name it out loud, but others had felt it.

The sommelier once stopped mid-pour and whispered, "Someone's praying." A child reached for a napkin and then paused, said it was "too bright." An elder couple—María and José—sat in silence for twenty minutes once, not speaking, just breathing. Later, María explained, "It's not that the patio feels sacred. It's that it reminds you: *you are.*"

Elizabeth never tried to label it.

But she could feel it too.

Especially when the wind came off the canyon in slow braids, wrapping scent around memory. Sometimes it was roasted citrus. Sometimes juniper. Sometimes the faintest hint of mesquite smoke and candle wax and something older—like cedar kept in a locked drawer.

Magnus Pollee muttered something unprintable as he adjusted the lantern over Table Three. The light had started to flicker, not from wind, but from the copper wire he'd re-routed last Tuesday in a rush. He stood with his boots caked with dried mud on a low bench, sleeves rolled to the elbows, hand steady.

"Should've just kept the oil lantern," he said to no one, then added, "but George wants the electrical."

His brown-on-brown dachshund, sat below him like a guardian angel in miniature, tail tapping in time with the guitarist's tuning. She just watched—and her owner would call her Honey.

The bottle wall behind them caught the low flame of the lanterns. Green and amber glass strung on old clothesline wire, each bottle a leftover from a night nobody remembered clearly. Some still had labels: dusty Rioja, a pale rosé with the name smeared into a watercolor bleed. Magnus had wired them into place years ago after a delivery fell off the back of George's mule cart. He'd turned the mess into a mosaic.

"Better than sweepin'," he'd said at the time. Now it was landmark.

Elizabeth watched him twist the lantern's screw with practiced ease, then step down, barefoot on the warm flagstone. The stone held heat like intention. Not blistering—just enduring. Laid in irregular patches, each slab the color of memory: ochre, rust, dust-pink, sun-glazed gold. A mosaic of permanence and error.

Magnus ran a hand over one of the posts—timber so weathered it looked carved from the bones of the building itself. "Still standing," he said, satisfied, and gave Fergus a nod.

Brooke passed him, balancing a tray of blue-glass candleholders.

"Don't touch the bar lights again, Magnus."

"I'd never," he deadpanned.

"Unless they ask me real nice."

She snorted and kept moving.

Elizabeth didn't need to signal him. Magnus knew the rhythm. Knew when to blend in, when to vanish. He didn't try to modulate the moment. He honored it by keeping the structure sound.

He'd reinforced the stage last spring. Rehung the south string of lights after a dust storm took them down. Sanded the bar smooth without being asked. Never asked to be thanked. Just said, *I work. That's the job.*

A guest leaned toward the bottle wall and asked where it came from.

"Accident," Magnus said.

"Most good things are."

And then he was gone.

Elizabeth let her eyes follow the line of the bottle wall, the curvature of the adobe, the slight lean of the old plank stage. None of it was symmetrical. All of it was remembered. The wind curled past the wine bottles and made them sing—a thin, reedy sound like a voice far off.

The patio was not perfect. But it was held. She called it the Threshold Air. It didn't ask questions. It asked for posture. You entered the patio differently—a little straighter. A little slower. As if the air had rules. As if the moment was about to begin. Elizabeth nodded.

It always does.

The guests came early on Tuesdays. They lingered longer. Couples took the outside tables even when it got cold, just to be near the music. Elders came to remember, young ones came to forget, and Elizabeth—

Elizabeth came to listen.

Clara stood near the back fence, wrapped in a shale-colored shawl that caught the breeze but not the chill.

The shawl had belonged to her mother.

Elizabeth had only seen her wear it on nights like this—when the sky was more velvet than void, and the air carried something unnamable between blessing and reckoning. Clara didn't wear the shawl for warmth. She wore it for memory. The threads had seen things. Held things. Been present at births, at deaths, at Tuesday rituals where laughter turned into silence mid-song.

Clara didn't stand at the fence for show. She stood because that's where she felt most useful. She wasn't watching Elizabeth. She was watching the moment. Guarding its perimeter. Not like a soldier, but like a witness making sure the story was being told right.

Her eyes flicked from the stage, to the long table, to the woman setting candles. Every detail mattered. Not because she needed control— but because the evening deserved its integrity.

And Elizabeth—

Elizabeth welcomed the scrutiny.

There weren't many people left who understood the weight of beauty when it asked to be held steady. But Clara did. And when their eyes met across the drift of candlelight, Elizabeth saw it:

That nod.

Not soft.

But approving.

Like a baton passing through breath.

She simply watched—first the stage, then Elizabeth. Her expression wasn't soft, exactly, but there was recognition in it.

Clara had once said—half-drunk, half-prayerful—that some people tended houses, some tended people, and some tended the space between.

"That's the trickiest," she'd whispered.

"It has no title."

Elizabeth had remembered that.

And tonight, watching Clara's stance—not stern, but sovereign—she felt the full weight of what it meant to hold that in-between. To carry the ache and the music. To make sure the space stayed porous enough for spirit, but strong enough for structure.

The elders called it threshold-keeping.

Clara never used the term.

But she embodied it.

The way she shifted just enough to give space to the musicians warming up. The way she let her shawl catch the wind, not to fight it but to translate it. The way her silence deepened the sound around her.

Elizabeth realized she wasn't just looking at Clara. She was mirroring her. Without meaning to, she had taken the same stance—feet apart, shoulders relaxed, eyes soft but alert.

They were both tending. Not just to the ritual. But to what the ritual allowed. Memory. Mystery. And that impossible thing Sam once called joy without cost. That thing they both knew didn't exist. And guarded anyway.

A nod from one woman tending a legacy to another.

She had once laughed at this very ritual. Years ago, when the band had been smaller—and *she* had been larger, belly full with Sam's third child. Elizabeth had spilled wine on her apron that night and cursed under her breath. Clara had laughed—not at her, but for her. It was a permission Elizabeth hadn't known she needed.

Above, in the uppermost pane of a darkened window, a figure stood still as glass. Sophia. Watching.

She always chose that window.

Not for vantage. Not for symbolism.

But because it overlooked everything and revealed nothing.

Sophia didn't haunt. That word was too human, too full of intent and ache. What she did was closer to resonance. Like a note held in a closed piano. You didn't hear it—but everything else was tuned around it.

Elizabeth had long stopped looking away.

The first few months, she had ignored the silhouette. Had told herself it was reflection, or shadow, or stress. But one Tuesday—months into grief, deep into a bottle—she had looked up, really looked, and nodded.

The figure had not nodded back.

But the wind had changed direction.

Sophia never interrupted.

She witnessed.

And what she witnessed, she anchored.

Tonight, her presence steadied the back half of the ritual—the part after the music started, when memory got slippery and wine got honest. The figure in the glass was still as ever. But the room?

The room remembered to keep its posture.

She watched and witnessed.

Not out of envy or grief, but reverence. For the room. For the ritual. For the way something beautiful had been returned, again, to the ground.

Sam's corner table sat empty tonight. Not abandoned. Appointed.

That table had become more than a seat. More than a place-setting. It was a constellation now—fixed, unspoken, known. No one asked to sit there. No one offered it to a guest who didn't know. Even children veered around it instinctively, as if some deeper code in their bones whispered: *Not here.*

It hadn't been declared sacred.

It had become sacred by use. By rhythm. By loss.

Elizabeth had once tried to remove the second glass. Just once. On a night the rain threatened and the wind pulled sideways. She'd stepped toward the table, hand outstretched, and stopped cold.

She could feel it, that deep inner sense—like when a voice falls just out of key and the body tenses in reply. The table needed its symmetry. Its duet. Even in absence.

Especially in absence.

So now, she left the bottle. Left the glasses. Wiped the surface, never too dry. Let the condensation form on its own, like breath returning. It was the only table she didn't reset. Because it reset her.

His chair still faced west, where the light left last. Two blue glasses stood side by side—one full, one not. A bottle of cognac rested between them. She left it untouched. Touching it would have made it ordinary. A gesture too close to performance.

That bottle wasn't a drink. It was a placeholder. A presence. The only object in the entire patio that refused metaphor. It was just what it was—a bottle waiting for the right hand to reach it, and that hand no longer lived here. The staff knew not to clear it. The guests knew not to pour from it.

Brooke once placed her hand near it and said,

"It feels like someone already claimed it." Then never did so again.

Elizabeth let it sit.

Night after night, Tuesday after Tuesday, its level unchanged. Sometimes sweating. Sometimes dry. Always centered.

Sometimes she thought the bottle aged differently than the others. As if the air around it moved in a separate time signature. She didn't test the theory. There were mysteries you didn't interrogate. Only respect.

A hush descended—not silence, but sync.

It was the kind of hush that held weight.

Not the absence of sound, but the agreement of it.

Even the cicadas paused. Even the wind took a quieter route through the mesquite. You could hear the flick of a napkin being unfolded, the tiny shift of a shoe adjusting under a chair, the creak of a wine cork slightly too long in the bottle.

Every movement became intentional.

Not out of control.

Out of reverence.

This was the moment the ritual knew itself. Not through announcement or cue—but through alignment. As if the patio exhaled and the canyon responded in kind.

Elizabeth paused mid-step, not because she had to. Because she wanted to feel it pass through her. This hush wasn't an interruption. It was an invitation.

To listen.

To remember.

To ready.

Clinks aligned. Laughter curved toward harmony. Forks paused mid-air. Then the first note. The horns burst like the canyon had opened. And the room—the building, the people, the sky—shifted. Just a little. The guitarist wore black, with silver at the cuffs. He wasn't the usual one. But the rhythm accepted him.

That's how you knew it was Tuesday—the ritual didn't demand familiarity. It demanded coherence. And this man, with a voice like silk pulled against stone, found his place before the first verse ended.

His cuffs caught the light—silver, but not polished. A little tarnished. A little real. Like the kind of adornment passed down from a grandfather who never gave compliments, only tools. When he sang, people forgot their plates. When he paused, they remembered who they were eating with.

And in that space—between note and next—Elizabeth felt something loosen in her ribs. The space that came when both had lived in the same room long enough to start speaking the same language—a shiver from the chilled air—butterflies swarming whispfully. She didn't know his name. The canyon had already accepted him. And so had the sky.

His voice was rough silk, and the melody was old, older than Elizabeth, older than the adobe, maybe even older than the canyon. Children danced. Grandmothers wept. Strangers found rhythm without names.

Elizabeth moved slower.

Sophia watched.

Mateo came out with a tray of carnitas and roasted quince. He raised one brow at the stage.

"They're good."

"They're right," Elizabeth said.

He grinned.

"Same thing."

She watched him retreat to the kitchen, then turned back toward the crowd.

It was easier, sometimes, to watch them go.

Not out of detachment.

Out of trust.

Mateo knew the beat of the night better than anyone except maybe Sam. He didn't ask for cues—he moved with the room. Knew when to step in, when to let the candles speak, when to pull back before the music swelled.

Elizabeth often marveled at it—not his timing, but his restraint. He never tried to lead the ritual. He supported it. Which, she'd come to learn, was the harder thing.

In the early years, she'd tried to orchestrate everything—the timing of the cognac pour, the lighting change between sets, the exact moment for the bread to arrive. But beauty didn't bloom under command. It needed room.

And tonight, the room had exactly that.

A ritual is not repetition. It is recognition—again and again.

Scroll

THE SPIRAL APPEARS

Balcony One - Outdoor Patio

She watched Mateo's silhouette disappear through the building arch, felt the hum of the guitarist's next phrase, and turned again toward the pulse of the patio—not to manage it. To witness it. Like the building did. Like Sophia did.

Like something much older had always done.

The band was into their second set now—slower, darker tones threading beneath the brighter brass. It wasn't mournful. Just deeper. Like the canyon when the light left it.

Sam had called this place a mouth once. Not a grave, he'd said. A mouth. It was an image she returned to more often than she admitted. The mouth. Not devouring. Receiving. Not consuming. Composing.

It helped her understand the way this place held stories—not like a book, but like a body. Scars, muscle memory, places of soreness and strange strength. People didn't just dine here. They exhaled here. They let go of burdens not by setting them down, but by having them sung into something bearable.

That's what the mouth did.

It digested.

And sometimes sings.

Even when the sky above was indifferent—stars spinning with no regard for grief—this patio, this mouth, remained loyal. It never forgot who had laughed here. Or wept here. Or loved so completely they had no words left afterward.

It remembered Sam. And Aris's hands when he built the stage.

And the shawl Clara wore when her water broke in spring.

And the night George hung his first lantern, whispering to no one, "May this light outlast me."

The mouth never said thank you.

It just kept opening.

And remembering.

She hadn't understood it then.

It had sounded indulgent—Sam at his most poetic, most infuriating. Always spinning metaphors from salt and steam. But later, years later, when she stood in the patio alone after everyone had gone, she finally felt it.

The echo.

The pull.

Like the earth itself wanted to taste what had happened here.

The patio didn't consume memory—it metabolized it. Turned joy into heat. Turned grief into root. Held it, not like burden, but like ingredient.

When the wind moved just right, she could smell the meals Sam had ordered and left unfinished. Could hear the echo of his boots scuffing the edge of the stage. Could almost feel the way his shoulder bumped hers in that casual, familial way he had—like punctuation.

And when she thought of his metaphor now, she no longer dismissed it.

The patio was a mouth.

But it didn't bite.

It remembered.

A place that tasted what you gave it, and never forgot.

Elizabeth had laughed at him then.

She had called him dramatic.

But only because he was right.

And that kind of truth always came wrapped in mischief with Sam—he never offered it plainly. He wove it into jokes, buried it in flirtation, let it smolder beneath a story that sounded too good to be factual. But the truths, when they surfaced, had teeth.

That night, when she laughed and rolled her eyes, he hadn't defended himself.

He just smiled like someone who had already been proven correct by time.

And maybe he had.

Now, she saw it everywhere—the mouth of the place. The way it opened toward the canyon, receiving every sound, every song, every grief. The way it waited for people to offer themselves. Not loudly. Just honestly.

There was a reason people cried here and didn't know why.

A reason forgiveness got whispered over carnitas and old quarrels dissolved at the bottom of blue glasses. This wasn't a restaurant. It was a vessel. And Sam had seen that from the beginning. Even if he never said so outright. He lived it into being.

But later that same night, she'd found the copper rings he'd left on the bar, still warm. He was always like that—doing something wild and then walking away like it had been ordinary.

Now, when the music shifted, she felt it too.

There was always a moment—small, nearly imperceptible—when the music stopped being performance and became something else. Like the night needed a language and the band had found it.

The shift wasn't in tempo or pitch. It was in intention. In the way the violin began to feel like thread, stitching memories together beneath the skin. In the way the horn didn't announce, but reminded. And in that moment, Elizabeth always paused her breath.

She let the air come in differently, like a guest she hadn't greeted yet. She let the ache under her ribs surface. The one that didn't have a name, only a temperature. It came on these nights. Only these nights. The ache of too much held and not enough said. She didn't cry. Not anymore. But she did listen harder. Because something in the music always knew her name. Even when she didn't speak it aloud.

The mouth, hungry. Not for food or song or applause—but for memory. For ritual. For the cost of joy. She glanced at Sam's table.

Two glasses. One full, one not. The bottle of cognac, sweating in the warm air. His chair still faced west, where the last light clung to the ridge. She hadn't touched any of it. It had become its own kind of altar. Not one with candles or flowers—those would have made it smaller. More graspable. No, this was an altar of restraint. An altar of not touching. Because the not-touching was the prayer.

To leave something exactly as it had been left—glass, bottle, chair— was to honor not the person, but the interruption. The unfinish.

Sam hadn't planned his last visit. Hadn't given a speech or written a letter. He'd just left. One week he was there, the next he wasn't.

And this table—this arrangement—held that rupture.

Elizabeth couldn't explain it, not even to herself. But every time she walked past, she felt the ache of pause. The echo of an unfinished toast. The vibration of a joke that hadn't landed yet.

Grief was often too loud.

But this—

This was quiet grief.

Grief that stayed exactly where you left it, waiting for you to circle back. No need to resolve it. Just to know it was still warm. She wouldn't. Because the moment something else. It belonged to the space between. Between sip and song. Between Sam's laughter and his silence. Between what they'd built and what they'd lost.

Elizabeth knew better than to reach into that space. Some silences weren't meant to be filled. They were meant to be witnessed. That's why she stood a little to the side. That's why her hands stayed at her sides. That's why she never let her gaze rest too long on the bottle.

To honor someone like Sam, you didn't replicate them. You let the space they carved remain open. An invitation. And the cognac?

It was for George.

And the Jack Daniels?

It was for Aris.

But the wine. All the wine

The wine was for Sam.

In the far corner, two men argued softly in Greek. It was always Greek in that corner. Not always the same men. Not always the same dialect. But the cadence was unmistakable—tight vowels, rolling consonants, the kind of argument that was more music than menace. Elizabeth didn't speak the language, but she recognized the rhythm. It was the sound of home voiced sideways. Not claimed, but remembered.

Sam used to love it. He'd lean toward their table with a smirk, guessing at translations.

"He says the wine's too dry." "No, she says his poetry is." "No, he says the lamb's not as good as his mother's." None of it accurate. All of it forgiven.

The men in the corner had never stopped coming, even after Sam died. They brought their own wine now. Asked for less. Stayed longer. Elizabeth sometimes wondered if they even noticed the music, or if they were part of its root system—old, underground, essential. Their voices braided with the strings. She liked it that way. It made the evening feel multilingual.

Lyric in tongue, abstract in time.

A woman read a worn book at a table meant for six. Someone left a note under a wine glass that said, simply, *Forgive me.* No one claimed it. Then something shifted. Not visibly. Not to most. But Elizabeth felt it—the way the temperature thickened for just a second, the way the pitch of a trumpet note bent too wide and then righted itself like a spine.

A guest tripped on a loose stone near the stage and laughed. The stone never stayed put. Elizabeth had fixed it three times. Mateo, twice. George tried to grind it down entirely, but the building refused. There was something honest about a patio that shifted beneath you. Something earned.

Sam used to call it the *truth stone.* Said if a guest could trip and laugh, they were ready to be part of the ritual. If they scowled, they weren't listening yet. Elizabeth hadn't believed him at first. But over time, she saw the pattern. It was a kind of test, that stone. A small, quiet invitation to fall just enough to notice where you stood. Not to humble. To awaken.

And when that guest laughed tonight—truly laughed, not nervously— Elizabeth felt a thread pull tight between years. Sam had laughed like that, too. Not always because things were funny. But because sometimes, it was the only way to keep things from collapsing. A trip. A laugh. A small, sacred error that made the evening more human..

Magnus reappeared wiping his hands on a rag that had once been a handkerchief, then a potholder, then something else entirely. Honey patiently waiting for him, seemingly knowing not to follow her owner inside the building.

He didn't speak—just checked the lantern posts, one by one, like a farmer counting fence rails before a storm. The glass in the blue candleholders trembled faintly as he passed, a sign the wind had shifted.

Elizabeth watched him pause at the far post—the one Sam had carved a mark into during a summer nobody liked to remember out loud. Magnus touched the wood. Not reverent.

"That one's leaning again," he said, voice low.

"I'll brace it after the last song."

She nodded. No need to thank him. He'd already moved on.

Honey stopped at Sam's table, gave the bottle a single sniff, then sat. Not begging. Not guarding. Just being.

Elizabeth felt a tug in her chest.

Magnus knelt beside the dog, adjusted a wobble in the stone with the heel of his palm.

"Still doing your job, huh?" he muttered to the stone. "Good lad."

Then he rose, dusted his knees, and gave the cognac bottle a nod—not to drink, not to toast. Just a nod. Man to moment. Witness to weight.

Clara watched him from the fence line. She didn't smile. The shawl around her shoulders fluttered, caught the starlight like netting. Magnus gave her a short tip of the chin—acknowledgment without exchange. Then he turned back toward the dark, toward the side gate he'd fixed last fall when the latch came loose and the wind threatened to undo the entire evening.

The latch hadn't failed since. Honey followed, nails clicking softly on the stone, a beat behind. They didn't look back. They didn't have to. The work was done for now. The ritual, still breathing. The stars blinked. The ground sighed.

Elizabeth stepped back instinctively, boots scuffing the edge of the plank stage. The stage had always held more than music. It held intention.

Built in a single weekend, with borrowed tools and a keg of desert beer, it shouldn't have lasted. The boards weren't perfectly cut. The frame wasn't level. But it stood. And in standing, it remembered. Every footstep, every stomp, every silence between notes—it recorded them all, like a ledger kept in rhythm.

Aris had chosen the placement.

A bottle of Jack Daniels.

Off-center.

Atop the wall of bottles

Facing the canyon.

He said it made the sound feel more honest. That was his word: honest.

Elizabeth hadn't understood at the time.

But now, she stood where his boots once had. She felt the uneven slant beneath her soles. The groove where he'd hammered the final nail with a flourish and a dare. The faint echo of songs sung for no one and everyone.

She didn't step onto the stage.

She let it hold the moment without her.

Because that, too, was part of the music.

Knowing when not to enter.

Some inherit land. Others inherit the space between.

Scroll

THE COGNAC BREATHES

Balcony One - Outdoor patio

She reached down and let her fingers find the corner where Sam had once carved his initials. The wood, warm from the day, had taken on a second heat—deeper, pulsing.

There was a new mark beneath the S.

Elizabeth hadn't seen it appear. She cleaned this corner every week. Rubbed oil into the wood. Whispered to it sometimes, when the guests had gone. She would have noticed a new mark. But here it was. A spiral. Small. Precise. Seemingly fresh with intention. The kind of mark someone makes after deciding, but before explaining. It hadn't been there before. And it was unmistakably his.

Sam had drawn spirals into napkins during meetings. Into the fog of windows on cold mornings. Into the sand with the heel of his boot while telling stories too old to be funny. Always spirals. He said they were the shape of memory. Of home. Of whatever came after language ran out.

This one was different. It was carved. Clean lines, shallow enough not to disrupt the wood grain, deep enough to remain if the stage burned. Her breath caught. Slow and deliberate. In alignment.

Like something had folded inward, and now the music could begin again. A spiral. Fresh. Waiting.

The music surged behind her—the guitarrón growling, the violin diving into a final chorus. Glasses lifted. Candles leaned in the breeze. Someone, somewhere, whispered a name that no one answered.

Elizabeth looked up. Sophia's silhouette was gone from the window. Clara stood with her arms folded now, her face unreadable.

The cognac bottle gleamed like a promise unfulfilled.

Elizabeth bent slightly and placed her hand flat against the wood. Her hand hovered first. Not hesitation—recognition. The warmth rose through the grain, slow and deliberate, like something waking. Not heat from the sun or stage lamps. Something older. Something beneath. She didn't press down all at once. Just the heel of her palm, then each finger. The spiral met her skin with a familiarity that ached. It wasn't metaphorical. It was physical. This wood knew her.

Knew her grief before it had a name.

Knew her silences before they became habits.

Knew how many times she had returned to this corner just to remember how time moved through people.

Sam had made that possible.

Because he lived in a way that turned architecture into memory.

Now, her fingers rested in the center of the spiral, and the air around her stilled. Attuned. It felt a tuning fork in her chest, and the patio responded.

Yes, said the grain.

Yes, said the air.

Yes, said the mark he left behind.

Just contact. Skin to memory.

Then she rose, walked to Sam's table, and poured a second glass of cognac—not for herself, not for the bottle's sake, but because the moment had asked for it. She set it beside the first. Perfectly aligned.

The glass touched down with the softest sound. A landing. Like it had been expected.

Two glasses now—one full, one full again. The symmetry was not just visual. It was emotional. Like a promise had been acknowledged on both ends, even if only one was living.

She didn't name it. Didn't whisper anything sentimental into the cognac. The ritual did not need speech. It needed presence. And alignment.

Two glasses, side by side, mirrored and unmoving. One holding time. The other holding what had been lost inside it.

Sam would've laughed at the poetry of it. And then ruined it with a joke about agave and Greek gods. But he would have noticed. The exact angle. The condensation forming at the same rate. The flicker of candlelight bouncing between them.

She stepped back again, slowly, like one does after lighting something sacred. To honor its burn. Two full glasses. A symmetry.

From the back fence, Clara watched. Elizabeth returned to her place near the bar and stood very still. Stillness was not absence.

It was listening.

She didn't fidget. Didn't scan the tables. Didn't perform watchfulness for the sake of appearance. She just stood—boots grounded, shoulders low, eyes soft.

From this stillness, she could feel the shifts that went unnoticed by others. The second vibration in the violin string. The catch in Brooke's throat before she laughed. The exact moment the cognac bottle adjusted to the air.

Stillness gave her access. To the music beneath the music. To the grief behind the ritual. To Sophia, watching. To Sam, waiting. Because they were here, still—just rearranged. Rewritten into the air, the echo, the timbre of the evening.

And when Elizabeth stood still, they could find her.

Because she listened.

And in that listening, the building breathed easier.

The sky leaned closer.

And the memory, ever spiral-shaped, began to sing back.

The song ended. Applause burst like a shaken jar. The band bowed. Someone whistled. The building remembered. And on Tuesday nights—it sang. It sang low. Not melody, but resonance.

The kind of sound you didn't hear in your ears, but felt in your chest, your knees, the space just beneath your sternum. The kind of sound that aligned you to something much older than language. Much deeper than loss.

She let it move through her. The memory wasn't hers alone. It belonged to the floorboards and the far window. To the stone Sam tripped over the first time he danced with Clara. To the wind that circled the patio and never forgot its route.

Each Tuesday added a layer to that song. A vibration.

And tonight, that vibration swelled—rich, round, precise. As if the room had finally remembered every note it had ever held and was humming them all at once. She closed her eyes. To stay. To root. To feel how everything he'd touched was still warm. And how everything she was becoming still answered to his name.

Then, quiet again. The instruments were still, their strings cooling. The candles flickered like they'd heard something they couldn't repeat. Plates cleared. Voices softened. Even the stars adjusted, a few degrees brighter, as if applauding in their own celestial register.

Elizabeth didn't look back at the table. The moment had passed—but not left. It had folded inward, stitched itself into the grain of the patio. Into the cognac. Into the glasses. Into her.

Tuesday would come again. But this Tuesday, this breath, this note— they would not return in quite the same way. That was the cost of memory. And its gift.

She reached for the final candle, shielding it from the wind, then let it go out between her fingers.

No ceremony.

Just closure.

A ritual, gently sealed.

He didn't haunt it. He tuned it.

Scroll

THE BAR

Balcony One – The Hour of Second Pours

The bar was carved from a single slab of pine, thick as a butcher's block and polished to a soft, amber sheen. Brass rails curved up from the floor like question marks, catching the light in lazy arcs. Behind the counter, glassware hung inverted like frozen bells, and liquor bottles stood in reverent rows before a deep-set window that framed the last light of the desert.

The walls were blood-warm, textured, and matte—earthy red. Cynthia had insisted on the color, saying it was the only way to bring Santa Fe inside without losing the shadow. Elizabeth had rolled her eyes at the time. But she had to admit—it held.

Stained glass windows filtered the sunlight into long, colored ribbons that stretched across the bar top, shifting with every hour. When the air turned still, you could hear the glasses hum faintly, like the room held a tuning fork somewhere beneath the floorboards.

The ceiling above was pressed tin, dark and ornate—each square a stamp of pattern, like someone had tried to trap sound overhead.

It was not a bar designed for speed or noise. It was a bar designed to listen. And it listened in layers. Not just to the clink of glasses or the shuffle of boots across the scuffed tile, but to the unsaid. The breath before confession. The silence between names. The heartbeat tucked beneath laughter.

Some places gather dust. Others gather stories. The bar gathered vibration. Each groove in the wood held a tale half-told—fingers that traced a lover's name into the condensation, knuckles that tightened around a glass before letting go. It remembered who asked for the good rye without saying why. Who always left before the music started. Who drank only when the wind blew west.

And it remembered Elizabeth.

Her presence was quiet, but it marked the room like a tuning note. When she moved, the bar adjusted—less like a host, more like a witness giving her space.

Tonight, it held its breath with her. The way one soul acknowledges another through the grain of shared ritual. The bar knew its purpose. And it had never forgotten hers.

Elizabeth ran a cloth along the grain in long, slow strokes. Each stroke carved her back into presence. The cloth met wood with reverence, not efficiency—her palm a metronome that kept time. This wasn't cleaning. It was returning. A motion that steadied her spine, softened her breath, reminded her that the world—even when fractured—could still be touched into coherence.

She moved like someone tuning an instrument. The bar responded in kind with subtle shifts: a brighter glint along the brass, a deeper hue in the amber polish, a tighter hush between glass and wall. As if the whole room recognized the rhythm and adjusted itself to match.

These were her small devotions. They had no name. No audience. But they were seen. By the wood. By the room. By something older than habit and deeper than routine. She didn't pray. Not aloud. But the cloth moved as if it believed reminding herself the world could still be put in order.

Brooke entered from the kitchen hallway, quiet. The hush followed her like steam from a pot—not loud, but present. She had learned the bar's rhythm the hard way: not through instructions, but through correction. The room didn't forgive dropped trays, forced chatter, or careless steps. It wanted presence. Intent. Stillness wrapped in movement. And she had learned. Her steps were nearly soundless now, her breathing matched the space. She knew which floorboard groaned near the till, which tap hissed even when off, which wineglass had the chip no one noticed but her. She had begun to understand that this place didn't just host the living. It hosted the remembered. And sometimes, the difference wasn't obvious. She paused by the till—not out of confusion, but deference. As if asking the room for permission before speaking. Her voice, when it came, was careful.

"You need me to wipe down menus?" Brooke asked.

Elizabeth nodded without looking up.

That nod was its own language. It said yes, of course. But it also said: I see you. I trust you. I know what you're doing costs you something. Around here, those words mattered more than pleasantries.

Elizabeth didn't speak unnecessarily in the bar. Each word spoken in that space had a resonance, and she treated them like ingredients— measured, intentional, precise. The nod served the same purpose.

Brooke received it without blinking, then moved. Like the room itself had whispered instructions in her ear. The bar noticed this.

Elizabeth felt it—subtle as a muscle twitch. The bar appreciating the balance. The fidelity. The continuation of something ritualistic and real.

A low voice murmured from behind the bar.

"Tell Brooke she left the back tray half full."

Magnus slid a coaster beneath a sweating glass, then placed it exactly in line with the edge of the rail. His apron hung lopsided, boots dusted from the alley, collar open just enough to say he'd been moving crates before the shift.

Elizabeth didn't look up.

"She knows."

"She always knows,"

he muttered, mostly to the cognac bottle, then set a new napkin down with the same care a man might fold a flag.

He wasn't loud. Wasn't fast. But his presence had weight—baritone steadiness in a room tuned to alto.

Brooke reentered behind him, glancing at the coaster.

"That yours or mine?"

"Depends," he said.

"You gonna pretend I'm wrong again?"

She smirked and nudged his shoulder as she passed.

Magnus collected three empties from the near corner. Didn't linger. Just moved like someone who knew how the air should feel when it was working right. The bar noticed him too. The way it noticed a tuning fork before sound.

Elizabeth caught his eye just once as he turned for the kitchen. He gave a short nod. A smile. She returned the smile. And as always, he was here.

Then he vanished behind the curtain.

In her periphery, the mirror shimmered with presence. Light, memory, atmosphere—all bending slightly, as if the room had just exhaled.

Then the glass on the bar vanished.

And everything shifted.

Brooke set a water glass down near the till, turned to grab a rag—and when she turned back, the glass was gone. She froze. There was no sound. No clink. Just absence.

Then—It was there again.

Same glass. But now full. With water. The rim beaded with condensation. Brooke stepped back.

"That ain't normal."

Elizabeth looked up, unimpressed, stacking menus onto the pass.

"You know what's not normal?" she said.

"Running doubles on three hours of sleep and a candy diet."

"I didn't touch it."

"I know."

They were quiet.

The mirror on the opposite side of the bar flickered—a gentle double-take of light. A reflection that almost matched the motion in the room—Sophia, though she hadn't been called that in life. The building named her differently.

Panagiota had died.

Sophia remained.

Sophia's shape stood there for less than a breath.

Gone.

Brooke didn't scream. But she reached for the menu stack like it was something to hold onto.

Elizabeth turned back to the bar, pressed her palm to the wood.

The grain throbbed.

The room remembered.

* * *

Later, Brooke would find herself standing in the walk-in with no memory of having walked there. The metal door ajar, her breath fogging against the sealed air, hands cradling a bottle she hadn't meant to touch.

She would blink and see the glass again (the one from the bar) resting on a crate of oranges. Full. No condensation. Ice melting slowly. She took a single step back. The door whispered closed behind her. She did not scream. She whispered,

"*Please.*"

To what, she wasn't sure.

Back at the bar, Elizabeth felt a shiver run through the wood. She didn't stop wiping. The motion was her anchor. But she felt it—that edge. That subtle slant in the air. Like gravity had chosen a new direction and hadn't informed the room. The bar's energy changed not with thunder, but with tilt. As though the floor beneath her boots belonged to a different hour than the one overhead.

She caught a glimpse of her own hand in the brass rail's reflection—warped, stretched, unfamiliar. Moments like these didn't frighten her anymore. They reminded her.

This was the cost of staying open. Of refusing to wall off the places where time thinned. The bar sat on more than foundation and adobe—it rested on memory, sedimented in layers. Some of it hers. Some of it far older.

And every so often, the old layers rose. She could almost hear them then—whispers in a dialect not of voice, but of breath. The room adjusting its posture. The ghosts (if that's what they were) rethreading their presence through the present.

Elizabeth steadied herself with the cloth. She knew the signs. Something was listening back.

The bar had seen things. Heard confessions. Held secrets that never made it to language. It would hold this too. It had held worse. In grief that pressed so sharply into the wood it left invisible notches. Elizabeth sometimes ran her hand along the bar and felt echoes of those old impressions—like Braille for the soul.

This was what people didn't understand. The bar didn't just absorb stories. It catalogued them with fidelity. It remembered the woman who returned every Thursday for seven months, then stopped coming after a man ordered her usual drink. It remembered the laughter that followed silence too quickly. The joy that frayed at the edges. The secrets passed in folded notes and the resolve hidden in unblinking stares.

Elizabeth never called it haunted. That word was too flat. The bar was attentive. And tonight, it was listening hard.

Brooke returned with a stack of folded towels. She didn't mention the walk-in. Elizabeth didn't ask.

"I'll inventory the shelf,"

Brooke said, already moving. Her voice was even, but her hands were too precise.

Elizabeth nodded.

She didn't need to ask what Brooke had seen.

They had both learned the same truth here—one not written on menus or spoken across shifts. Some rooms had pulse. The bar's pulse didn't race. It hovered.

Brooke moved methodically to the shelves, but Elizabeth could feel the tremor in her stillness—the microhesitation between each movement, the breath held just a beat too long before release.

There was no need to break the silence with explanation.

In Balcony One, silence was a kind of intimacy.

And in the bar, it was almost sacred.

They worked like women in a storm cellar—not speaking of the wind, but hearing it in every nail that held the roof. The glass incident wasn't the first. And it wouldn't be the last. But it meant the room was active. And the bar had decided to open another layer.

Someone dropped a spoon in the back. Everything normal. Everything askew. Elizabeth reached for a bottle she hadn't touched in years.

Pomegranate wine. The kind Sam used to bring for late shifts, when the air outside turned metallic and the conversation bent philosophical.

She uncorked it without thinking, poured a small measure into a tasting glass. She held it to her nose.

The scent knocked loose something sharp and citrusy in her mind— sunlight on copper, laughter under duress.

It was the kind of memory that didn't belong to any one moment, like a rhythm familiar and unresolved—that fluttered in the chest before the brain could assign meaning. Sam had poured that wine once under protest.

"No philosophy without sweetness,"

he'd said, tipping the bottle like it contained sermon.

Elizabeth had rolled her eyes and taken the glass anyway. It had been late. The kitchen closed. The lights dimmed. And the air thick with things no one was ready to name.

The scent of pomegranate had mingled then with burnt sugar and tired laughter. The kind of night that pressed itself into the furniture without leaving a mark you could show.

She hadn't tasted it since. Hadn't needed to—until now. The memory was enough. And yet, tonight, the scent asked to be held again.

She turned toward the mirror.

Her reflection was there. It moved when she did.

But for a moment—half a moment—it wasn't her face.

It was the room's.

Elizabeth exhaled.

She whispered into the stillness:

"Who are you—you don't remember, do you?"

The mirror did not answer.

But the bar—the bar was listening.

She thought, briefly, of a letter she never sent. A name written in careful cursive. Folded once. Slipped behind the wine. She'd kept it, even after the flame had taken her life. But not her name. The name had stayed. Stayed in the grain of the bar.

In the bend of her wrist when she poured. In the way she listened for voices that weren't supposed to speak. She never said the woman's name aloud. Names, here, were more than identifiers.

They were frequencies.

To speak one aloud was to activate a current—to risk bringing the full charge of memory into the room. Some names had been spoken too often, worn thin by grief or gossip. Others were still sharp, still wet with meaning, and best left sealed.

This one?

This one hadn't been uttered since the night she was killed. Elizabeth had loved her. Loved her deeply. But that night—she couldn't protect her, even though she was a perfect shot. There was fire and smoke. The smoke from that fire had lingered for days. Not in scent—but in shape. It twisted up into the sky and curled along the horizon.

Elizabeth had watched her lover disappear in the smoke, in the fire. The wildfire had engulfed most of Pine Valley. The two women were hunting together, but the fire raged faster than they could run. This was Elizabeth's ache. The ache was quieter now. Like everything else the bar had taken in. But the bar knew it. And the bar never forgot.

The wine sat untouched beside her hand. Elizabeth stared past it, gaze drawn not to the mirror this time, but to the bar top itself—its wood darkened in one patch, a spot near the tap where years ago someone had branded an initial. The mark was long faded. She hadn't thought of it in ages.

But now it burned, faintly. Like someone had just pulled the iron away.

She didn't move.

Behind her, Brooke shuffled bottles—label out, caps tight, fingers steady. But the rhythm was too careful. Too deliberate. As if she were reciting lines she didn't believe.

Elizabeth let her hand slide down the bar's edge until her fingers touched the underside.

There.

A chip in the wood. Her doing. From a night she wouldn't speak of.

A man had leaned in too close, too long. She'd jerked back. Glass slipped. Broke. She hadn't told anyone. But she'd pressed her palm hard enough to splinter the varnish.

Now she traced that scar like Braille.

Some nights, when the bar was closed and the staff had long since gone home, Elizabeth would find herself back at that spot—fingers grazing the underside like she was reading a passage no one else could see.

The scar was barely visible now.

But it hadn't faded.

It had settled—like sediment that refused to dissolve, no matter how many times the current swept over it. She hadn't meant to leave a mark. Not then. But the bar had accepted it anyway. Catalogued it. Wove it into its grain like thread into tapestry.

She wondered, sometimes, how many others had left their own unspoken inscriptions. Not on purpose. But through accident, or emotion, or need.

She wondered if Sophia's hand had ever slammed down in frustration.

Or if Sam had ever scratched a name into the surface, then sanded it down the next day.

The bar would remember it all. It was built to hold what others buried. A shadow shifted. Not Sophia. Just the idea of her. Lingering, curious. As if even she wasn't sure what came next.

Elizabeth leaned in, voice low.

"This place," she said,

"knows more than it tells."

Brooke looked up.

"What?"

"Nothing."

Elizabeth turned toward the shelves, reaching for a rag to polish the quince bottle. Her hand froze. Tucked between two bottles of rye was a small, worn notebook. Clothbound, green, edges frayed. She hadn't seen it in years. Didn't even know it had made the move when the new shelves were built.

She slid it out slowly. The fabric cover caught slightly against the lip of the shelf, like it didn't want to leave. Brooke noticed.

"What's that?"

Elizabeth didn't answer.

She opened it to a random page. Ink bled across yellowed paper. She flipped back. There, scrawled in a tight, familiar hand:

"Don't forget what this room does."

No name. No date. Just the sentence. And beneath it, a pressed sprig of sage—crumbled to dust the moment she touched it. Behind her, a shadow flickered again. This time, Sophia was not in it. But the stained glass window had changed. It was still glass, still patterned.

But the light it threw?

Blue.

And it was night.

It was the kind of blue that didn't belong to any hour. The kind of hue you might find in a dream just before waking—unplaceable, but full of weight. Elizabeth felt it immediately. The bar had done this before. Shifted its palette, its palette, its pitch, its time signature. To accommodate what needed saying. To shelter what couldn't be said.

The blue refracted off the bottles like memory off bone—angled, soft, but undeniable. Even the dust in the air looked sacred in that light. Elizabeth did not move. Did not speak. She simply stood still long enough to feel what the room was trying to offer.

And then—one breath later—the light changed again.

Blue light painted the bar like water—thick, impossible, gently wrong. It pooled around Elizabeth's feet and rippled when she moved. She didn't remember walking backward. But she had. One step. Then two. Until her shoulders touched the edge of the wine rack.

She blinked. And the room changed. A stillness so complete it erased the present. The bar was empty. Not just quiet. Vacant. No Brooke. No clatter. No hum. Just Elizabeth. And the book in her hand, now closed.

She opened it again. The pages were blank. All of them. Except the very last.

"What you bury will wait for you. Especially in a place that remembers."

The sentence pulsed like a heartbeat. For a moment, the world narrowed—not into darkness, but into texture. The texture of her own breath, shallow. The weight of her hand, trembling. The pull of memory, tight as a laced corset.

She hadn't realized how many layers she'd worn tonight. This room—this bar—had always demanded composure. But the book's last line had reached beneath all that.

"What you bury will wait for you."

She whispered it again, this time to herself. As if the repetition might grant clarity. It didn't. But it did grant gravity. And gravity—when held just right—could be a kind of answer.

Her thumb rested on the book's edge. She could feel the stitching in the spine. Imperfect. Human. The kind of imperfection that made a thing true. This wasn't just memory surfacing. It was the past checking its alignment. Elizabeth closed the book. Her hands were shaking. She wasn't afraid. But she wasn't untouched. The distinction mattered. Fear was a spike—sharp, immediate, fleeting. This was something else. A saturation. Like rain soaking into wood—not all at once, but deeply, unavoidably.

She knew the feeling. Had felt it the first time she touched Sophia's mirror. The first time Sam handed her a drink without speaking. The first time she locked eyes with Cynthia across a table and realized she wasn't being looked at—she was being seen. Tonight had that same voltage. Something was trying to complete a circuit. Elizabeth stood still. Whatever this was—memory, ghost, the building itself—it was searching for a conductor. And she was willing.

She looked up at the ceiling. She was alone. But her reflection wasn't. The mirror displayed a second Elizabeth—same clothes, same hair—but her face was turned slightly toward the bar, toward the place where the glass had appeared. It wasn't mimicry. It was memory manifest. A version of her that had once stood there, years earlier—jaw tight, hands shaking, adrenaline still cooling beneath the skin. A night that had never made the ledger. Never found its way into anyone's retelling. But the bar remembered. It didn't need chronology. It needed presence.

This second Elizabeth wasn't haunting. She was anchoring. Showing her what still lived inside the walls. Inside herself. The version that had stood tall after the heartbreak—after the loss. The one who didn't weep because breaking didn't feel allowed.

Now, they stood together.

Not exactly facing.

But not apart.

Time folding in on itself like paper warmed by flame.

Elizabeth resisted looking at the mirror. But something pulled her eyes toward it. She saw herself whispering something.

Over and over.

Mouthing words Elizabeth couldn't hear.

Elizabeth moved closer.

The whispering stopped.

The mirror image blinked—half a beat too slow.

Elizabeth pressed her palm to the glass. It was warm. And then—so gently she almost didn't feel it—the surface gave. Just a breath of give. As though cotton had been stretched over breath. Her fingers sank half a centimeter before the mirror caught her back. The give in the glass was not just a trick of perception. It was permission withheld. As if the boundary between now and then, here and there, could stretch—but not break. Not yet.

Elizabeth pulled her hand back slowly, fingers tingling. She'd expected chill. What she felt instead was a softness. Warm. Pliant. The same temperature as breath on skin.

The mirror, like the bar, was a witness. But its allegiance was different. Where the bar grounded, the mirror reflected. It transported. Offered fragments. Glimpses. Echoes.

And sometimes, if you looked long enough, it offered invitations.

But not without cost.

Elizabeth exhaled and looked past her own reflection to the place where the second self had stood. Empty now. The room, as always, made space. Behind her, the stained glass flickered. A presence shaped into silence brushed past. Elizabeth turned. The bar's frequencies had deepened.

Elizabeth knew enough to recognize the change wasn't arbitrary. It was response. Some rooms echoed. Others absorbed. But this one—this bar—answered. It didn't offer solutions. It didn't fix or forgive. But it held. Held laughter, lies, longing, loss. Held names never spoken and touches never claimed. Held her.

Now, it held something new. Or perhaps something old, returning.

Sophia's absence.

Sam's memory.

Her own weight, centered between them.

Elizabeth stood in the hush and let the shift continue. Just letting it land. A crash. Not violent. But sharp enough to break the air.

Elizabeth jerked back from the mirror. The reflection snapped back into place—hers, whole, normal. She turned.

Brooke stood frozen in the doorway, a broken glass stem in her hand and its bowl in shards on the tile.

"I—" Brooke started.

"I didn't drop it."

Elizabeth nodded slowly.

"I know."

They stood in silence, the space between them full of static.

The blue light had faded. The stained glass glowed amber again, as if the last few minutes had been a dream wrapped in memory, folded back into the walls.

But the book was still on the bar. And the mirror still hummed. And the glass on the floor had no dust. Just one perfect spiral, etched into the base of the stem. Elizabeth stepped forward and picked it up.

"Don't throw this one out," she said.

Brooke took it with both hands.

"Why?"

Elizabeth's fingers brushed the spiral at the base. And she thought— not for the first time—of the hand that used to hold hers under the bar. That hand had known exactly how long to linger. The kind of touch that steadied breath, that recalibrated silence.

She'd never spoken the name aloud in this room—not because of shame, but because of reverence. The bar had listened to their silences more than their sentences.

It was a love not defined by longevity or label.

But by the way it altered time.

Minutes thickened.

Rooms reshaped.

Glass held its breath.

Even now, years later, the echo of that touch lived in the grain. The bar didn't remember feelings. It remembered contact.

Elizabeth let her fingers rest there a moment longer, palm open. Then let go. The way she'd memorize her laugh. The way they never said it out loud. But some things didn't need chronology. They needed acknowledgment. The bar wasn't asking for her to name it. It was asking for her to carry it differently. To stop treating memory as archive. To begin treating it as companion.

Sam knew this. So had the one whose name she never spoke. They'd each left a mark—absorbed.

Elizabeth stood still and felt the quiet press of presence. Something loosened. A grief she hadn't realized was still knotted behind her ribs. And she—without ritual, without theater—let it. The letting wasn't loud. It didn't claim space or demand witness. It moved like pomegranate syrup—slow, red, sacred.

A breath let out she didn't know she was holding. A softening beneath the sternum. The bar didn't change. And yet—she felt shifted. Like the spiral etched into the glass stem.

She thought of Aris, the man who'd chosen that mirror—who had hung it with his own hands long before the building was complete. A man whose name the bar knew, whose choices still echoed like footfalls in a familiar hall.

Elizabeth imagined Sam there—just once, just briefly—seated at the end of the bar, elbows on wood, gaze direct. And not alone.

For a flicker of a moment, Elizabeth saw Sam—a silhouettes, not a specter.

His presence once tethered to this room: a laugh, a scent, a gesture left behind.

His form leaned into the silhouette of another—the woman Elizabeth would not name. Like chords resolving—Sam's tilted smile, the breath of the woman who once kissed her wrist in the dark, a giggle long faded but never erased.

Each had left a thread.

And the bar had braided them together.

The ache in Elizabeth's chest wasn't grief anymore. It was gravity. A quiet invitation to be part of the pattern. She let the moment pass through her.

When she opened them, the bar was as it had been. But her place in it had changed. The bar wasn't something she moved through. It was something she now moved with.

She reached for the bottle of wine again. The glass stem trembled.

She thought of Brooke, of the steadying she offered without realizing. Of Mateo's silences, Cynthia's pigments, George's timing. Each of them stewards of something more than a building.

Elizabeth had always thought herself the anchor. Now she saw: she was the hinge. The one who turned between memory and moment, between echo and utterance.

She let out a breath. One that sounded, finally, like her own. Whatever haunted this room was not separate from her. It wasn't trying to speak through glass or shadow. It was speaking through her choices. Her rituals.

Her refusal to abandon the bar.

In that moment, Elizabeth understood: this was not a room of memory. It was a room of transmission.

What entered here transformed.

Not always cleanly. Not always kindly.

But undeniably.

And she—witness, keeper, hinge—would go on tending the flame.

Even when the light bent strange. Especially then. The clock above the wine rack ticked once—audible, singular. But no time displayed

Brooke reentered, the stemless glass now rinsed and drying in her apron.

Neither spoke.

The bar no longer pulsed.

Elizabeth returned the bottle to the shelf with rhythm.

The room exhaled.

One blue flame above the pass guttered slightly, then steadied.

Brooke leaned against the counter.

"Glass inventory still says we're one short."

Elizabeth nodded, not looking up.

"We're not missing it," she said.

"We're carrying it."

Some rooms keep their promises by never speaking them aloud.

Scroll

THE KITCHEN

Kitchen – During the Second Set, Late Spring 1919

The knife hadn't fallen.

Brooke remembered that.

Brooke hadn't meant to pause. But she did—half-step between the prep table and the pantry, towel in hand, unsure what she was waiting for. The kitchen wasn't quiet exactly, but it held a certain gravity. The kind born of music, of rhythm. Of something repeating itself with care until it became its own kind of knowing.

She watched Mateo. Her father was a chef and admired Mateo – the kind of admiration reserved for those who move as if they belong to a place more deeply than the blueprints allow. He stirred with no urgency, only fluency. The oil responded like it trusted him.

Brooke had worked other kitchens. None of them listened like this one.

She could feel it: the way the walls didn't echo but absorbed; how the counters seemed to inhale the clatter and release it softened. The bread warmer clicked once. Mateo didn't startle. He reached for a clove, cracked it clean, and dropped it into the pan without breaking the hum of his movements.

He moved with the kind of grace you don't expect from a man built like an old oak—slow where he meant to be, quick where it counted.

He'd been reaching for the thyme when the knife slipped from the counter.

And he caught it—hand out, and there it was: steel against callus, danger met without drama.

Brooke – a towel in her hands, a stack of warm plates beside her, and eyes too full of knowing.

"Smells the same," Brooke said, softly.

He didn't ask what she meant. Just said, "Memory always does."

She bit the inside of her cheek.

The smell in the kitchen was always the same—roasted cumin, charred citrus, heat curled into something edible. But it wasn't the scent Brooke remembered most. It was the hush. The kind of quiet that meant someone was working with their whole self. Mateo cooked like that. With his back straight, his hands sure, his breath held between gestures. Watching him now, Brooke didn't feel nostalgic—she felt anchored. She'd only been here a few seasons. But something about the way he stirred the sauce, the way the towel hung over his shoulder, made her feel like she'd arrived somewhere older than both of them.

She moved to the counter, fingers grazing a wooden spoon. It was worn to a shine at the grip—smooth from years of turning, of tasting. She didn't know its full history. It was the kind of object that carried memory without asking permission. Mateo passed her a lemon without looking. She took it, sliced, squeezed. Fell into rhythm.

The second set had started upstairs—she could hear the hum through the floorboards. Horns. Applause. Laughter. A stomp in rhythm. Someone calling for another round.

Down here, the air was thicker. As if the kitchen was braising the night itself.

The kitchen itself was a contradiction Mateo loved—a fusion of old bones and new fire. Along the far wall sat the original cast-iron range, ornate with floral scroll work and fire-blackened edges, its chimney angled like a shoulder against time. Mateo still used it for baking—bread mostly, and slow roasts that needed more presence than precision.

Beside it, gleaming like a recent guest, was the new gas-powered stove installed one year after Balcony One opened to the public. George had approved the upgrade reluctantly, but Mateo had grinned like someone given a new heartbeat. It wasn't about convenience—it was about control. The flame answered him instantly, obedient and hot… a language he already spoke.

Copper pots hung above both stoves, each one blackened differently— some from open fire, others from the blue lick of gas. Between them, the kitchen held an equilibrium. Sweat contract of old and new. A conversation.

Brooke caught the way Elizabeth's eyes lingered on the steam rising from the bread warmer. It wasn't about doneness. It was something else— an inventory, maybe, of what couldn't be written down. She'd seen Elizabeth do that often: read the room the way some people read tea leaves, as if even the air could be translated if you knew what to look for.

"Did you always know?" Brooke asked suddenly, not sure what she meant until the words were already out.

Elizabeth looked over, not startled. "Know what?"

"That you'd be here. That you'd stay."

There was a pause. Not long. Just long enough to weigh the honesty.

"I didn't know," Elizabeth said. "But the building did."

Brooke absorbed that. Let it settle beside her ribs like warmth from the oven. She wasn't sure she believed in places knowing things. But she believed in people who listened well. And Elizabeth—she listened in layers. To walls. To weather. To the unsaid.

From the far counter, Mateo cleared his throat gently. "The kitchen asks for love," he said, half-turning. "And respect."

And with that, the scent of roasting garlic curled into the air like punctuation. Final. True.

Mateo lifted the pan and tilted it, letting the fat skim off the edge with practiced grace.

"You want to taste?" he asked, not looking at her.

Brooke stepped forward. Nodded.

She tucked the towel into her waistband, more out of ritual than need. The heat from the pan carried something ancestral, though she wouldn't have used that word. Something more like *returning.* As if the act of being handed food by someone who had shaped it returned her to some ancient gesture of trust.

Mateo's hands, steady and precise, still bore the marks of his work: small burns healed silver, calluses rubbed smooth at the center. They moved without flourish, without show. Every action declared that presence was the ingredient that mattered most.

Brooke accepted the piece of meat like a communion wafer. Not because she believed in anything particular—but because something about the moment made belief feel momentarily possible.

He handed her a piece with the tongs, still sizzling. She held it in her palm, blew gently, then tasted.

Heat bloomed.

Spice—*home.*

And behind that, something she hadn't expected.

Peace.

It caught her off guard, that peace—like a doorway she hadn't seen and wasn't sure she was allowed to enter. She stood still for a breath, as if any motion might spook it. Around her, the kitchen ticked on: the low simmer of broth, the faint hiss of the warmer, Mateo's gentle steps as he turned toward the pantry.

But Brooke didn't move. Not yet.

Because the flavor in her mouth wasn't just memory. It was permission. To pause. To feel safe in a room without needing to prove she belonged there. And in that stillness, something in the walls exhaled.

She looked to Mateo. He hadn't noticed her hesitation.

Or maybe he had.

And was giving her the space to stand inside it.

Mateo reached for the salt with his left hand.

Paused.

Just long enough for Brooke to notice.

The air around the stove shifted. Warmer, somehow. Denser. Like someone had opened the oven and let memory pour out.

A window fogged.

Above the sink. Brooke glanced at it.

There was no one there.

But the condensation traced the shape of a hand before it vanished.

Mateo didn't flinch.

He just adjusted the flame beneath the pan, nudged the spoon clockwise, and began humming again—but not the lullaby from earlier.

This one was older.

Brooke tilted her head. "What's that one?"

Mateo didn't look up. "She liked it."

"Who?"

He didn't answer.

But he nodded. Once. Toward the stove.

And the flame flickered blue.

Just for a breath.

The back door creaked.

Elizabeth stepped into the kitchen, wiping her hands on a linen towel she hadn't needed to carry. Her eyes scanned once—Mateo at the stove,

Brooke mid-step, something still hanging in the air like a half-spoken sentence.

She moved with familiarity, not rush.

Paused near the high window.

Her fingers brushed the glass.

Still warm.

For a moment, no one moved.

Brooke remained mid-step, unsure whether to retreat or advance. Elizabeth stood, hand just inches from the fogged glass, as if listening through the pane. And Mateo kept stirring decisively. He knew better than to disrupt what didn't want interruption.

The kitchen's warmth thickened with presence. Like something had entered through time itself. Older. Wiser. A feeling sewn into the floorboards, into the simmering broth, into the steam that curled like script above the pan.

Elizabeth's voice dropped low, almost inaudible.

"She comes here, sometimes."

Brooke's breath caught.

"Sophia?"

Elizabeth didn't answer.

But the silence felt like yes.

Mateo exhaled. His shoulders eased. The air shifted again—less tension now, more reverence.

And beneath it all, the humming returned. Not from Mateo. From the walls. A faint, steady vibration, like a tune remembered rather than played.

No one spoke.

But they all knew.

Sophia had passed through.

To watch. To listen.

To witness.

Brooke straightened. "Did you feel that?"

Elizabeth looked at her. Steady. "Some rooms hold warmth longer than others."

Mateo didn't turn. Just kept stirring, humming that older tune.

Elizabeth crossed to the prep table and unwrapped a loaf of bread. Sliced it without looking down. Placed the pieces in the warmer. She moved like someone tending coals.

Brooke relaxed—just a breath.

The kitchen exhaled.

And the flame held steady.

Brooke stepped toward the cooler out of instinct. Her fingers brushed the metal latch, cool and familiar. She paused to feel the way the chill radiated outward. Every surface in this kitchen told time differently. The tile beneath her feet still held the warmth of the midday sun, while the copper ladle on the hook had already turned cool, anticipating night.

She glanced toward the pantry—once, briefly—as if expecting a whisper to emerge. Perhaps a sense that something waited in the wings of the familiar. Kitchens had their own ghosts, not the spectral kind, but the echoes of service, of burned fingers and saved sauces, of lessons learned mid-shift.

She turned back, caught Mateo watching her—aware. He gave a small nod, the kind that said: Yes, you're here. Yes, you belong.

Brooke nodded back, then adjusted the stack of plates because her hands needed something to remember.

Steam curled up from the stock pot in a thick ribbon, rising toward the ceiling before diffusing into the quiet hum of the overhead vent. The smell was layered—onion, bay leaf, marrow—each note a marker of time passed and attention paid. Mateo tilted the lid slightly, not to stir, but to listen. A good broth, he'd once said, sings before it boils.

Brooke leaned her hip against the counter. "You ever cook alone?"

Mateo didn't answer right away. He set down the tasting spoon, wiped it once, twice. "Alone is different than quiet," he said.

She considered that. Looked down at the damp edge of her apron. "I think I used to like quiet more than I do now."

He met her eyes then. Not for long. Just long enough to share something not meant to be unpacked—just placed, gently, like a bowl on a shelf.

Outside, the faint echo of applause drifted down. The second set had truly ended.

And the kitchen, once again, began to listen.

Brooke turned toward the pantry, drawn by a subtle shift in the room's rhythm. As she approached, the scent of dried herbs and aged wood enveloped her, grounding her in the present. She reached for a jar of cumin, its label faded but legible, and measured out a spoonful, adding it to the simmering pot.

Mateo glanced over, his eyes acknowledging her action with a silent nod. "Good choice," he murmured, the corners of his mouth lifting slightly.

Brooke smiled, the warmth of the moment settling in her chest. The kitchen's cadence resumed, each movement and sound weaving into a tapestry of shared purpose and quiet understanding.

Brooke leaned against the counter for a breath, letting her gaze drift to the knife rack. One blade was missing—Mateo's favorite. He never said it aloud, but she'd seen how his fingers lingered over the handle before he drew it. A gift, maybe. Or a memory. Tools like that didn't come new into a place like this. They arrived with stories, already worn into the steel.

She turned back to the table, spotting a small bowl of lemons beside the bread. She picked one up, rolled it between her palms. The skin was thick, pocked, imperfect—the kind of citrus you got from a neighbor's tree. She imagined Mateo accepting a crate at the back door, nodding once, adding it to the unwritten inventory of gifts that kept this kitchen alive.

"Smells like uncle's farm," she said, slicing the lemon. The juice bloomed on the board.

Mateo didn't respond, but he reached for the halves when she was done. Squeezed them directly into the sauce. Not wasteful. Exacting.

The sound of laughter from the balcony that lived above the kitchen softened.

In the kitchen, the walls held quieter echoes—ones meant to be absorbed, not repeated.

Outside, the wind pressed gently against the adobe, like a visitor too polite to knock. Inside, the vent above the stove gave a single groan and then settled. Mateo didn't look up. He was wiping the counter in slow, looping motions, each pass drawing a quiet circle of calm.

Elizabeth stood with one hand still on the bread warmer. She hadn't meant to pause. But something about the moment—the way the scent curled upward from the dish, the way Brooke had just breathed out like letting go of a decade—had caught her mid-movement.

There were nights when the kitchen turned holy.

She'd felt it once before, the week Sam died, when Mateo cooked through the storm—broth and biscuits, bone-in cuts braised down to their secrets. No one had spoken much that night. The kitchen had borne the grief in silence, its warmth a kind of cradle.

Tonight wasn't grief.

But it was still something.

Brooke moved past her, fingers brushing against a canister that wasn't quite closed. She tapped the lid into place, unconsciously.

Mateo hummed again—quieter this time. As if the song were not meant for them.

But for the room itself.

A low click came from the back of the kitchen—one of the racks settling, or perhaps something else adjusting itself into place. The kind of sound that didn't startle but stirred, like a page turning on its own.

Brooke glanced at the cooler door. It was closed, of course. The latch hadn't moved.

And yet.

The temperature shifted. Barely. A breath cooler near the tiles, like a window had been opened in a memory she couldn't place.

Mateo broke a small sprig of thyme and dropped it into the pot. "Not everything needs an explanation," he said.

Elizabeth lifted an eyebrow. "But some things deserve one."

He nodded once. "That's why we cook."

Brooke reached for the wooden spoon again, the one with the softened handle and the faint crack near the tip.

It felt warm in her hand.

The kitchen, she realized, remembered silences. The held breath before the next thing. The hush before the news.

She stirred once, counter-clockwise.

And somewhere behind the pantry door, the sound of laughter flickered—short, unsure, familiar.

Then gone.

Mateo pulled the pan from the heat.

The smell was layered now—meat and memory, salt and something sweeter. He covered it with a clean towel and nodded, once, toward the warming drawer.

Elizabeth passed him the bread without a word.

Brooke watched them move, wordless but fluent, like musicians passing phrases back and forth across a quiet score.

She folded the last towel. Stacked the plates. Wiped her hands on her apron, though they were already clean.

The pantry door clicked shut behind Brooke, soft as breath. Inside, the air was cooler, lined with cedar shelves and jars labeled in Elizabeth's tight script—paprika, tamarind, bay. She paused for a beat, allowing her eyes to adjust, letting the hum of the kitchen fade to a lower frequency.

In kitchens like this, there were sanctuaries within sanctuaries: the shadow behind the oven, the silence inside the walk-in, the stillness of the pantry. Places where breath came back. Where the rhythm of the line didn't press so loud.

She let her fingertips trail along a sack of pomegranates, its surface dimpled like old linen. Her father used to say you could tell the soul of a place by how it welcomed pomegranate seeds. Cheap kitchens bought them juiced. Brave ones cracked each one open. The best ones—he said—found the seeds one by one.

Here, the labels were both precise and unnecessary.

She opened a tin of dried lavender. The scent was immediate. She didn't know who kept it there. Probably Cynthia. Maybe George. But the smell made her throat tighten. It reminded her that someone had loved something enough to keep it.

She shut the lid gently.

This pantry wasn't large. It didn't need to be. Everything fit. And what didn't fit was carried, instinctively, by those who worked within it. Memory, after all, was not measured in square footage.

She took a breath. Then another.

The pantry door creaked open, and Brooke stepped back into the kitchen. The warmth embraced her, the familiar scents of simmering spices and baked bread wrapping around her like a comforting shawl.

Mateo glanced up, a subtle nod acknowledging her return. Elizabeth, still at the prep table, offered a brief smile before returning to her task of slicing herbs with practiced precision.

Brooke moved to her station, her hands finding their rhythm once more. The clatter of utensils, the sizzle from the stove, the soft hum of conversation—all blended into a symphony of purpose.

She reached for a bowl, the cool ceramic grounding her. As she began to plate the next dish, her movements mirrored those of her colleagues—fluid, intentional, and in harmony with the kitchen's cadence.

In that moment, Brooke felt it—a sense of belonging. Forged in the shared language of service and the unspoken understanding among those who found solace in the kitchen's embrace.

From upstairs on the balcony, a burst of laughter rolled down through the floorboards. Someone clinked a glass. The second set was ending.

Elizabeth glanced toward the stove. Then the window.

Then the space where nothing had been. Mateo wiped his hands, laid the cloth flat on the counter. Brooke stepped backward, toward the swinging door, her breath steady now. Just before she left, she turned back once.

The kitchen was quiet.

But not still.

It was listening.

Outside, the second set gave way to clinking glasses and fresh laughter, but inside the kitchen, something had changed.

The warmth deepened. As if the room had drawn something in, tasted it, and tucked it into the folds of its memory.

Mateo lingered at the stove, one hand resting lightly on the edge of the counter. Elizabeth didn't leave. She stood near the bread warmer, one hand on the towel she'd forgotten to fold, as if holding the last note of a song that wasn't quite finished.

Brooke, halfway through the door, turned back again.

There was no sound—only the kind of silence that holds shape.

A plate clinked gently in the rack.

A shadow leaned ever so slightly across the prep table—too tall to be Elizabeth's, too wide to be Brooke's, gone before it settled.

The oven clicked. The flame didn't shift.

Then—

From the window, a wisp of steam curled inward. From breath. From return.

And Brooke, who had learned never to speak to what you don't understand, whispered only this:

"She liked it."

And the kitchen held it close.

The difference between cooking and alchemy
is only who you're feeding.

Scroll

THE BASEMENT

Balcony One – Beneath the Zitting Room

The door was visible, but locked. Hand crafted by George. He never wanted anything to waste. The door made use of the corner of the Zitting room – space not wasted – a simple closet he would say.

The door remained locked.

Only a few had a key.

And Elizabeth did.

Her hand found the bolt handle, the latch no blueprint had marked.

It opened. But not to a storage closet.

To something else—

with recognition.

There were only two who had ever felt that recognition. Not seen it. Not even believed it. But felt it.

Sophia had known. Not when she lived—not entirely. But in the moment of her passing, when the veil split as a silken fabric, the basement became real. Not constructed. Manifested. Woven from the breath between her last and what followed. She hadn't walked it with her feet, but with her memory. And that was enough.

Now, it lived beneath the Zitting Room—the place that honored Sam's life, the place of Sam's naming, the place of layered losses. But the basement was hers. It was continuation. A chamber not built by hands, but by remembering. Sophia had visited it since. Sometimes often. Sometimes in form. Enough to lend it her silence. Enough to make space.

Elizabeth did not know all this, not in facts. But she felt it. In her spine. In the give of the latch. In the way the air did not resist her presence, but responded to it.

This was not a portal.

It was a manifestation.

Balcony One was quiet—music finished, glasses cleared, laughter thinned to murmurs upstairs. Brooke was finishing inventory. Mateo had already gone to the back.

Elizabeth was alone.

Not lonely.

Just alone.

She didn't check over her shoulder. Not this time. The Zitting Room behind her was empty, but it wasn't absence she trusted—it was rhythm. The sound of the building at rest: a wine bottle settling against another, the low groan of wood remembering its shape, the soft click of Brooke's ledger closing upstairs.

She moved by feel and someone else's memory. The groove beneath the back stair had never been marked, but Elizabeth's palm fit into it like a held breath. Her fingers somehow knew.

In the earliest days, she'd tried to ask about the basement. Mateo laughed. "There is no basement," he said, laying a copper tool flush against the molding.

She had nodded. Then waited a full month before trying the door again.

Now, it yielded under her hand like an inhale.

The hush on the other side wasn't silence. It was the kind of stillness that fills a room already listening.

And tonight, the basement was listening early.

She opened the door.

The hinge didn't creak. It rarely did. The building wasn't dramatic. It simply revealed.

Cool air drifted up like a sigh from the earth.

It didn't smell like dust or damp, the way basements were supposed to. It smelled… expectant. Like the air hadn't been disturbed but had been waiting. A patience older than the house itself.

Elizabeth stood. Knowingly. She had been here before, but no one else knew. There were stairs, not a closet, and they required something. Attention. Reverence. As if the staircase were in the cathedral, the weight of each step mattered.

The first time she came down here, she hadn't known why. Only that the scent of quince had reached her where she stood in the pantry and tugged something behind her ribs. She hadn't told anyone then. Not even George.

Now, as her hand traced the wall's curve, she could feel where the plaster thinned. Where stone took over. This wasn't architecture. It was intention. The house had moods, and down here—beneath the noise, beneath the blueprints—it had memory.

She stepped again.

And the air thickened like cloth.

She stepped onto the first stair.

The wood held her.

Second step.

Then a pause.

Something shifted behind her—barely audible. Not a footstep. Not wind.

Just the memory of motion.

She turned her head.

Nothing.

Except—

A faint whiff of quince.

The smell of something buried. Preserved. Waiting.

She looked down.

Into the dark that wasn't dark, just deeper.

And descended.

She descended slowly.

The stairs were quiet—they remembered.

Each step seemed to respond to her weight not with resistance, but recognition.

As if someone else had walked this way before and left the imprint of a slower gait. Older. Tired. Not fearful.

At the third-to-last step, she paused.

A soft warmth met her ankle. Rising—not from the air, but from the grain of the wood itself. A warmth that defied the chill.

She exhaled. "*I know,*" she whispered.

It wasn't an answer.

Just an offering.

But her hand stayed there.

She paused at the threshold.

The air in the basement was cooler than memory but warmer than expectation, like it had been waiting for her specifically.

She reached the basement floor.

Dirt-packed. Stone-lined. Not modern. Not meant to be seen.

The walls bore no plaster, no paint—just the raw bones of the earth, as if the house had grown downward into the soil, seeking something older than itself.

The stones were veined with a black mineral she couldn't name. One line, she realized, traced like veins in marble. Another curled like a sleeping woman's spine.

Along the base of the far wall, moss traced a seam where stone met stone, thriving in the absence of sunlight.

A single beam, rough-hewn and darkened with age, stretched across the low ceiling. It wasn't structural—at least not in the conventional sense. Elizabeth had the sense it had been placed there not to hold weight, but to hold memory.

Elizabeth moved slowly, letting her hand skim the top of the half-wall that separated something she didn't understand from the rest of the room. Dust coated everything—fine, undisturbed, like snow that had decided to lie still for a decade.

And yet—beneath it—something shimmered.

She leaned closer. A faint, almost imperceptible glint along the mortar.

She remembered the smell.

Char and thyme. And the faintest whisper of quince.

Near the back wall in a corner, propped against a shelf warped by heat and time, leaned a small Byzantine-style icon—unsigned, save for a faint scrawl and the number 1892. A copper leaf embedded in the corner of the frame – small, curled slightly outward. Like a thumbprint pressed into gold.

The image was unmistakable. The Panagia, the All-Holy Virgin, seated in full view, holding the Christ child in her lap like a flame passed hand to hand. Her robes were layered in deep red and midnight green, and behind her, the background blazed gold. Around her clustered strange-winged beings: a lion, an ox, a man, an eagle—faces turned not outward, but inward. Some bore eyes on their wings. Some had no bodies at all—only faces, suspended in the haloed hush of heaven.

The Christ child held an open book in his left hand. But the text was illegible—not faded. Just unreadable, as if meant only for those who had already forgotten how to question.

Her expression was unreadable.

She reached forward once, touched the edge of the icon—not the woman—and whispered the first word that came to her mind.

"Sophia."

The room, somehow, exhaled.

It was only then that she noticed what wasn't here.

No mirror.

Every room in Balcony One had one. Sophia had insisted—mirrors to anchor light, to hold memory, to watch.

But not here.

This was the only room in the house without a mirror, and Elizabeth felt it like a cold draft down her spine. Not fear, exactly. But exposure. As if without reflection, the room could see her more clearly than she could see herself.

She moved slowly, her hands trailing the air as though it might take shape around them.

The air was thick with the scent of earth and something else—something metallic, like the tang of iron or the memory of blood. It wasn't unpleasant, but it demanded attention.

Elizabeth stepped carefully, her footsteps muffled by the packed dirt. She moved with respect, as one might navigate a sacred space.

Behind her, the air shifted.

A whisper rose—

And she understood it.

Stay.

Elizabeth closed her eyes.

She remembered the first time she'd felt Sophia in this house—dismissed it as superstition, scolded herself for softness.

But this was not softness.

This was structure.

And it had weight.

She turned toward the deepest wall.

The quince scent was stronger now.

But so was something else.

Soil.

Like something had been planted.

And never dug up.

The farther Elizabeth moved from the stairs, the less the air behaved.

Temperature no longer followed logic.

There were no walls, but there were edges.

No corners, but clear thresholds.

The floor beneath her shifted—like something once solid deciding it no longer needed to be.

She didn't panic.

She simply stepped slower.

This was not fear.

This was reverence.

She touched the back wall—or what should have been one.

Marble, then not marble.

It pulsed beneath her palm.

The scent of quince swelled and then receded, like a wave refusing to break.

Somewhere above her, a chair scraped against the floor.

Someone laughed.

The building went on.

As if this room did not exist.

As if she were not standing in the part of the house even the blueprints knew nothing about.

She turned once—just once—to see the staircase.

It was still there.

But it looked smaller.

As if it belonged to someone else's life.

She moved forward.

Not toward anything.

Just away from where she had been.

The floor beneath her feet shifted again—not lower, not broken. Just different.

Softer.

As if something had been buried there.

The light—what little there was—no longer cast from behind her. It seemed to rise from the ground itself, thin and amber, like the memory of candlelight.

Elizabeth knelt.

She didn't know why.

Only that her knees found the earth without command.

Her fingers reached forward and touched something smooth.

Metal.

Curved slightly at the edge.

She brushed away the loose soil.

A cross.

Small. Bronze. Its arms flared, like a blooming flower or a wind-stirred flame.

It wasn't ornate. But it bore lettering.

Greek.

ΦΩΣ. ΖΩΗ.

Light. Life.

She didn't know the full translation.

She couldn't read Greek.

But she knew the meaning.

Not intellectually. Not doctrinally.

In her chest.

In the way her hand curled around it like it had been waiting for her palm.

It was warm.

Not from the earth.

From memory.

She rose, cross in hand.

The room didn't shift.

But something inside her did.

Clarity. Inheritance.

She looked up.

The staircase was still behind her.

But she did not rise.

Not yet.

She did not stand.

Not yet.

The cross lay quiet in her palm, warm against her skin. But she felt, unmistakably, that it had belonged to someone. *George?* She thought. But the presence around her did not confirm, as though her question was wrong.

She closed her hand around it.

She rose slowly, letting her palm rest once more on the ground before pushing herself upright. The earth pulsed faintly—like the settling of flour after the heat rests.

She turned to the wall again.

And found a seam.

It ran shoulder height across the stone—neat, intentional, like someone had stitched two eras of foundation together.

She ran her fingers along it.

Stopped at the center.

Something metallic met her touch.

A hinge.

Small. Delicate.

Meant to open if invited.

Elizabeth leaned close. Rested her forehead against the stone.

The air here was deepest.

Elizabeth drew back.

Somewhat out of fear. But mostly out of respect.

Whatever this was—this hinge, this seam, this breath beneath the stone—it was not hers to open.

Not yet.

She knelt once more.

Placed the cross at the base of the wall, letters upward.

Like an offering.

Like a promise.

The room did not shift.

It held.

She stood, turned without haste, and walked back across the packed dirt floor.

Each step felt easier now—aligned.

At the stairs, she paused.

Touched the banister, then the air just above it—where the warmth still lingered from her descent.

She didn't look back.

She ascended, stair by stair.

They each seemed to disappear as she moved upward.

She reached the Zitting Room.

The door closed behind her with no sound.

Only certainty.

Some doors do not open to be passed through.

They open to be witnessed.

To be remembered.

To remind Balcony One that it has a soul.

Some rooms are not built. They are remembered into being.

Scroll

THE MIRROR

Balcony One – Just Before the Mirror Spoke

The mirror in the waiting room wasn't original to the building. Elizabeth knew that much.

It had been brought in by the George, or so the story went—salvaged, just the mirror, from a shipwreck or monastery or some forgotten estate on the Aegean coast. No one could say for sure.

It was just a mirror—salvaged, unremarkable. Until George cracked it with the ring his mother had given him. The fracture bloomed like frost, and something passed. Not seen. Not said. But felt. The mirror drew a breath that day. And Sophia become more than memory.

It didn't behave like a mirror.

Elizabeth had stopped looking in it long ago.

She stood before it now.

Her hands still carried the scent of earth. Her knees ached slightly from where she'd knelt.

She paused near the kitchen threshold, reaching to untie her apron—and caught herself in a reflection that hadn't been there yesterday.

Not a mirror. A steel kettle on the high shelf, polished more than it should've been. But the shape was unmistakable. Oval. Warped. Watching.

Elizabeth narrowed her eyes.

Her own face, bent slightly sideways in the metal curve, didn't move when she did.

Not a delay—more like a question.

She didn't blink.

The reflection did.

Then returned to stillness.

She reached for the apron's knot again, slower this time.

The reflection stayed put.

She let her breath steady.

Then turned her back—not out of fear, but instruction. Like she was obeying something older than impulse.

The cross she'd left behind in the basement was already starting to feel like a story she hadn't told yet.

She wiped her palms on her apron. The hem was damp.

This mirror hadn't always been here.

Or rather—it had. But not at first.

She remembered the waiting room before its presence. Back when it was just a coat rack, two cracked chairs, and a chess table. Nothing reflective. Nothing watching.

Then one day—it was there.

Mateo claimed he didn't hang it.

George said, "It was always part of the plan," and never clarified.

Brooke, pragmatic as ever, assumed Elizabeth had put it up during one of her night shifts. "You're the only one who moves things in silence."

But Elizabeth hadn't.

And she hadn't asked.

Because shortly after that, more mirrors began to appear.

The narrow one along the staircase, tall and clouded.

The double-pane near the bar that caught no light at noon but glowed faintly around midnight.

The circular glass in the bathrooms, rimmed in brass—just large enough to see a pair of eyes.

She had tried, once, to count them all.

Eleven, she thought. Then thirteen. Then eleven again.

One mirror always seemed missing.

Or new.

She stopped counting after that.

The mirror reflected her. But not the way glass should.

There was a delay—subtle. A lag in breath. A slight off-angle in the shoulders. Her reflection's mouth was tight. Her own had softened.

She narrowed her eyes. The reflection did not.

In the background, for just a flicker, someone passed.

Not behind her.

Behind the reflection.

Elizabeth didn't turn.

She waited.

Sophia never rushed.

Light from the sconce above was swallowed into it—dimmed, then stilled. Shadows didn't fall correctly. Angles bent. The line where Elizabeth's arm met her torso folded slightly inward, as though she were stitched together by a seam the mirror remembered but she had forgotten.

Her reflection blinked.

She hadn't.

Still, she didn't move.

She could feel the wooden floor beneath her feet, but the reflection stood on stone.

Cold. Wet. Familiar.

The mirror, she realized, was not showing her.

It was showing what she carried.

A flyer—creased three times, tucked behind a register drawer. From years ago. A suffragette meeting she never attended. The name of the woman who invited her blurred, but the ink of the word *Come* still legible.

The mirror held it like a photograph.

Then it blurred.

Replaced by candlelight.

And the edge of a dance floor.

Two women—barely outlines—moving slowly. Hands at each other's waists. Breath shared. Not dramatic. Not defiant.

Just present.

Elizabeth exhaled once. A tremor in her throat. The only proof she was still watching.

The mirror didn't ask for more.

It only waited.

Elizabeth moved—just enough that her breath touched the glass.

Each room had its own mirror now.

In the Zitting Room: a long oval, framed in black walnut, its surface slightly tinted like dusk. The top bore a faint etching—three blooms barely visible unless the light struck at an angle. Elizabeth didn't know what kind of flower they were. She hadn't asked. Mateo once called them "funeral roses." But he said it softly, like the mirror might overhear.

In the walkway above the stairs: twin rectangles, hung across from each other. They never reflected the same image. One always seemed a moment behind, the other just ahead. Brooke hated walking between them. Elizabeth found it soothing—like being held between two breaths.

In the bar: a tall, beveled mirror behind the shelves, so aged it blurred the bottles into streaks of color. It never reflected the patrons clearly. Faces bent slightly sideways. Eyes looked away. Yet when Elizabeth stood before it alone—just polishing glass or resetting coasters—she sometimes saw a hand rest beside hers. Not touching. Just… mirroring.

On the patio: a circle, no bigger than a dessert plate. Hung high, tucked above the doorframe. No one noticed it except Elizabeth. It never reflected the space. Only the sky. No matter the time of day, the mirror held a soft cerulean glow, cloudless and clean.

Each mirror was different.

But all of them watched.

Or waited.

"I never said her name here," she whispered.

The mirror didn't fog.

It didn't ripple.

But the candlelight behind the dancing women flickered once. As if someone had inhaled sharply, then caught themselves.

"I folded the flyer," she said. "But I kept it."

Her voice was low—not ashamed. Just buried. Like something spoken across a great distance, through time that had calcified.

"She asked me if I wanted to come. And I did. God, I did. But I couldn't."

A beat.

"No. That's not true."

She lifted her chin, met her own eyes.

"I didn't."

Behind her reflection, the dance continued. Slow. Safe. Sacred.

Something inside her moved.

Something released.

Like the last thread of a knot finally pulling through.

The glass shivered.

Just enough for the light to shift across Elizabeth's cheekbone—like someone brushing a strand of hair behind her ear.

And then—

The women in the reflection paused.

One of them—braver, perhaps—tilted her forehead toward the other's.

They didn't kiss.

But they didn't move away.

And the candle behind them flared, then stilled.

From just behind the glass—neither above nor behind—came the voice.

Soft. Even.

"We were both hidden."

A simple truth, spoken without apology.

"But you... you stayed visible."

The mirror held still.

Then—

A faint flicker at the edge of the glass. A child's laugh. Not loud. Not clear. But there.

It echoed the kind of sound Elizabeth remembered from open windows in summer—someone else's joy, just far enough away to make you ache for it.

Her breath caught.

The mirror didn't shift. But something moved inside her.

"We watched from separate rooms," the voice said. Still soft. Still even.

"And I named her after the scent of spring."

Elizabeth didn't know who *she* was.

But the word pomegranate bloomed behind her ribs again. Not the scent—this time, the feeling of it.

The voice didn't continue.

Some truths, it seemed, only needed to be said once.

Then silence.

The dance dissolved.

The stone floor beneath Elizabeth's reflection returned to wood.

Her shoulders aligned again.

The crease in her blouse fell correctly.

The mirror now showed only what was present.

Elizabeth.

And behind her—

No one.

Just the room.

Just the waiting.

She watched the candlelight settle back into the mirror's edge, its arc still catching something older than flame.

Elizabeth had once asked George about it.

Years ago.

They had been standing in the Waiting Room, George rolling paint between his palms, not yet applied to the walls.

"Did you hang this?" she had asked, nodding at the mirror.

He'd looked at it for a long time before answering.

"Yes," he said.

She waited.

"Do you see this ring?" he'd said, holding the brush. "My mother gave it to me. From John—the man she married. He gave it to her."

He turned the ring slightly – he wore it on his pinky finger.

"The mirror caught on it once. It cracked."

He paused again, quieter now, like the words weren't meant for the air—

"Something seemed to connect. Between the ring… and the mirror. Like it would remember."

Elizabeth had nodded then, and left it alone.

But now—

As the light in the mirror bent around her cheek again, soft and sure—she understood.

It wasn't hung to reflect.

It was hung to witness.

The mirror didn't move.

But the light did —slipping across Elizabeth's temple like a hand smoothing down her hair. The kind of gesture no one had made in years. Not since—

She didn't finish the thought.

The reflection behind her flickered.

And then—nothing.

Only herself again.

Standing as she was.

And still, somehow, different

Elizabeth turned from the glass.

The room felt unchanged. The light steady. Her own reflection returned to its proper angles.

But just as she reached for the door—

she paused.

Something behind her.

She looked once more.

And the mirror—

wasn't the same.

Another mirror had joined the room.

It sat on the side table near the doorway—a small square of tarnished silver with corners curled like old parchment. It hadn't been there when she entered. She was certain.

The glass was dim. Dust rimmed the edge, as if it had waited a long time to be noticed.

She stepped closer.

This one didn't show her face.

Just the large archway behind her—stretched, elongated. Familiar, yet strangely bent. As if the corridor remembered someone taller. Slower. Older.

Her hand hovered, then fell away.

Just watched.

The reflection held.

Then, slowly, as if unspooling a long-forgotten reel, the archway began to shimmer.

The image stilled.

She turned toward the door again.

When she looked back—

the mirror was gone.

Just a frame—

Cast iron.

Blackened at the corners.

A frame she had seen before.

In the bar?

No—

in the kitchen.

Or maybe—this frame had once held a mirror.

Still.

Waiting.

Some mirrors do not remember what you looked like.

They remember what was watching you.

Some mirrors do not remember what you looked like. They remember what was watching you.

Scroll

THE HAUNTING

Now – Balcony One, Before Hours

It began with the floorboards—one long exhale from the bones of the building.

It was the kind of creak you almost didn't notice. A stretch of wood relaxing into its own grain. But it wasn't underfoot. It came from behind her. Far back—somewhere near the hallway that ran between the host stand and the staff bathroom.

Elizabeth reached for the old percolator on the stove and set it to brew.

She was alone in the building. Not unusual for Elizabeth.

George had gone to Hurricane for supplies. Rosa was late. No customers yet. No music. Just light. The late winter sun angled through the high windows, catching in the dust, turning the air gold and granular.

She turned back to the counter and started wiping.

The smell hit next.

Something hard to name. Like citrus, but not bright. Like cardamom, maybe, or an old drawer that used to hold perfume. It moved past her like a breeze—but there was no open door, no window shift. The air just—changed.

She froze, cloth still in hand.

"It's just morning smells,"

she told herself.

"Settling."

She glanced at the front door. Still locked. Checked the windows. Still closed. Her body was still, but her breath had shifted—shallower now, like the air didn't want to leave her chest. She shook her head and kept wiping.

But then she saw it.

One of the chairs at Table Five had been pulled out. Not far. Just enough to look used.

She was certain—absolutely certain—she had straightened every chair after close the night before. George had trained her that way. "Clean lines," he always said. "You set the chairs like you're setting intention."

She walked toward it. Slowly. Placed one finger on the backrest.

The wood was warm.

No. Not warm. *Touched.*

She let go and stepped back. Her stomach tightened—not fear, exactly. A kind of remembering. Like déjà vu, but reversed. Like she'd been *watched here before.*

She turned to the server station, pulled the drawer open for silverware—and stopped.

The spoons weren't right.

The large spoons—four of them—had been flipped upside down. Neat. Precise. Not clumsy like someone had dropped them. Placed. *Deliberate.*

"Maybe I did that," she whispered aloud. "Maybe I…"

But she hadn't.

She walked to the window again, touched the glass. Cold. Looked out. Empty gravel, wind in the mesquite, one crow hopping along the fence line.

Then behind her—fabric on fabric. A brush of movement.

She turned fast.

No one.

Light shifted again. The air felt—convex. As if the space had pushed inward.

And then, just for a breath, she saw the figure.

Standing in the hallway shadow. Still.

Not male.

A woman. Long hair. Shoulders back. Not threatening—but not kind either. Watching.

Gone.

Elizabeth stood there, hands tingling.

She didn't feel afraid.

She felt—*noticed.*

And in that moment, something inside her settled, even as her chest stayed tight.

This wasn't just energy.

This was someone.

And she wasn't a stranger.

George came in through the back.

Keys clacked on the prep table. The screen door slapped once. Her hands were steady, but something behind her ribs felt angled, listening.

"You here?"

he called.

She answered without turning.

"Front."

Footsteps. The easy, heavy gait of someone who built the place plank by plank. He appeared in the doorway, already shrugging off his jacket. But he paused mid-motion. His eyes swept the room.

"You feel that?" he asked.

She didn't answer. Not yet.

He stepped in fully and looked toward the hallway—right where she'd seen the presence.

"It's Sam,"

he said. Like a conclusion. Like the answer had been waiting for the right question.

Elizabeth turned then, slowly.

"But Sam is dead, George."

She looked at him. Measured. Then said,

"You think it's him?"

George nodded. "Every once in a while, when I open up alone. That cold by the walk-in? That's Sam. Always was. Always that same note—fun, full of joy."

Elizabeth stared past him toward Table Five.

"I used to talk to him,"

George added, quieter now.

"After he passed. Just in case."

Elizabeth shifted her weight. The air felt different now—warmer, like heat from a hand not her own.

"It's not him,"

she said.

George blinked.

"Sorry?"

"It's not Sam."

The words didn't come sharp. No edge. But no apology either. She wasn't offering a theory. She was naming a truth.

George crossed his arms. Looked at her harder. Not unkindly. But with caution, like approaching a steep incline.

"What makes you say that?"

She searched for language that would land. "It's not cold. It's quiet. Watching. Unsure, confused. Trying to understand—lingering."

She paused.

"She's not trying to be heard. She already is."

George tilted his head, like trying to see her at a different angle.

"She?" he asked.

"Yes."

Elizabeth's voice didn't waver.

"She."

George stepped toward the server station. Picked up a spoon. Turned it over. Set it down again. The small sounds filled the silence like punctuation. He walked a slow loop around the room. Past the bar. The corner table. The hallway mouth. Elizabeth watched him scan the floor, the walls, the light. When he returned, he said,

"Where'd you feel her?"

Elizabeth gestured, hand low, toward the chair at Table Five.

"She sat?"

he asked.

"She watched."

George stood quiet. The windows buzzed faintly in their frames. Wind outside. A shift of dust. He didn't speak for a long while. Then:

"You sure it wasn't just—leftover feeling? We get a lot of that in here. Energy echoes. You know?"

"I know,"

Elizabeth said.

"This wasn't echo."

George looked at her for a long moment. The way someone looks at a painting they've seen a dozen times—only this time they notice something they hadn't before.

He nodded. Slow.

"Okay."

She narrowed her eyes, cautious.

"Okay?"

"I've been wrong before,"

he said.

"Doesn't happen often. I'm Greek you know."

Elizabeth folded the towel in her hands. Set it down. She didn't smile. But she no longer felt alone.

George moved toward the kitchen, then paused at the doorway.

"You said she's watching. You think she's watching me?"

Elizabeth considered.

"I think she's watching with you."

George turned back, exhaled. Then walked on.

And neither of them mentioned the chair.

They moved together, unspeaking, across the dining room.

Elizabeth's shoes made no sound on the floor. Neither did George's. The wood swallowed noise. Absorbed it. Even their breath felt muffled—as if the air was thick with dust they couldn't see. They passed Rosa' hostess station.

The adding machine clicked—three times. A slip curled out. George reached for it, then stopped. It wasn't numbers. It was a word. Printed like it didn't belong.

"That's not possible," he said.

Elizabeth took it gently. "No. But it's still here."

He led her through the arch toward the bar. The air felt wrong—like it had curdled. He moved on, faster now, into the Zitting Room.

Halfway through the Zitting Room, the temperature dropped. Not a breeze—an absence. Her breath fogged. George's didn't. She noticed. He reached the door to the storage room. Pulled out his keys and unlocked the latch.

It opened an inch.

Then stopped.

He frowned, pushed harder. Nothing. The air here was strange. Too still. Too full. Like the room wasn't empty, even if the furniture said otherwise.

George jiggled the latch.

"We keep this open. Always."

"Let it be closed," she whispered.

He looked at her, then back at the door.

From inside came a soft knock.

Three quick taps. Then nothing.

They both froze.

George flinched. Not visibly. But his hand jerked—twice, like a tap from below.

He looked down. Nothing touched him. But the sting bloomed across his knuckles all the same. He tapped his own skin. Softly. Once. Twice.

"It was the way my mother taught manners. Quiet. Specific. Never yelled. Just—bam. Bam. Bam. Bam. Bam."

Elizabeth nodded once.

Something had connected with George. But she didn't know what.

George stepped back. The hallway narrowed around them. Elizabeth's fingers brushed the wall. Cold as stone.

They turned and retraced their steps.

Only—when they exited the bar, they weren't in the dining room.

They were in the kitchen.

But they hadn't crossed the swing doors. There were none behind them.

George spun. Looked back.

No hallway. Just flatware and prep tables.

Elizabeth pressed her palm to her chest. Her heart was steady. Too steady.

"This isn't normal," she said.

George didn't answer.

The walk-in door creaked. They turned together.

It opened slowly. No one behind it. The lamps inside flickered, but didn't fail.

They stepped closer. George reached out—slow, careful. Opened the door fully.

Inside: cold shelves. Lettuces. Egg trays. Nothing wrong.

Except—

The light flickered again. For half a second, Elizabeth saw movement. Behind the milk crates. A flick of hair.

Gone.

George looked at her. He saw her see it.

They backed out, closed the door.

The adding machine clicked. Twice.

Two new slips.

George tore them both.

One read: *You saw me.*

The other: *Now I see you.*

George whispered, "What is this?"

She turned slowly.

"Something you built around grief," she said. "But not just yours."

They crossed back through the kitchen—though the door should've led to the alley, this time it opened onto the front dining room.

George stopped. Stared.

"Okay," he said. "That's not right."

The air was warmer here. Music played. Soft. Greek—Cynthia's playlist. A laouto, light drums, a woman's voice almost breaking.

Only—the speakers weren't on.

Elizabeth walked to the center of the room. Turned a slow circle.

She looked toward the restrooms.

"Something's wrong with the mirror," she said.

George followed her gaze.

The mirror above the waiting entrance was crooked. Slightly, but definitely. George had mounted it himself.

They walked toward it.

As they neared, their reflections blinked out again.

Gone.

The room remained.

This time, something else appeared.

A table. Set for one. Candle lit.

A plate: lamb bones, picked clean.

A wine glass: half full, red.

And behind the table—a woman.

Not young. Not old. Long hair. Greek. Shoulders soft. Face not visible, but posture unmistakable.

Watching.

Elizabeth stepped closer. Her breath fogged the glass.

The figure looked up.

No face.

Just the outline of it.

And then—it was *her own face* staring back.

Elizabeth staggered back. George caught her elbow.

The reflection reset.

Normal again.

They stood in silence.

Elizabeth touched her chest again. Her breath shook now.

George said,

"This isn't the building."

Elizabeth shook her head.

"No. It is."

He looked at her.

"Then what the hell is happening?"

She didn't answer.

Because the candles were flickering again.

This time—every flame in the room.

And a piano—began to play, but there is no piano in Balcony One.

Three notes.

Then silence.

Then a child's voice—a boy—clear, sharp, frightened:

"I didn't mean to."

George's face went white.

He turned his head—slow, deliberate.

The voice was familiar to him. A young boy. An orphanage.

Somewhere behind them: tap. tap. tap.

Five in a row. Quick. Measured. Like knuckles on the back of a hand.

George flinched. Looked down. His right hand curled inward.

"Did you—hear that?"

Elizabeth nodded.

He rubbed his hand, the skin between thumb and forefinger.

"She used to do that," he said softly. "Hard. Just enough to make you stop. Look up."

He shook his head like trying to chase off a memory, but the look in his eyes said it had already landed.

"I haven't felt that in fifty years," he muttered.

George stepped back from the waiting room mirror. His face was drawn tight—like it had been pulled inward.

Elizabeth watched him.

She didn't move toward him this time.

She let the space hold them.

A faint ticking sound began near the server station. George turned. The wall clock. Its hands spun once—fast—then stopped. Wrong time. Noon, even though it was still morning. He rubbed his palms together.

"It's like the building's trying to tell us a story we forgot."

"No," Elizabeth said. "It's trying to tell us one we buried."

The mirror behind her flickered.

George noticed but said nothing. Elizabeth stepped to the center of the room. A shaft of light cut across her shoulders—thin and gray, even though the sky had been blue minutes ago.

Elizabeth turned toward the mirror.

Their reflections had returned—but not fully.

She saw herself. And behind her, posture stiff, face hidden. A woman, half-shadowed, shrouded in flame and smoke.

She turned around.

No one there.

Elizabeth gazed upon the figure as if trying to discern the truth.

The adding machine clicked by itself—three times, then stopped. No paper came out.

Elizabeth's jaw tightened.

A draft moved through the room. But no door had opened.

George waited. Elizabeth continued to analyze the figure with her eyes, breathing through her nostrils as if in a trance.

Elizabeth turned to him. Her face had shifted. Not shocked. Not sympathetic. *Knowing.*

The mirror rippled faintly. A shimmer—not light. Memory, maybe.

George stood beside her now, watching.

"This doesn't feel like Sam," he said.

"It isn't," she replied, in a softer, otherworldly voice.

He waited.

She watched the reflection.

It showed a table again. One place set. A single bloom in a chipped glass. A meal untouched. Wine spilled.

She spoke quietly:

"She's not here to scare us."

She sat down in one of the waiting room chairs. The wood groaned under her. The sound was strange—like it had been stretched.

The mirror behind him reflected the room again.

Empty.

Elizabeth watched his hands. They were trembling. He didn't seem to notice.

The floor creaked behind them.

Neither turned.

Elizabeth whispered,

"That's the ghost."

George exhaled.

"She's here because something stayed," Elizabeth said. "Not her. Not her soul, exactly. But what wasn't spoken. What got—absorbed."

George rubbed his temples.

"So this is what? Residue?"

Elizabeth looked at him.

"It's what memory becomes when it has nowhere to go."

Elizabeth nodded toward the mirror.

"She's watching because she *knows.*"

He nodded slowly.

Then: a sound behind the hostess desk. Not loud. Just a clink.

They both turned.

On the edge of the podium, half in shadow, sat a small cobalt goblet, ringed with white Greek lettering.

George stared at it.

"I thought we lost that," he said.

Elizabeth didn't speak.

The mirror flickered again.

This time, it didn't reset.

Their reflections were—layered. Doubled. One over the other. Past and present pressed together but *misaligned.*

George stepped forward.

He touched the mirror.

Slid his finger across the silver crack he made accidently with his pinky ring.

His hand blurred.

He pulled back.

"I think you called her here," she said.

George looked at her.

"She's not haunting the building," Elizabeth continued.

"She's haunting the *unspoken.*"

The adding machine clicked.

One final slip spat out.

George didn't pick it up.

Elizabeth did.

She read it aloud: "*You're not alone.*"

George stepped forward—picked it up, then reached for the cobalt tumbler. The glass was dry. Cool.

"I brought this from Nafplio," he said. "Didn't mean to. Was in my coat when I left."

He looked at her.

"I never told anyone that."

Elizabeth didn't smile. Just said:

"She knows."

He set the glass down gently.

Then, from the server station: a faint ticking.

The wall clock spun once, then stopped—off by hours.

George looked up.

The building exhaled.

Elizabeth looked at George.

He looked back.

And for the first time since they met, they saw *through* each other.

As haunted.

And haunting.

"It's like the building's trying to tell us a story we forgot."

Elizabeth's voice was quiet now.

"No. It's trying to tell us one we refused to carry."

Behind her, the mirror flickered again.

George said,

"I feel like I've been talking to ghosts my whole life."

Elizabeth nodded.

"But this one," he added, "feels like she's listening back."

They didn't move.

The building exhaled again—soft, slow, settling.

And in the dining room, one sconce blinked twice, then steadied.

George looked at her.

"I think there might be more than one."

Elizabeth shook her head in denial.

"No, there can only be one."

They didn't leave the building.

They sat at Table Five with two mugs of coffee gone cold. The adding machine didn't click again. The mirror held. The piano stayed silent.

Elizabeth didn't ask if he was okay. George didn't offer answers he didn't have.

The light shifted across the floorboards, slow and amber. Outside, the wind picked up again. A dry, scraping sound against the window—branches or time.

"She's not done," George said finally.

Elizabeth shook her head. "No."

"But she's… quieter."

Elizabeth was looking at Cynthia's painting on the far wall.

George followed her gaze.

"She ever tell you her name?" he asked.

Elizabeth looked back at him.

"Not yet."

He nodded.

"You think she will?"

"I think she's waiting for us to ask."

They sat in silence.

"You think she's angry?"

"No," she said.

"She's exact."

He stood. His body stiffened at the knees.

"I should check the walk-in."

Elizabeth didn't rise.

George hesitated at the edge of the dining room.

"You staying?"

Elizabeth nodded. "Yeah."

He stepped toward the kitchen, but before he left, he turned back.

"If she ever tells you her name, will you tell me?"

Elizabeth touched the linen on the table.

"Not yet," she said.

He nodded once. Then disappeared into the back.

Elizabeth lingered.

Not afraid. Not alone.

Just listening.

And beneath her breath—without knowing why—she whispered,

"*I see you.*"

She wasn't the echo. She was the one doing the listening.

Scroll

THE POMEGRANATE

Balcony One – Just After the Haunting

The next morning, the air was quiet again.

George moved through the kitchen alone. Meant to inventory ginger, maybe. Or fix the floor tile near the walk-in. But something paused him near the dish bins. It was the smell that caught him first. Just a trace of something sweet and low and slow… syrup forgotten on the back of the stove.

It had started near the dish bins.

Not the smell—the sensation, as though someone was breathing in reverse, just behind his ear.

George had paused there, one hand mid-air, fingers dripping with rinse water, blue eyes narrowed toward nothing.

Then the second shift: a patch of warmth beneath his left heel, as if a floorboard had been set under the sun.

He stepped off it instinctively. Back on again. Warm. Definitely warm.

But only in that one spot.

It wasn't strange enough to concern himself. Not yet.

Not with the rest of the kitchen humming as it should—the lazy thud of the freezer seal, the intermittent drip near the prep sink, the clink of dried rosemary still sitting in the strainer.

Then—another change.

The scent.

Pomegranate.

And George, not one for poetic nonsense, found himself thinking of the Trifili's pantry. The dark blue jars. The marble shelf. The way the sun slanted only through one window, but always found the pomegranate first.

He shook his head once.

Focused.

Still dishes to count. Linens to stack. One more sweep before the first crew arrived.

He moved to leave the kitchen, toward his office.

And the scent moved with him.

George paused, one hand holding a wrench, the other ghosting over the archway frame.

He shifted his weight off his left heel—still sore from a crack in the tile he meant to repair. He had planned to fix it, then leave it, then show up at midnight with a box of grout and a bottle of a new soda called Coca-Cola from the Salt Lake run – like it was a date with destiny.

Behind him, the kitchen lamp hissed softly, wick trimmed low. The glass chimney caught a flicker of motion that wasn't his.

George ignored them.

The scent was still there. Sweet. Slow. Settling.

He closed her eyes.

It wasn't lavender. It wasn't wine.

It was—

Pomegranate.

He hadn't smelled pomegranate since he was six.

Not since his mother used to prepare the seeds before dawn in the back kitchen of the Trifili family's house in Athens.

The windows fogged. The tiles always a little sticky. His mother kept the pots going humming her favorite static.

Not pomegranate jelly, or jam. But syrup.

Jars of pomegranate syrup meant for barter—sealed with wax, cooled on the floor by the sink. He'd pressed his cheek to one as a boy. Said that it smelled like gold and rose tincture.

Now he closed his eyes.

Not to remember.

To feel.

The scent curled through the kitchen.

He remembered pressing his face against the old glass jar, warm from sun, and whispered that it smelled like gold and secrets.

It was real—he could still feel the knot in the wood on the floor—but no one else remembered it quite the same.

And the smell.

Not just pomegranate. But polish. Beeswax. Wood heat. A cinnamon oil rubbed into the floor by hand every October.

There, on the lowest shelf near the kitchen's far wall—just behind the flour sacks—sat a bottle.

Short. Squat. Dark brown glass. Stoppered tight.

It hadn't been there yesterday.

He would've seen it.

He always saw things others missed. That was why he was in charge.

The bottle didn't glow. Didn't hum.

But the air around it felt… curved.

Like the moment just before a song starts, when everyone inhales at once.

He crouched slowly.

The floor beneath his knees was warm.

His fingers hovered first.

Then closed.

The bottle was heavier than it looked.

The glass was smooth, almost waxy, like it had been rubbed with oil or breath.

He lifted it, turned it in his hands.

His thumb traced the bottle's curve twice.

There was a groove—not a flaw, but a choice—just beneath the neck. It reminded him of the spiral bands his mother's ring, the one John Trifili once wore.

He pressed his finger there. Held.

A hum rose—not sound. Not pressure.

Just vibration.

The kind he'd only felt twice before: once while sailing from Greece to America the first time, we he was a young boy and started the ship head on fire. And once at the cemetery in Athens, the day of his mother's funeral, when he stood still enough to hear the rain hit each rusted nail individually.

He could feel it—the way the weight settled not in his hands, and behind his sternum. Like breath taken too deeply, or song remembered too late.

The scent pulled him further.

Not memory now. But memory's echo.

His mother's voice—faint, not present.

But this was not that jar.

This was something else.

Something unpromised. Something unclaimed.

And it had found him.

Syrup.

The same slow scent of pomegranate, yes, but not fresh seeds. Not jam.

Preserved.

And something else.

Smoke?

No—singing.

A chord his body remembered but his mind did not. A hum in his teeth. A catch behind his ribs.

The type of singing he remembered at the Opera house owned by the Trifili family, in Athens.

The bottle was warm in his hands.

He looked toward the kitchen door.

Still quiet.

The others wouldn't be back for a while—not yet.

George shifted the bottle in his hand, thumb resting on the stopper.

It wasn't cork. It was glass too—fused or fitted, he couldn't tell.

It didn't seem sealed, but it wouldn't budge.

He braced it against his knee and twisted gently.

Nothing.

Then—

a soft pop.

Like breath released from a held note.

No smoke. No hiss.

Just scent.

Richer now.

Thicker.

Pomegranate, yes.

And honey.

And something like myrrh.

And behind it all—

a note of iron. Old. Cold. Like dried blood on a spoon left too long in the drawer.

George pulled back, blinked, shook his head once.

But the smell didn't fade.

It filled the kitchen, curling into the linen, the flour, the grain.

He felt it settle in his mouth.

On his tongue.

The air tilted.

And for a heartbeat—he wasn't alone.

Not a presence. Not quite.

More like the memory of someone standing just behind him, a second before they speak. A memory of a woman, bitter, who once beat him. A woman who also loved him.

He pressed the stopper back in.

Not all the way.

Just enough to still the scent.

The warmth lingered in his palm, like a hand he hadn't realized he was holding.

George stood, bottle cradled at his waist.

Looked once more toward the door.

Still quiet.

He left the kitchen, crossed the dining room, and stepped into his office.

There he saw a wooden crate he had forgotten about. Dust curled at the edges.

He eased the bottle onto the crate.

Tucked it under a folded cloth.

Pressed his fingers to the linen once.

Just for a second.

He didn't pray.

Not in the way his father did.

But he did press his fingertips together like it meant something.

Just for a second.

The cloth beneath his hand was soft with time. The stitching was uneven, the thread a little too bright. It grounded him.

Earlier that week, George had repaired a floorboard in the bathroom. He always hummed while he worked. Nothing exact—just a tune that circled a few notes, like water around a drain.

He didn't know why he'd hidden the bottle.

Only that showing it would've broken something.

Rhythm.

There were things George understood with his hands before his thoughts caught up.

He stood slowly.

He didn't look at the crate again.

Didn't check the seam of the shelf. Didn't smooth the dust.

Some things, once set down, ask not to be disturbed.

He moved toward the window above his desk.

And caught himself checking behind him—not for people.

For presence.

The office had changed.

Like someone had exhaled just before he stepped in with the bottle.

Then—the door opened.

Hannah.

The manager he had hired.

She didn't flinch.

She tucked the clipboard higher under her arm, squared her shoulders. Her voice when she spoke came from the stomach—not practiced, but true.

And still—he could feel the bottle in his palm. Like something had been passed to him.

And not taken back.

He took a breath, looked at Hannah, and smiled.

The office remained.

The air had cooled.

And outside, somewhere near the bar, he heard the first note of a broom being pushed across tile.

George straightened his spine.

Hannah stood in the doorway, sleeves rolled, one brow lifted slightly—not in surprise, but recognition.

She didn't ask what George was doing.

She didn't look at the linen on the crate.

Didn't tilt her head.

She just stepped inside.

And sat at her small desk, next to George's.

"Smells like something warm in here," she said, her voice easy. Measured.

Not curious.

Not accusing.

Just… aware.

George nodded.

Swallowed.

"Just finishing inventory," he offered, too quickly.

Hannah didn't press.

She set down her clipboard on the desk and began writing.

George moved toward the office door to leave the room.

"Be sure to log the ginger. Mateo keeps overordering."

He mentioned to Hannah as he moved.

Then—

"Some things have a way of showing up when they're needed."

He didn't smile.

Didn't glance back.

Just walked out, quiet as he came.

Hannah sat still, holding the silence like a thread. Her fingers holding the pencil as she tapped it on the desk. She turned slightly, catching the last of George's steps as they faded into the main dining area—steady, unhurried. He always moved like that. As though he was balancing something invisible.

Hannah didn't know what it was, exactly, but she'd noticed that stillness before. Especially when George passed by her desk, always with a hand on the edge of the ledger shelves—not for support, but for orientation. As if George's presence gave her direction, whether she named it or not.

George moved through the dining hall, through the bar, onto the patio, and toward the back of Building One. George found a chair he was refurbishing and sat. The scent of the pomegranate signaled a flood of memories. His mother, the family who raised him, and his father. There were many things he had forgotten but now remembered. The tall spiral staircase with a wrought iron railing that led to the roof of the Trifili home. The lemon tree. The thorns.

He didn't think his mother wanted to beat him. But she did. He didn't assign weight to it. He just believed she was trying to survive. He was mischievous. He caused problems in a house he wasn't born in. She wanted to appease the Trifili family, but they only saw her as lower class. But they loved George as their own.

He remembered leaving the Trifili household. He didn't know why, but his mother wanted to survive on her own. He took to the streets. A thief, but still just a boy. His mother couldn't handle him any longer and left him in a boys orphanage. The syrup unsealed the memory. What he'd boxed away behind pride and time began to flow back, slow and bitter-sweet.

The air had cooled as the sun began to set, but his chest still carried heat. The memories flooding back almost consumed him, but not quite.

He thought of the bottle of pomegranate syrup, he hid under linen on top of the old crate.

And stood up, walked toward the patio.

There was a stack of napkins needing folding.

Tables that needed to be set.

The sound of Hannah humming—off-key, unhurried—from the bar.

He knew she had left the office, so he quietly returned there.

The scent of pomegranate had faded.

But it had not left.

It had simply chosen to wait.

The kind of sweetness you don't name out loud.

The kind you carry without knowing.

Until something calls it back.

Outside the sun had nearly slipped behind the ridge.

The office window lit for a final moment, catching the glass just enough to flash. A shimmer—soft, nearly imperceptible—ran down the side of the building and across the bougainvillea's stem.

Somewhere in the kitchen, Mateo was cooking, absent-minded. Rosa was out in the main dining area finalizing bills for the last customers. George turned his face slightly toward a black and white photo framed, sitting on his desk. The photo was of him, as an adult, walking with his back to the camera. He was walking down a path in Greece, holding the hand of his aged mother. She had long, thick flowing hair, golden white, holding a purse in one hand, and her sons in the other. George carried a camera strapped to his shoulder. He is a photographer, but Cynthia took this photo.

The photo looked back at George. Fading. The smell of pomegranate lingered.

*
**

Some sweetness doesn't bloom for the table.

It waits – rooted, unseen—

Scroll

THE OFFICE

Balcony One

The double doors rise tall from the plaster wall between the kitchen and the bathrooms—just visible from the main dining area, framed in cypress with hand-pounded brass handles that stay cool. They open wide and sure, the way a room does when it knows it belongs. Hannah presses her weight against the carved frame, steadying her breath before stepping inside. When it gives, it's with a breath as air moves rapidly from underneath the door. The light inside is thinner than it is in the rest of Balcony One, like it knows not to intrude.

Three desks form the quiet constellation of the room. George's near the back—heavy, carved, brought from Athens. Cynthia's to the left—smaller, her ledger stack always squared. And Hannah's near the door, her clipboard resting in perfect reach. The desks don't match, but they belong—as if each woman, each man, etched a different part of the same map.

The room breathes with their presence, layered and quiet. A shared interior where names are remembered by touch, not title. The desk waits. So does the ledger. And so does George—though he wouldn't admit to waiting for anything.

There's no electric lamp on the desks. Just heavy glass oil lanterns, bases ambered with age. The chairs behind them don't match anything else in the building—Greek, carved, or whatever could be salvaged. The drawers hold ledgers bound in butcher twine, slips of paper in Greek and English, some signed only with initials. In the corner, a cabinet leans under the weight of what George never displays: photos. A young boy, shirtless, standing in the sun beside a lemon tree. A marble balcony. A woman with a scar just visible above her neckline, staring past the camera.

On the wall: one photo framed. George in front of the Blue Parrot. The sky behind them cracked with heat. Long hair. On the island of Crete.

The office sits between the kitchen and the bathrooms. It was never drawn on the original blueprints. George built it from scraps left over from the kitchen extension—cypress planks, sandstone offcuts, two hinges without matches. He said every restaurant needed a quiet mouth, a place where the noise of decisions could go to die. Cynthia added the filing shelves. Hannah brought in the third chair. Now it belongs to all three.

The room smells of ink and smoke. Not from cigarettes—but from the oil lamps rested quietly on each desk, the glass chimneys always a little sooted. On the desk: ledgers, correspondence in both Greek and English, and a fountain pen chewed near the base. There's no calendar. No clock. Just a worn leather blotter and a drawer that sticks every third time.

There were two immigration packets in the bottom drawer—one yellowed, one creased but cleaner. George kept them both, though he rarely opened them. The first held the documents that brought him to America at ten years old, pages stamped and notarized in ink that bled through the paper. The second bore the strain of his forties, when the Blue Parrot folded and he returned not as a son but as a man with failure pressed into the seams of his passport. "It felt like immigrating twice," he'd once muttered to Cynthia, not bitter—just amazed by the circularity of it. "Same weight. Same waiting. Just fewer illusions."

Cynthia never flinched when he said things like that. She only nodded, then made sure the envelope went back in the drawer.

After they married, it was Cynthia who insisted they return to Greece—more than once—so he could see his mother before she died.

By then, his mother had moved with John Trifili to a small mountain village near Delphi. They'd built a house there—no electricity, no running water, but a working telephone and a view so quiet it felt like prayer.

John had died suddenly, just a few years after he married George's mother. But the house still held traces of him—music, a stack of old records, the faint scent of pine resin in the kitchen wood.

His mother's voice changed when she saw Cynthia—softer than it had been in years. George never forgot that. The way something in her face unknotted, just for a moment.

He didn't open the immigration files anymore. But he didn't throw them out either.

He kept them for accuracy. Not nostalgia.

To remember what it took to leave.

And what it meant to return.

Behind his chair, the wall is lined with photographs. A few of his mother—facing away from the camera, her profile caught mid-turn. A wedding photo from one of the Spendlove boys. A black-and-white snapshot of the Blue Parrot's opening night in Crete—white jackets, strong brows, tables with linen pressed too flat. And beneath it, in smaller frame, the letter from the Trifili family bearing the red seal that brought him back from the orphanage in Kalamata.

It's not a shrine. George would bristle at that. But it is a reckoning space. A place where names aren't softened for American mouths. Where he is still Yiorwos, still a boy who made messes in drawing rooms and got whipped with lemon thorns for it. A place where the mirror on the far wall doesn't reflect his face so much as catch the shape of the man he became in spite of it all.

He keeps one bottle in the cabinet—tsipouro, from a cousin he barely knows. Sam Zitting's name is scribbled on a folded paper beside it, underlined twice. Not debt. Not warning. Just a reminder: that even grief, if seasoned right, can feed someone.

Sometimes, late at night, George sits in the dark with the door cracked, listening to the kitchen settle.

This is when she comes. Not his mother—he doesn't believe in ghosts. But something of her. A feeling in the temperature shift. A hush in the beams above. The way the ring on his hand grows cold, as if remembering what it once cracked.

He rests his palm on the desk. Not in reverence. In habit. The way she once pressed his hand against the railing before stabbing it, over and over, because he'd ruined one of Katherina's canvases. Because he'd drawn mustaches on gods.

He hadn't cried then. He will cry now as he remembers.

He remembers the orphanage's long corridors. The cold bathhouse. The scent of wet wool and disinfectant. The silence of boys who knew better than to speak. And he remembers the day the Trifili carriage came. The way the woman held his chin like it wasn't a question. "You'll come now," she'd said. "You've been returned."

He still doesn't know what she meant. But some nights, in this office, he thinks it was less about return and more about inheritance. Not land. Not name. But the burden of memory—and the choice of what to do with it.

He moves through the double doors, the sound small but final. He continues into the main dining room with the slow precision of a man who no longer rushes—who understands that legacy is not what you build, but what you refuse to forget.

The gas sconce hisses faintly. He crosses the dining room, then touches the banister of the stairway, then through the bar and into the Zitting Room. He paused. Looked at the frame of the Zitting Room closet door. Every board, every bolt, he set himself. Not perfectly. But with weight. With hand. With memory.

Some nights, Mateo finds him here, sitting in the dark, murmuring in Greek.

There is no plaque for George. No portrait. No founder's story etched into brass. But on quiet Tuesday nights, when the mirror hums and the candles burn uneven, you can feel it. The shape of a man who stayed. Not for fame. Not for redemption.

But to witness what might yet be redeemed.

What is salvaged is not always broken.

Some things are kept not to be restored—

but to remember what still holds.

Scroll

THE SIGN IN THE ARCH

Balcony One – Before the Room Had a Name

Before the name, there was the arch.

Not planned. Not drafted. Just… inherited.

George hadn't meant to build a room. He was extending the bar, that was all. It had outgrown its footprint. He sketched it on the butcher paper that lined his desk drawer. Not blueprints. Just marks and estimates. Arrows, circles, and the weight of his own handwriting.

The arch was an accident. A miscalculation in elevation against the old adobe. It created a pocket—an alcove that didn't quite belong to the bar and didn't quite want to be closed in. Cynthia saw it first. She walked through the half-framed space one morning, coffee still steaming, and said, "Feels like a room." Then she kept walking.

George stood in the doorway longer than he should have, dust in his hair, tape measure slack in one hand. The curve had formed naturally. The load wanted to rest there. The bricks had taken to it. He wasn't about to argue with that.

So he gave it shape.

No name.

Not yet.

The room opened slowly. Not like a door—more like a lung. It breathed as it grew. The walls leaned gently inward, not perfectly plumb, but true to their own balance. Each table placed was not just furniture, but a kind of punctuation. A booth curved the opposite wall of the arched windows, perfectly positioned to catch the evening sun. The floorboards creaked in a different rhythm than the rest of the restaurant—slower, as if each step had to pass through memory first.

George didn't speak about it much.

But Sam noticed.

Of course Sam noticed.

He leaned against the unfinished frame that first Friday, thumbs tucked into overalls, grinning like a man who'd seen the bones of a thing before it wore its skin.

"What's this then?" Sam had asked, jerking his chin toward the raw opening.

George shrugged. "Just an overshoot."

Sam's laugh filled the half-room like varnish on wood. "Hell of a good overshoot."

They didn't call it anything for months. But Sam started sending regulars back there anyway. "You'll like it," he'd say. "It's quieter."

Elizabeth had taken to wiping the sills twice as often. Rosa lined the baseboards with eucalyptus twigs, just for scent. No one asked her to.

Something in the space invited more.

One afternoon, Mateo left a broken violin on the windowsill. A guest had abandoned it—claimed it was cursed, no joke. But Mateo thought it deserved better than the dumpster. So he leaned it gently against the glass. George didn't move it. Neither did Sam.

They didn't speak of ghosts then. Not yet. But everyone who sat in the unfinished room lingered longer. Ordered slower. Sometimes left notes.

George caught one once—tucked between napkins. A scrawl of pen on receipt paper:

This room knows my name.

He didn't show it to anyone. Just folded it, once, and placed it in the drawer near the bottom of his desk.

Still no name.

But something had begun.

It wasn't until the night Sam stayed late—after close, when the sinks were drained and the world outside had gone quiet—that George traced the edge of the arch with his hand. The stucco was still raw, unpainted. The light from the kitchen spilled over his knuckles.

He was alone. Or mostly.

He thought he heard the violin hum.

That was the first time he imagined the sign. Not what it would say— he hadn't come to that yet. But he saw the shape of the letters. Not printed. Not stamped. Carved. With weight. With pause between each one.

He didn't draw it.

Didn't speak it.

Just stood in the archway with the memory of Sam's laugh still hanging in the beams, and let the idea take hold.

The room wasn't ready to be named.

But it had already started remembering.

It was a dry winter. The kind that pulled paint from walls and moisture from joints. The patio heaters worked double shifts, and the regulars drank their red wine slower, like the glasses were warming stones instead of stemware. Cynthia kept extra shea balm in the office drawer for everyone's hands. Rosa burned citrus peel behind the bar. Even the floorboards seemed brittle—like they needed coaxing to hold the weight of so many unspoken things.

George felt it in his fingers. Not arthritis exactly. Just… withdrawal. His hands craved the grain of wood the way some men crave drink. He hadn't built anything in months.

It was Mateo who mentioned it first.

"The booth plaque came loose again," he said, balancing a tray on one shoulder. "Second time this week."

George grunted. Didn't look up.

Mateo waited a beat. Then added, "The varnish is pulling away from the west arch. Might want to sand and reseal."

George just nodded. But he heard it. More than heard. He felt it like a hinge shifting in his own chest.

That night, long after close, he walked the floor barefoot, candle in hand. The restaurant was quieter than usual. Not still—never still. But hushed in the way of old buildings that remember too much.

He stopped beneath the arch.

Ran his thumb along the curve of the frame. The stucco was crumbling slightly where the light always caught it at sunset. Not much. Just a powdering. But enough.

He stepped into the room—Sam's room, though no one said it like that.

And looked up.

The sign was there. Of course it was.

ZITTING ROOM, hand-carved, letters beveled at the corners, slightly uneven the way only true craftsmanship can be. He had made it the week after Sam died. Late one night. With wood from a tree that had fallen in the Virgin River floodplain. Walnut, dark and heavy. The letters took hours. He sharpened his chisel between every vowel.

He hadn't planned to name the room. But the moment Sam's obituary ran, George found himself back in the shop, drawing the letter Z without meaning to. It came out too wide the first time. Too regal the second. But the third—slightly tilted, bearing its own weight—felt right.

He carved it slowly, like a prayer offered backwards.

That was the same week he hung the portrait.

Sam in tall grass, holding the pheasant like he'd just apologized to it. George wiped the frame with oil before hanging it, then stepped back, hands on hips.

He didn't cry then. Not quite.

But he did sit on the booth's edge for a long time.

Didn't light the lantern. Didn't pour a drink.

Just let the dark settle and waited for something he never named.

He didn't want a shrine.

He wanted a remembering.

So he named the room. Not with ceremony. Just with the sign.

The next night, people noticed.

Regulars paused. Staff lingered. Cynthia ran her fingers beneath the sign once, quietly, while passing through. Brooke whispered something under her breath near the booth. Rosa placed a fresh cloth under the salt and pepper. Mateo made sure the candle in the back corner was lit before the guests arrived.

No one said Sam's name aloud.

They didn't have to.

The room had learned it.

George stood in that same archway now, years later, thumb pressed into a nick near the Z. The varnish was fading. The wood wanted tending. So did he.

He would refinish the sign that weekend. Quietly. Without telling anyone.

The sign was not a memorial.

It was a continuation.

A naming that never stopped echoing.

The wood had been waiting.

George found it behind the old shed near the wash, where the cedar slabs were stacked like unread letters. This one was different. It had a natural curve, as if the tree had leaned toward something before falling. A knot sat at its center, rough and dark. He ran his fingers over it, palm flat. There was a grain to the silence.

He brought it to the back of the building without telling anyone. Set it across the two sawhorses. Lit the lantern. Let the night settle around it.

The carving took longer than expected.

It wasn't the lettering. He'd done that before. What slowed him was the curve—how the grain of the wood resisted the phrase, how it pulled the chisel a little off every time he got too sure of himself. He started over three times. Let the knife rest between cuts. Sipped water. Thought of Sam.

Sam would've hated the idea of a room named after him. Would've laughed it off, told George to name it something Greek, or something foul. "Name it after your mother," he'd once joked. "She's got the stronger constitution." George didn't laugh then. But he did now.

He'd already made the first pass:

The Zitting Room.

That was the easy part.

But the wood didn't feel finished. The bottom edge needed a second line. He didn't know what it was until his hand wrote it without asking.

Let us raise a glass with Sam.

It wasn't fancy.

It wasn't final.

It was… enough.

He etched the words deeper than the first line. Let them hold. There was something about the phrase—how it didn't say "to Sam," but "with Sam." As if he were still there. As if the toast could still find him.

The next morning, just after dawn, he sanded the whole thing smooth. Oiled the wood with what he had left. Mateo walked past once, didn't say anything. Just nodded and kept moving. Cynthia came later with a mug of tea and didn't ask what the sign was for.

George didn't explain.

He just carried it to the arch.

Mounted it with care.

Three bolts.

No ceremony.

Only weight.

Only presence.

By the time service started, the smell of cedar still hung in the Zitting Room. The light caught the curve just right—glinting along the bevel of the "S" in Sam. Guests paused beneath it, unsure why. Some looked up. Some didn't.

But every one of them sat a little straighter that night. Every toast landed heavier. Every clink of glass held just a fraction more memory.

And in the corner of the room, George stood for a moment. One hand on the booth's edge. Not smiling. Not weeping. Just holding the quiet.

Let us raise a glass with Sam.

And so they did.

That night, the building held its breath.

It wasn't ceremony. There were no candles, no crowd. Just George—alone in the Zitting Room, long after the last guest had left, when the chairs were stacked and the wine glasses were drying upside down like questions.

He didn't turn on the overheads. Just the wall sconce to the left of the arched window, the one Sam liked to sit beneath. The light hit the new sign at a slant, enough to draw the grain forward, make the carved words glint like wet stone.

"Let us raise a glass with Sam."

He'd wiped the wood three times already. Not because it was dirty. Because he couldn't stop touching it.

That phrase—it hadn't come from a speech.

But that phrase—"Let us raise a glass with Sam"—had stuck. Not to commemorate. To continue. That was the difference. It wasn't for Sam. It was with him.

Now, in the Zitting Room, the grain of the sign caught fire under the amber light. The edges still smelled of tung oil and cedar. The iron nails sat flush, handmade by a blacksmith George met in Toquerville who still believed in heating things until they confessed their true shape.

He sat at Sam's table.

He didn't speak.

But something in the room answered.

The scent came first. Not pomegranate, not quince. Not even cognac. Something rounder, duskier. Like earth after rain and citrus crushed beneath foot. Not one scent—an accumulation. A memory in composite.

The picture still hung by the arch. Sam with the pheasant. George had hung it that morning, after polishing the glass with a rag he'd found folded in the register. He'd stared at that photo for too long—long enough to remember Sam's posture.

He hadn't been a perfect man. That wasn't the point.

He had been present.

And presence—that was what this room remembered. That was why the adobe curved differently here. Why the windows caught light longer. Why the echo of laughter always seemed to turn once before dissolving.

George closed his eyes.

He let the memory come.

Of Sam's voice on the stairs. Of the way he ordered wine by the year, not the label. Of the last Tuesday, when he didn't show. When the chair stayed empty, and the air turned dense, like the beginning of a storm.

George hadn't cried then.

But he did now.

Just one breath, exhaled too hard.

Enough to mist the edge of the table.

He reached forward. Touched the inlay.

It wasn't copper.

It was the scrap left from the bar, the one Mateo almost threw away, the one Sam had once leaned against so long it bore a shadow.

Elizabeth had suggested inlaying it after the funeral.

But George had been the one to glue it.

He'd sat right here, at midnight, with the epoxy setting and his hands trembling. He hadn't prayed. But he'd whispered.

"Still with us."

And meant it.

Now the copper caught the light like a pulse.

George tapped it once, a soft rhythm.

Let us raise a glass with Sam.

Let us remember how it tasted—what he left behind in the glass, in the booth, in the breath that followed his jokes.

Let us stay.

Not in sorrow.

In presence.

And George had built the sign not to close the memory—but to mark where it entered.

He stood.

Touched the frame.

Let the wood answer.

The Zitting Room didn't reply with language.

Only light.

Only warmth.

Only the slow hush of adobe breathing in.

And the faintest trace of laughter from a chair no one had touched.

Not since Sam.

Not yet.

Time softened the corners, as it always does.

The sign had dulled—its sheen now tempered by dust, by fingerprints, by seasons of Tuesday light filtering through the west-facing windows. The letters still read the same. "The Zitting Room – Let us raise a glass with Sam." But the wood held more than words now. It held weather. And weather, like grief, does not ask permission to change.

George continued to keep it polished.

He wiped it now and then. Checked the bolts. Ran his thumb along the bottom edge where the resin had pooled too thick on that last coat.

The room had absorbed the memory.

Sam's laughter still lived in the grain. Not replayed—integrated. In the slant of the light. In the pause before a toast. In the way people shifted their bodies slightly inward when they entered, like they were stepping into a story already in progress.

New guests didn't know the name.

They saw the photo. Maybe read the plaque. Asked about the pheasant. Sometimes smiled at the idea of naming a dining room after someone local.

But they stayed longer in here.

And spoke softer.

And, more often than in other rooms, they cried.

George noticed, but didn't say so.

He watched from the bar. From the corner booth. From the hallway near the kitchen where the mirror didn't quite align.

It wasn't sadness that drew them in. It was something else. Something rarer.

Permission.

The Zitting Room gave people permission to carry what they hadn't named yet. And to lay it down without needing to explain.

Some called it the most haunted room in the restaurant.

George corrected them once, early on.

"It's not haunted," he'd said, wiping down the copper edge. "It's hospitable."

They'd laughed, not unkindly.

But he meant it.

Hospitality isn't performance. It's presence. And presence, in its truest form, leaves an imprint. Sam had known that. George still carried it.

Even now, long after the copper dulled and the photo faded, he felt the pull.

Especially on Tuesdays.

Especially near sunset.

He'd come into the room when the tables were empty, when the staff had stepped out for breath or smoke, when the music from the patio softened and the lights hadn't yet turned. He'd sit at the edge of the booth—not Sam's, never that—but the one just beside it.

And listen.

Sometimes nothing happened.

Just stillness.

Sometimes the chair across from him shifted—half an inch, maybe less.

Sometimes a glass had been set there without explanation.

He never asked who placed it.

He never moved it.

On the anniversary of Sam's death, Cynthia left a small branch of cedar tucked behind the copper seam. No note. No flourish. Just a gesture.

A week later, it disappeared.

That's how the Zitting Room worked.

It didn't demand ritual. It responded to it.

George had once said that Sam didn't die in this room.

"But part of him never left," Elizabeth replied. She had been cutting stems for the side table, her hands full of lavender and time.

George nodded. Didn't speak.

But that night, he sat a little longer at the edge of the copper. He poured a single shot of tsipouro. Didn't drink it. Just let it catch the light.

Then raised his glass anyway.

Not to memory.

To continuation.

To the way Sam still stirred the wine in the stemware. Still pressed his boot against the table leg. Still waited for George to finish the story he always left halfway through.

That was the thing about Sam.

He never gave you endings.

Just invitations.

And the Zitting Room—this room that bore his name, not in granite or gold but in the soft bend of adobe and the warmth of cedar—held the invitation open.

George didn't write the name above the door for mourning.

He wrote it for return.

And return, he had come to believe, was not the opposite of loss.

It was its echo.

One that curved inward, slow and warm, like a spiral.

Some names are not etched in stone.
They are carried in the silence between laughter—
and the places we return to when the toast is ready.

Scroll

THE FLOWER LEFT BEHIND

Balcony One

The sun had begun its slow descent—casting angled light through the western windows, warm against the red walls. The restaurant was alive. Voices from the bar. Plates clinking in the kitchen. The low hum of a broom brushing tile.

But the Zitting Room was empty.

Brooke stepped inside, quiet as she could. She hadn't been asked to clean it. Wasn't even sure why she'd come. In her apron pocket, a single bougainvillea. She hadn't meant to pick it.

The flower had caught her attention only after she'd bent to wipe the windowsill near the kitchen's south exit. There, half-shaded and out of season, one bougainvillea bloom curved against the wall, low to the earth and still touched by dew. Brooke didn't think. She reached for it the way you do when you recognize something—not from memory, but from rhythm.

Her mother used to say that some plants found people, not the other way around. That bougainvillea, in particular, remembered grief with a kind of gentleness. Brooke didn't think of that as she snipped it. Just noticed how the stem fit easily between her fingers. Perfectly soft. Like something waiting to be held.

She wrapped it in a square of dry cloth—one of Rosa's—without a word. Slipped it in her pocket before the others could ask. She hadn't decided what to do with it. Only that it wasn't to be left behind.

Cut from the side yard that morning.

Still dewy.

The Zitting Room never felt empty.

Even when no one was in it.

The walls curved in that particular way adobe did when it aged well—softened, thickened, breathing slightly. Light from the windows fell in golden diagonals, warming the floorboards like a waiting lap.

The tables were half-round, tucked beneath the arched windows.

Opposite them, two booths nestled into the wall like resting thoughts.

And beyond them—

a door.

Tall. Arched.

More decoration than passage.

Dark wood inlaid with curling iron.

Most assumed it was ornamental.

Brooke had asked once.

Elizabeth only shrugged.

"It remembers things," she'd said.

And that was all. On the wall next to the archway leading into the Zitting Room, hung the portrait. Sepia-toned, framed in rough pine. Sam

Zitting in tall grass, a pheasant in one hand, a rifle in the other. His cap was crooked. His gaze was not.

Just present.

Brooke stood in front of it for a moment longer than she meant to. She had felt that before. The sensation of being noticed without expectation. A rare, quiet kind of attention. It reminded her of the way Elizabeth sometimes looked at her. Like she was listening to something Brooke hadn't said yet.

Brooke never read into it. She didn't have time for that kind of interpretation. But she remembered once, just a week ago, handing Elizabeth a folded cloth at the end of the shift—fingers brushing by accident—and how Elizabeth's breath caught almost imperceptibly. A pause so small, it might have been a trick of timing. Brooke just moved past. But something about the exchange had lingered, unsorted.

Now, standing in the Zitting Room, under the weight of the sepia gaze and the soft breath of the bougainvillea, Brooke felt it again. That quiet watching. She adjusted her apron without meaning to. Cleared her throat into the stillness. And stepped forward.

The table beneath the left arched window had been polished so many times it caught the afternoon light like metal.

They called it the copper table, though it wasn't copper—not truly.

Just memory, burnished into wood.

Sam had always claimed it.

Never by word—just by presence.

Even now, the table seemed to hold the shape of him.

The way he leaned back.

The way his laughter curved across the glass.

The way people lowered their voices when they sat there.

Brooke crossed the room, careful not to disturb the quiet. The flower was still warm from her pocket.

At the table—his table—she paused.

There was already a glass there.

Simple. Clear. Heavy-bottomed.

Someone had rinsed it, but not yet put it away.

She didn't think.

She just slipped the stem into the water.

Watched it settle.

It looked small against the wood.

But right.

Folded her hands in front of her apron.

Let the quiet settle.

The bloom held for a moment longer than it should have.

Its stem, freshly snipped, stood straight in the slender glass. The petals were full, unbruised. Fragrant. A single breath of bougainvillea—cut early, before the heat of day could lean in.

Brooke didn't pray.

She didn't whisper.

She simply placed the flower and stepped back.

A quiet instinct.

A nod of respect for someone she'd never met.

She didn't notice the way the air shifted behind her.

The subtle contraction.

The inhale that wasn't breath.

Sophia hovered near the window.

She remembered another bloom—long ago—when the building was still raw adobe and open beams. She had tucked a Sego lily into the crook of the door, behind a nail that wasn't flush. No one had noticed. But the next day, George asked who'd lit the back lantern early.

The girl would never know her name. Not her first one.

Panagiota had lived.

Sophia… watched.

A memory shaped by grief.

Her eyes—not misted, not spectral, but watching—lingered on the flower.

And then on the girl.

There was a soft ache in Sophia's chest.

Not pain.

Just… recognition.

A gesture made too late.

But still made.

The kind of thing that matters more because no one told her to do it.

Sophia did not move.

She only watched.

Sophia's gaze followed the girl's hands—the way she moved without fanfare, without explanation. It reminded her of the early days, before Balcony One had a name. Before the walls were colored or the menus printed. Back when gestures meant more than intentions.

She could feel the pulse of the room—how the offering, unasked and unframed, shifted its center of gravity. This wasn't grief. Not fully. This was reverence. The kind that didn't belong to gods or names or bloodlines.

She had once left flowers too.

Not in vases. Not in public.

After the mirror cracked and let her through—after George brushed it with the ring still warm from her hand—

She began to mark the place.

Not with words. With lilies.

Wild Sego blossoms tucked beneath floorboards, behind beams, in the curve of a doorframe.

Not because she believed in superstition.

But because Balcony One welcomed her.

Because something in her remembered what it meant to keep watch.

She watched Brooke with the quiet ache of recognition.

She began remembering something about George. But the residue faded. She thought she had stood here once with scaffolding and dirt, but it was not her memory. Even though she had once stood here with Sam. But the memory was not hers.

Sophia couldn't remember.

She hadn't needed to remember fully for herself. Not yet. Some women built with words. Some with hands.

Her gaze returned to the flower. Its edges had begun to soften. But it was still standing. The light in the room shifted. Not dimmed—but lengthened. As if the sun itself were pausing. Stretching. One beam fell directly on the copper table. The bougainvillea caught it—just barely— and for a second, the petals looked translucent. Like tissue folded in prayer.

A hush gathered in the corners. The kind that doesn't come from silence. But from attention. Even the air felt pulled slightly inward. Not heavier. Just—held.

Outside the Zitting Room, a floorboard sighed. Not loud. Just enough to let the room know it was not alone. Brooke turned her head.

Through the edge of the doorway, she caught the blur of a figure. Elizabeth. Apron tied. Hair pinned. Walking steady, as always. She didn't pause. Didn't peer in. Just moved past with the ease of someone who already knew what had been placed on the table.

What had been seen.

What would be remembered.

Brooke watched until the steps faded.

Then turned back to the flower.

It had begun to wilt—just at the edges.

Not decay—

Just relief, beginning.

Some flowers do not open for sunlight.
They open for memory.

281

Scroll

THE DOOR

Zitting Room – Just After the Bougainvillea Faded

She hadn't meant to walk that way. But her body knew before her mind did. A faint sweetness still lingered in the air—bougainvillea, wilted but not yet dried.

Brooke had offered the flower that morning without explanation.

Elizabeth hadn't asked.

But something in her had noted it—quietly, like tracking the weight of a ring long since worn smooth.

All day, her hands moved as usual—broom, bottle, receipt, cloth—but her awareness lagged just behind. Not distracted. Tilted.

She didn't follow the scent.

She followed the feeling.

The way her father once traced fault lines in stained maps, fingers finding seams long buried.

The way George used to pause mid-step, turned toward a door no one had knocked on.

It wasn't memory guiding her.

It was something older.

Elizabeth moved through the bar, towel in hand, though she'd stopped wiping anything down ten minutes ago. The stained-glass windows behind the bar caught the evening light like a secret trying not to be seen.

Elizabeth had polished those windows once—years ago, before she understood how light lives differently in silence. She remembered the exact rag, the faint ache in her wrist. Magnus had laughed from the bar, calling it a fool's errand.

"You can't clean what wants to blur," he'd said.

But she'd done it anyway.

Now, she didn't clean them.

She watched them.

And sometimes, at dusk, she'd catch herself whispering—not words, just sound—as if trying to match whatever note the windows already held.

Three of them—narrow and pointed—rose in staggered succession across the back wall, each set slightly lower than the last. Amber, red, blue, green. The glass was thick and imperfect, casting not just color but distortion. The light they let through didn't fall in neat lines—it bent. Tilted. Like sunlight filtered through old memory.

They faced east, Elizabeth had always assumed, though the way they held the last of the light made time feel like a negotiable thing. The lowest window pulsed with a dull orange warmth, the topmost flickered violet, as if the three together formed an unholy trinity—not malevolent, but misaligned. Watching something no one else could see.

To the right, set into the south-facing wall behind the bar, a single large window. Unstained. Clear. The glass there didn't color the light. It surrendered to it.

In front of that window, the bar's bottles rose in tiered rows—three deep—each one catching the sunset like a prism. There were tall green ones with torn paper seals. Squat brown bottles shaped like apothecary jars. Thin, fluted ones that looked more decorative than drinkable. Tequila. Amaro. Cordials with labels in languages Elizabeth couldn't read.

The window behind them caught their shadows.

It didn't judge.

The whole wall was framed by cabinetry—dark wood, deep-toned, old but still formal. To the left of the window, rows of upside-down glassware: stemmed and stemless, some etched, some plain. To the right, a stack of ceramic mugs with uneven handles—each one the same, but slightly off.

Above them, the upper paneling bore carved flourishes—hexagonal inlays flanked by what looked like small wooden florets or pressed flowers. Fleur-de-lis, maybe, though dulled by time. Not decorative in a grand sense. More like something inscribed before language. Something meant to bless the bottles.

No one called her name.

No orders shouted from the kitchen.

Just the muted clink of a shaker being rinsed. A register drawer sliding closed.

Elizabeth passed slowly through the bar, the bottles and windows now to her left,

Nestled behind the layered bottles, the clear south-facing window opened—welcoming the light.

Unlike the stained glass behind her, which fractured the world into fragments of color, this window revealed it whole: a broad, unbroken view of the land that fell away into the mouth of Zion.

The canyon's lip curled in the distance, cradling the last of the sun. Clouds drifted slow and wide above it, burnished gold and lavender. If you stood still long enough, you could watch the light shift across the buttes—a silent choreography of shadow and flame.

The window wasn't just glass.

It was permission.

A momentary reprieve from the weight of walls.

A reminder that this place had not always been shaped by hands.

Behind the bar, the bottles stood like quiet witnesses to it all—rows of translucent color catching sky in their shoulders. Every now and then, a ray of light would thread between them and throw a perfect golden circle on the counter.

Elizabeth had never said it aloud, but she always felt that was Sam's favorite window.

Her steps made no sound on the wood.

To her right, the archway waited—curved and red, the entrance to the Zitting Room shaped like a held breath.

She didn't rush.

No one did, crossing that threshold.

The arch was low enough she had to duck her chin slightly. She did so without thought, as if bowing to something.

Inside, the light changed again.

Not brighter. Not dimmer.

Just quieter.

The booths along the far wall sat empty, their deep cushions still holding the impressions of whoever had lingered last. The half-moon tables under the tall windows gleamed faintly, though the sun had already left them. And across the room, the decorative door—

That's what everyone called it.

The decorative door.

Tall. Arched.

Crafted by George—

the psychic architect.

Set into the back wall like a secret that had agreed to be forgotten.

Most assumed it didn't open.

That it wasn't meant to.

But Elizabeth had always known better.

Tonight, it wasn't fully flush to the wall.

A line of shadow traced its edge—too narrow for light, too present to be dismissed.

She crossed the room.

No one called to her.

No glass clinked.

No chair scraped.

Only the faint scent of bougainvillea, returning again.

She stopped in front of the door.

She remembered catching a glimpse of Sophia standing here once, years ago.

Not speaking. Quiescent. Spectral.

Just placing her palm on the wood and closing her eyes.

Elizabeth hadn't asked.

Hadn't needed to.

Some things were passed down without words.

And some were passed down because no one dared to say them aloud.

Her hand rose slowly—familiar with this gesture, but never casual about it. Her fingers found the knot near center. Not a handle. A memory.

She pressed.

A click.

The wood gave way. Not with sound. With surrender.

The door eased open by a breath.

Beyond it—

darkness that wasn't empty.

Somewhere deeper in the stone, a memory stirred.

Not hers—Sophia's.

The air shifted like breath caught between notes. Elizabeth could feel it—like a thread pulled taut not by time, but by recognition.

She had read once, long ago, that the oldest parts of the earth remember music. That stone itself can hold the tone of sorrow, if shaped during a song.

Elizabeth stepped slightly forward, not down, not in—just toward.

The hum wasn't melody. It wasn't even harmony.

It was ache, in D minor.

A chord that had no beginning.

And no need for one.

Air that remembered stone.

Stillness that hummed with a tune.

No voice.

No words.

Only the shape of song.

Lingering like smoke after the fire has gone.

She didn't step forward.

Not yet.

But the air pressed differently here.

Not against her skin—

against her knowing.

The scent beneath the bougainvillea was stronger now.

Stone.

And something older than stone.

The stairwell was not fully visible, but she felt its shape.

A tilt downward.

A narrowing.

The way water finds the lowest place.

Elizabeth placed her fingers on the doorframe.

The wood was thick, warm at first touch, then cold a breath later – like memory resisting being summoned. George had built this door himself. Iron stars pinned its edges, and a wrought iron grate, inset at eye level, offered no view – only a feeling. He'd said it was patterned after the one on his grandfather's house in Athens.

His mother, Panagiota, had brought him there once—just once—when he was still small. She'd stood before a similar door with an iron grate and tried to explain who she was. Whose son George was. What had been promised.

But the man behind that door rejected her.

George never let anything go to waste.

He had built this door for storage. But he made it beautiful. Made it remember.

And when Elizabeth placed her fingers to the latch, she felt not the entrance to a closet—

But a story that had waited too long to be acknowledged.

Then something in between—like touching a memory still deciding how it wants to be remembered.

From deep below, a shift.

No footsteps.

No movement.

Just presence.

A thread of something passed along her shoulder.

Sophia.

Not close enough to speak.

But near enough that the air tasted different.

Elizabeth did not call her name.

She never did.

Names had a weight in this building.

You didn't use them unless you were willing to carry what answered.

A sound rose.

Not in English.

In Greek.

Barely a hum.

Not heard—registered.

The way the body remembers water long after you've left the river.

Her hand dropped from the frame.

She could have stepped back.

Could have let the door close.

Could have walked away and counted it enough.

But she stayed.

Not to see.

To feel.

The stairwell below seemed to breathe once

—the air pulsed.

Not with sound.

With awareness.

Elizabeth remained at the threshold.

Her hands at her sides.

Open.

She didn't reach for the light.

There wasn't any.

The dark inside the stairwell wasn't hostile.

It wasn't hollow.

It felt... tethered.

As if something in it had been waiting not for discovery—

but for witness.

She stepped closer to the opening.

Not onto the first stair.

Just near enough that her breath stirred the edge of it.

She felt it again—

the pull.

Not magnetic. Not emotional.

An ache.

Some part of her she rarely acknowledged recognized what lay beyond the door.

She had felt it before.

Not the basement, not the door—but the ache.

A Sunday, late summer. She was bringing in the porch quilts. Elizabeth had paused, hand to the railing, and felt it—like a note struck deep in the earth, too low for hearing, but perfect for feeling.

She'd told no one.

Not then.

Not when it returned the night Sam died.

Not even when she saw Sophia's reflection ripple in the glass of the upstairs mirror, just once, as if trying to remind her of something she hadn't been old enough to know.

The ache had no name. But it had persistence.

And now it vibrated through her soles, up her spine, settling in her molars like the memory of grief too early mourned.

She did not step forward.

But she did not step back.

Not factually.

Spiritually.

There was no heat.

No chill.

Just that very particular sensation of standing near a story that had not yet been told.

And would not be, if she turned away.

A movement—

small, low, from the base of the stair.

A shadow shifting.

It didn't rise.

It didn't beckon.

It simply re-formed itself slightly, like fog adjusting to a body it once held.

She had known this moment was coming.

Had known it since Sam's death.

Since the Zitting Room started holding onto things longer than it should.

Since Sophia stopped answering from the mirror and started pressing against the floorboards instead.

She inhaled once.

Held it.

Let it out.

Her fingers brushed the edge of the open door.

The hum stopped.

Not cut short.

Concluded.

Whatever waited below had made its offering.

And now—

it waited for hers.

Elizabeth closed her eyes.

"Not yet," she said.

Then she closed the door.

Not all the way.

Just enough.

She turned from the stairwell.

The door eased shut behind her.

The Zitting Room received her in stillness—the slow settling of air after something has shifted and chosen not to announce itself. Her foot brushed the copper edge of Sam's table. Warm. Elizabeth didn't pause—

Until—

she saw it.

Near the corner, across from the copper table.

A mirror.

Not the same one from before.

This one was oval, darker in frame. New –newly arrived.

She would have noticed the difference.

It reflected nothing unusual—just the opposite wall, the lower third of a window, the curve of a chair's back.

She simply looked.

And for a second—

just a second—

her own reflection didn't meet her gaze.

The face looking back at her turned a beat slower.

Then caught up.

Elizabeth blinked once.

Then walked on.

She didn't look back.

She knew better than to stare at something still deciding what it was.

Behind her, the Zitting Room exhaled. A slow breath, drawn not in lungs but in wood and stone and story. Elizabeth let the sensation pass through her ribs before reaching for the archway into the bar. Her hand didn't tremble. But it hesitated. Briefly. Like she'd left something behind—something unspeakable but not unfinished.

In the bar, someone coughed.

A spoon clinked.

Life resumed its thread.

But beneath it all, beneath the floorboards and the walls and the moments, the ache lingered. Quieter now. But present.

Waiting.

Not for answers.

For readiness.

*
**

What waits beneath does not sleep.

It listens.

It remembers the names we have not yet spoken.

Scroll

SOPHIA'S RECKONING

Beneath the Zitting Room – After the Door Refused to Stay Closed

They buried her gently in the mountain cemetery near Delphi. Sweeping pines, the Church of St. Theodores, and ornate monument statues.

There were no hymns—just a low chant, a hand-carved cross, and George's hand closing gently over the ring on his pinky finger.

It had been John's once.

Given in promise.

Taken in grief.

Passed to her son on the last day he was hers.

She pressed it into his hand—no ceremony, just insistence.

"This is how you carry me," she said.

Not in words.

In a look that softened his ribs and steadied his throat.

When Panagiota died – she did not linger in the grave.

Not truly.

Because something in the ring had already begun to hum—

Memory.

And memory is how some women refuse to disappear.

A part of her came with George when he returned to Utah.

Not in voice. Not in body.

But in metal.

In weight.

In the slight crack she left in the mirror when he brushed past with the ring still new to his hand.

He never threw the mirror away.

George never let anything go to waste.

He built a frame from salvaged wood, mounted it beside the waiting room arch.

But the mirror pulsed three nights later.

Not with light.

With presence.

Sophia—that was the name she took in death.

Not the name John had whispered.

Not the name Panagiota carried in the olive fields.

But the one that fit her shape on this side of the veil.

Not a shadow.

Not an residue.

Something housed.

She did not haunt.

She remembered.

And through remembering, she built.

The mirror was the first.

But the others came after.

Not hung.

Found.

Each one held a fraction of her—

a tilt of the head,

a scent caught at dusk,

a flicker of lace in a room no one had entered.

She did not speak, but the rooms shifted when she passed—not in temperature, but in gravity.

The Zitting Room, especially, remembered her more than most.

It curled its corners when she stirred.

Dimmed its candles a second early.

Held scent longer than it should.

And beneath it—

where no door had been carved,

no latch hammered—

a space began to take shape.

Not a basement. The blueprints never showed a basement. George never carved it out. It wasn't planned. It just… appeared. Built not with hands, but with haunting. A room Sophia made—when mirrors were no longer enough.

A reckoning.

Built with the will to remain.

She hadn't been here in life.

But memory doesn't require physical permission.

She knew what a cellar should feel like.

The kind where women boiled pomegranate syrup at midnight.

The kind where secrets weren't kept—only stored.

This one was hers.

Not to possess.

To witness.

And when Elizabeth arrived—

drawn by scent, by silence, by a mirror that didn't behave—

Sophia watched.

As mothers do, when their children are long grown, but still carry the ring.

Presence is difficult to preserve. Especially in buildings. Especially in women.

So she stayed.

A presence—not as a ghost, not quite.

As pressure.

As the weight that settles in corners too quiet to sweep.

She had not expected it—this state, this soil-self. She thought she'd be done. Buried. Quiet. But memory doesn't surrender that easily.

The soil in Delphi was not loose.

It held shape.

Pressed into itself like bread without leaven.

She had felt it first not with her hands—

but her ribs.

The way the earth resisted collapse.

The way it remembered being moved, then packed again.

As if it knew it had taken something in and was deciding what to do with it.

There were stones, too, wedged like bones in the heel of the world.

She lay between two.

One smooth, one jagged.

She had names for them.

The smooth one remembered the small village near Delphi.

Its cool curve reminded her of the river she once crossed with a pack too heavy and a hymn half-learned.

The jagged one felt like Doxa, Δόξα.

Sharp. Blunt. Burned.

Insistent.

She did not sleep.

Time did not collapse here—

it stretched.

Like cloth too often worn.

She remembered being lowered down. Among the cypress trees and old marble, in the same village she had lived with John. I held her gently.

But not fully.

Because something pulled.

A thread across water.

She didn't resist. She didn't know how.

The ring had passed to George.

He had carried it across the ocean—his pinky now bearing the curve once worn by her husband.

And when he brushed the mirror in Utah—by accident, with the ring he wore—

it cracked.

Not from force. From recognition.

And something in her recognized him back.

Not with eyes. With memory.

She did not mean to follow.

But the break opened a door no one knew to close.

And through it, she came.

Not in form. In frequency.

A low hum the adobe began to absorb.

She did not know this place.

But she felt him.

And that was enough to stay.

She didn't know who she was, or where she came from. This was not her home—she had been buried in Greece. But something here kept her. And so she stayed, and manifested.

In the mirror.

Beneath the Zitting Room—

within the blue glass—

She waited.

Not out of vengeance.

Not out of confusion.

But because the air had shaped itself to remember her.

And memory is a stubborn kind of welcome.

The building above shifted over time.

Expanded. Contracted. Settled again.

She felt each winter's frost.

Each monsoon sigh.

And with every season, she grew quieter.

Not diminished.

Just… incorporated.

Balcony One did not sit on top of her.

It sat with her.

Her ribs became beams.

Her silence, insulation.

Her memory, mortar.

And when someone walked past her—

when their weight fell just right,

and their heart was open enough to feel what hadn't been said—

she whispered.

But Balcony One remembered her differently.

And when a place remembers you, it rewrites the rules.

There are no blueprints with her name on them.

No initials in the concrete.

No handprint in tile.

Not even the whispered lore of staff who want to believe the place is haunted.

She is not that kind of remembered.

She is the draft that never makes it to the final plan.

The breath held just before someone decides not to say the name.

When people talk about Balcony One's beginnings, they name Mateo. Ricky. Sometimes Cynthia.

And then George.

The psychic architect.

Not just the gypsy.

The receptor.

The man through whom the place dreamed itself awake.

He did not conjure Sophia.

But his grief made space for her.

His blueprints bent around memory he didn't know he was carrying.

The mirror cracked when the ring caught the frame—

and through that fracture, she came.

Not as Panagiota.

That name was buried in Delphi.

But something in the wood, in the adobe, in the air—

heard the shape of what he missed.

And made her.

Not from scratch.

From ache.

She was not erased from history.

She was excluded from narrative.

No initials in the concrete.

No plaque.

No room named in her honor.

Just air.

She used to think legacy was shaped like stone: engraved, enduring.

Now she knows it is shaped like breath:

repeated, or lost.

And breath is fickle.

She once imagined a daughter.

Or at least a niece.

Someone who would remember how her hands folded linen the Greek way.

Someone who wouldn't let her story slip behind someone else's headline.

But the women in her life died early.

Or were taught to forget.

Or would look down on her.

So when she came through the mirror—

she came not to haunt.

But to witness.

And when she saw Elizabeth for the first time—

She connected. A daughter she never had. Or someone who noticed she was there when no one else could.

Now, when the light hits the Zitting Room just right, and the blue glass catches it like water, and someone pauses without knowing why—she is there.

Not standing.

Not lingering.

Listening.

Folded into the curvature of the Santa Fe styled adobe. Tucked inside the quiet between glasses clinking and someone adjusting a chair.

But sometimes Elizabeth looks toward the booths

as if she expects someone to already be seated.

Sometimes Brooke stops mid-shift and feels the weight of something not scolding her, but watching.

Sophia has no shrine.

But she has air.

And in this building,

that's almost the same thing.

So she learned to stay silent without being gone. And she listened. To the patter of new boots on old wood. To the sigh of hinges that once held Sam's laughter. To the bar-back girls who knew something wasn't right but didn't yet know what.

She listened to Elizabeth.

The first one who didn't flinch at the cold draft near the mirror. The only one who spoke back—not in words, but with knowing.

George didn't understand Sophia was even there.

Not directly.

Not with names.

But every spring, when the bougainvillea began to bloom, he would walk to the back wall of the Zitting Room, press his fingers against the door he shaped after his grandfather's house, and stand still.

The staff assumed he was checking for stress fractures.

Or planning another repair.

Or just lost in thought, like he often was when the light came through the southern window too soft to ignore.

They didn't know he was counting the layers.

Measuring time by how the wall gave back its coolness.

Mateo knew not to ask.

That night, long after the kitchen had closed,

George circled the building like someone tracing a memory by hand.

Touching the doorframes.

Checking the floorboards.

Whispering things not meant for answers.

Not aloud.

But he placed a chair differently in the Zitting Room that week. Angled not toward the stage, not toward the window—but toward nothing in particular. Later, he built a shelf where no shelf was needed. Added molding to a corner that no one ever sat in. He said it was to balance the space. To honor the adobe.

What he didn't say—

what he never needed to—

was that he had once watched her tuck a flower into that same corner.

quietly.

Like a prayer she didn't expect to be answered.

Now, he trims that molding himself. Every season. No one else is allowed. He claims it's a skill thing. That no one else does it right.

But the truth is simpler:

She had noticed the corners.

And he refuses to let her be the only one who did.

Balcony One did not sit on top of her. It sat with her.

Scroll

PANAGIOTA

Αγάλι-αγάλι γίνεται η αγουρίδα μέλι

Slowly, slowly, the sour grape becomes honey.

In Greek, there's a word for stay:

μένω.

It doesn't mean haunt.

It doesn't mean wait.

It means to stay.

To dwell.

To endure.

To remain long after you've stopped asking for permission.

Méno.

She did not linger out of vengeance.

Or guilt.

Or some unfinished task.

She lingered because the silence was too wide without her.

Because there was an unfinished thread from Greece to Utah.

Because someone—her son—was remembering her in a way the earth could not hold. Remembering and reaching. And memory, when given form, becomes a pathway.

They buried her near Delphi, in the small mountain village where she and John had built their quiet life.

A humble house. A garden. A lemon tree that bore too early some years.

The Mariolato Cemetery marked her name, but not her story.

That stayed tucked in pine needles, smoke trails, and the curve of his ring.

The one she gave to her son after her husband John died. The same ring he wore on his pinky. The same one that caught the edge of the mirror in the waiting room.

It cracked—

Panagiota was not summoned in that moment.

She was remembered into place.

Balcony One gave her shape.

The walls breathed her in like a scent they had been waiting for.

She became Sophia.

Panagiota was not a bitter woman, at least later in life. But she was not a passive one, either. She had buried her rage long before she was buried. Pressed it into the folds of her apron. Tucked it into dough at dawn. Stitched it into hems no one looked twice at.

She was born into olive rows and ash-thick prayers.

Doxa.

A mountain village smoldered by war.

Her mother sang folk hymns with flour on her hands.

But Panagiota's path bent early.

The kitchen fire took her breast.

Left a scar and a silence in her bones.

They called it shame.

She called it survival.

Then came Evangelos.

A soldier with the kind of eyes that made promises even when his mouth didn't.

She loved him.

Devoutly.

Even after he left.

He wrote her letters. She kept them like relics.

Her family shunned her. So she took her path to Athens.

She found the house.

Rodinos. The father of the man who vanished. A home of iron railings and pressed tile, tucked in one of Athens' older quarters.

She knocked.

He answered.

She said her name: Panagiota. She held out the letters—Evangelos' letters. Signed. Folded. Full of promises.

She said,

"This is your grandson. These are your son's words."

Rodinos took the pages.

"I'll read them," he said. "Come back in a few days."

She did.

Same dress. Same child. Same hope.

She knocked.

He answered again, but colder. He looked at her like she was someone he'd never seen.

"I don't know you," he said. "Don't come back here."

She stood there.

"What about the letters?" she asked.

"There are no letters."

And he shut the door.

She didn't scream. Didn't beg. Just stood for a moment longer, then turned and walked away.

Later, George—her son, her storm-eyed child—would say the door at the back of the Zitting Room reminded him of that one.

The shape of it.

The way it could open through the eye level—iron-barred window, wide enough to offer a chance.

And just narrow enough to end it.

She knocked on doors across Athens. Seamstress, maid, cook—whatever work they'd give her. Yiorwos was nearly four. His hand still found hers in crowds.

Then one night in Pagrati—a neighborhood of neoclassical façades and opera ghosts—she knocked, and the Trifili matriarch answered. She took one look at her. At the boy. And let them in.

The mother owned the Athens opera house. Sharp eyes. Gloves without flaw. Her children were fractured brilliance:

Yana, the writer, pages always curled with smoke.

Katerina, the painter, ink-stained and unreachable.

And John—the son who returned from Berlin with an ear for frequency and built Alpha Studio, the first recording studio in downtown Athens.

None of them had children. And in Yiorwos, something clicked.

A boy with salt-shot hair and storm eyes.

They raised him like a mosaic:

Yana taught him syllables.

Katerina gave him color.

John played him records in the dark.

And the mother—she allowed Panagiota to stay.

Not as an equal.

As a maid. A body with chores.

But still: she stayed.

She lived in their basement like an echo still forming. Served in silence. Watched as her boy became their boy, their heir of everything but name. She cooked. She stitched. She endured. But bitterness bloomed in her bones. Not at them—at the shape grief had taken. At how love was never fair. At how even remembered women must be small to be permitted. By then she could read, but not write.

But when Yiorwos caused problems, like smearing ink across Katerina's paintings.

Or when he would walk up the spiral stairs to the lemon tree and pick off a blossom bud. She punished him. She would take a pen and stab the back of his hand—bam, bam, bam, bam, bam.

Panagiota loved fiercely.

But she punished fiercely, too.

The Trifili family adored George—their little clover boy. He drew laughter from Katerina. He helped Yana pick words for her poems. John taught him to run his fingers over reel-to-reel tape and listen for silence.

Panagiota watched from the kitchen. She served them. Dressed their beds. Smiled at their affection for her son.

But some nights, when the apartment fell quiet—after the last dish was dried, after George returned from a too-loud laugh in someone else's arms—her hands shook with a bitterness she couldn't name.

Sometimes she hit him.

Not once. Not lightly.

And not for disobedience—but for love misplaced. For loyalty she feared she was losing.

He would speak decades later of those beatings.

Sadistic, he said.

Punishment not for what he'd done, but for how close he'd grown to the family who had taken them in.

She didn't do it because she hated him.

She did it because she couldn't bear to be the shadow in her own story. Because shame, when unspoken, curdles in the body. And when it can't be screamed, it strikes.

Eventually, she made the choice. She packed what little they had and left the Trifili home. She told herself it was because she didn't want to be a burden. Told herself the family had grown weary of George's mischief—his ink-stained fingers, his noise, his interruptions. But beneath all that, it was jealousy. Not of what they gave him. But of how purely he received it. She had survived abandonment, exile, fire—and yet it was her son's laughter in another woman's arms that undid her.

Panagiota loved George.

But she didn't know how to let others love him too.

So she took him from the only home that had held them gently.

And tried to rebuild a new one with her bare hands.

She had made her choice.

But Athens had no mercy for single mothers. Especially those who'd once worked for families with operas and art and sound proofed rooms. She tried—seamstress, cleaner, cook. Anything. But George grew restless, wild with the energy of boys who've known love but not permanence. So she took him south, to Kalamata.

And left him at the orphanage.

He was 8 years old, or maybe 9.

A boys-only home that smelled of soap and stone and sour milk. There were no linens there. No books. No music. Just bottle caps used as currency.

Fists behind doors.

A bathhouse with open taps and cold water.

She thought it would teach him discipline. Maybe it would make him grateful. Maybe it would make him strong. What it made him—was alone.

But the Trifilis found him again. Brought him home. They took the time to write a ten-page letter. A letter to Evangelos and included a photograph of his son – Yiorwos. Geography and grief aligned at last. So Panagiota gave her blessing and Yiorwos crossed the ocean—to his father and his father's wife—and to the land that would remold both their names.

But she did not follow.

She stayed in Pagrati until her heart loosened.

She let him go.

Years later, she fell in love again—this time with John Trifili. Kind. Curious. A now retired sound engineer with calloused fingers and a soft voice. He gave her a ring. She gave it to her son after John died. He died unexpectedly not long after their marriage.

They buried her with the pines watching.

Quietly.

But the ring—

the ring remembered.

When it cracked the mirror, something shifted.

And Panagiota crossed.

Not from the grave.

From memory.

Balcony One received her like a body exhaling.

She didn't haunt.

She held.

Held the corners no one cleaned.

Held the air between someone's pause and someone's sigh.

Held the story that hadn't been given breath.

She became the scent behind the bougainvillea. The pressure near the mirror. The sound no one could name in the stairwell. She was not bitter, not anymore. But she would not be forgotten.

What George built, she answered.

Not with speech.

With presence.

She is not listed in the deeds.

But she is in every lintel.

Every shelf he angles just so.

Every corner no one dares rearrange.

Sophia is her name here.

The name the building gave.

Now, she does not speak often. But when she does—the building listens. Not just Balcony One. But the adobe. The beams. The air in the corners. The places women cleaned after hours. The spaces where grief was never written down. The alcoves where someone once hummed a song no one else knew.

This is what it means to linger:

Not to hover.

But to infiltrate.

Not to cry out.

But to be unignorable in stillness.

Méno.

Not a plea.

Not a warning.

Just the truth.

Sophia—

No.

Panagiota—

had been her first given name.

A Greek name, *Most Holy Virgin Mary*.

Παναγιώτα.

Just scattered in whispers, exiled for carrying a child alone, and folded into the crowded hush of Athens and Sparta.

Balcony One understood her new name. Not given by any man, nor etched in any book. The building itself called her Sophia—as if it knew what kind of spirit had come to stay. And like most names born in silence, she did not choose it. She became it.

It settled in her like stone under floorboards.

Softened by repetition.

She still does not understand why she remained. Only that she was not done listening. And that the one who loves her—the one with grief still warming in his hands—was not done either.

Panagiota watches.

Mother. Exile. Architect of memory.

What roots in silence will speak in stone.

Scroll

ELIZABETH DESCENDS

Behind the Bar – After the Last Glass Was Dried

The last glass had been dried.

Elizabeth flipped the bar towel over her shoulder and let her hand rest, palm-down, against the smooth wood. The room was still—not just empty, but emptied. No music, no chatter. Only the soft tick of cooling fixtures and the faint scent of pear brandy lingering in the air.

She didn't leave. She never did, not right away. The bar was her church, her ledger, her confessional. After hours, the bottles didn't gleam for guests—they stood like sentinels, stripped of charm, honest in the dark. Even the shelves seemed to breathe differently without eyes on them.

She moved along the counter in a slow arc, wiping rings that had already dried. Not to clean. To remember. Her rituals were hers. Not sacred—just practiced. Left to right. Wipe, check, straighten.

When her cloth reached the second shelf, her fingers stilled. There was a mirror tucked behind the Campari. Oval. Off-center. Framed in something that wasn't brass but remembered it. It hadn't been there before—or if it had, it hadn't been angled just so. The mirror didn't reflect her face. Just her hands. And only when they moved. She leaned back. Blinked. The glass had shifted. Like it wasn't trying to be seen—but trying to see.

Her hand dropped to her side, still holding the rag. The bar was quiet. But something in the quiet had changed. Not the silence of closing time. The silence of listening. She'd seen reflections play tricks before. A glass catching light at the wrong angle. A bottle echoing motion that never happened.

But this wasn't that. This wasn't cold. Nor warm. It had the feeling of breath—the trace of something that had just departed.

In 1907 she became the Sheriff of Washington County. Duly elected—under the disguise of Charles Worthen, a man. In 1909, she ran for sheriff again—and won. So the disguise needed to hold. The Mormon's had a saying that a man not married after a certain age is a menace to society. She couldn't allow Sheriff Worthen to be seen as a menace.

It was 1910 when she came home as Sheriff Worthen, removed her hat, removed her badge and sat—quietly. She was fully Elizabeth now. A woman was there—sweeping while dinner cooked steadily. The woman sat next to Elizabeth. She brushed the ash off Elizabeth's brow and placed a gentle kiss on her cheek. Elizabeth said,

"I don't want them to become suspicious."

The woman replied with a smile,

"Suspicious about what?"

"About Sheriff Worthen."

The woman wiped Elizabeth's brow once more time.

"What? That Sheriff Worthen is really a woman in disguise? Or that a woman happens to be the best damn Sheriff from the Rocky Mountains to the Mohave?".

Elizabeth looked at the woman.

"I think you need to marry Sheriff Worthen."

She smiled at Elizabeth and clutched her necklace,

"What a scandal, the Sheriff marries his housekeeper."

"Better than the Sheriff is a woman, and sapphic."

Both women laughed at that. Sapphic was their little joke. A tongue in cheek reference to their relationship. A relationship shunned in most of the country at that time.

"Elizabeth, are you asking me to marry you?"

"Will you?"

"And what of my daughter?"

"She will be adopted by Sheriff Worthen."

Elizabeth smiled

But now, now this woman was gone.

Not gone. Just gone quiet.

Sheriff Worthen died in that fire too—but the papers never knew it. And the daughter—the daughter came with Elizabeth to Balcony One. She remained in the background, for protection—and for normalcy.

The mirror didn't shimmer. But it held still in a way that made her aware of every nerve in her hand.

She folded the cloth, slow. Set it aside. The bottles beside it leaned slightly forward— not by motion, but by presence. As if the whole shelf were waiting.

The tallest one, the pear brandy, caught the edge of the mirror and refracted it, casting a warped oval that curled along the back wall.

She saw her hand again in the glass. Then—somehow—the back of her hand. She hadn't moved. But the mirror had. Like a door swinging inward on its own hinge. A breath she didn't realize she'd been holding slipped out—a quiet release.

In the heart of the glass, something flickered. Not a face. Not Panagiota. Not Sophia. Not even her own. Just a corridor. Narrow. Clay-walled. Lit from nowhere. Rooted in a part of the building that didn't exist.

She didn't startle. Didn't flinch. Only blinked once and watched it fade.

The bar shelves settled again. The moonlight from the southern window slipped in with a cooler angle. The stained glass to the east gave nothing. She stepped a little closer. Placed a fingertip near the mirror's edge. No temperature. But pressure. Like touching the surface of deep water.

And then: a word, not spoken—recognition. This mirror hadn't arrived. It had revealed.

The copper table.

The carving on the stage she never remembered approving.

The pattern in the plasterwork of the Zitting Room ceiling.

Balcony One was not showing her something new.

It was reminding her of something she had already known.

She pulled her hand back. The mirror tilted again. And this time, it showed her face. Not ghosted. Not aged or softened.

Just her.

As she was.

And behind her—something.

Not quite a figure.

More a presence pressed into shape.

She didn't turn around. The scent came first. Bougainvillea. She didn't have to name her. She'd already been carried.

The feeling rose again—Resonance.

The air thickened. But it wasn't oppressive. It was attentive. Like something was holding the space open just long enough for her to notice it.

She breathed.

Slow.

Centered.

The bottles rebalanced. The weight of the room shifted. And something in her began to match it.

She caught her own reflection once more—this time from the side. Face turned, softer than she remembered. A softness that had nothing to do with aging. And everything to do with no longer performing. Behind her, the mirror held space.

For her.

For someone else.

For a presence that was not Panagiota exactly.

But carried her shape.

The shape of someone watching, not as ghost or guide, but as mother might watch a daughter—the kind of watching that holds but doesn't correct.

No voice came.

No message.

Only a tether.

Not seen. Not spoken.

Felt.

A line of quiet knowing drawn between two women who had never met—but recognized the weight the other carried. Elizabeth adjusted a tumbler on the shelf. Just a hair. Out of instinct. Out of reverence.

The mirror did not move again. But the moment did. It opened, not wide—but enough. Enough for her to feel known. She moved, just enough to rejoin the room.

The bottles gleamed. The shelves exhaled. The air behind the bar returned to stillness. The mirror stayed. So did she.

Not in awe.

Not in fear.

In understanding.

Something had crossed a threshold—from being unseen, to being seen.

From being unheld—to being held.

What is passed down is not always given.

Some things wait patiently—

for the moment you are quiet enough to notice them.

Scroll

EVANGELOS

Then – New York Harbor to Cleveland, 1855

George arrived in America with salt on his shoes and a warning stitched into his name. Nine years old.

Three days before landfall, he'd gotten bored. Or angry. Or some mix of both. The steward had been short with him. The toilet was clogged again. George stuffed a handful of toilet paper in the bowl, lit it with a kitchen match, and slammed the door. He called it a "scientific experiment."

It didn't do much damage—just smoke and panic. But the captain found out. Had a steward sit beside George for the rest of the voyage. A quiet man with soft hands and a ring on his thumb. He didn't scold, just watched. Ate his meals beside him. Slept in the bunk across the hall.

The steamer had coughed him up onto the New York docks—where Evangelos met him. It was snowing. He did not kneel. Did not hug. Just took the boy's duffel and turned toward the station.

George followed.

There was no home in New York. Only the train. Fourteen hours inland to Cleveland, the window icing shut halfway through. George stared out the window at fields too wide to understand. He asked what kind of food Americans ate. Evangelos said, "I'll show you."

In Cleveland, the restaurant smelled like grease and vinegar. Evangelos didn't take George home first. He took him to the restaurant.

George had expected something grand. Instead, it was a five-stool counter, one booth, and a griddle older than the floor. The cash register stuck when you opened it. The light over the back door flickered.

A woman walked in. Evangelos ordered stew, lamb, baklava for all of us. The woman was his wife and pregnant. And when the time came due, George's little half-sister was born.

George fell in love with the baby immediately.

He was a good protector of his little sister.

Evangelos worked at the National City Bank of Cleveland. The rest of the time, he read—stoically, voluminously. Plato, Pausanias, politics. He moved through the house like he was just borrowing it. No clutter. No mess. Not even a photograph.

His wife was kind in a distracted way. She served George lentil soup and called him "little brother," even though she was no sister. No mother, either. But she made space for him. That counted.

Still, George watched for his father's shadow in every room. Measured the silence between footsteps. Memorized how long Evangelos lingered at the windows.

There was no welcome. Only accommodation.

By spring, George had learned how to navigate the train line between Hudson and the city. When they returned home, George would sit at the kitchen table looking at ledgers.

George stayed. Longer than anyone expected. Long enough to stop flinching when Evangelos left without saying goodbye. He learned to read. Fluently. Widely. Evangelos insisted.

"A man without language is a mule with no bridle."

He never raised his voice, but George felt the disappointment like a draft through a cracked door.

In the city, the world was shifting—post-war bustle, new immigrants, new tensions. George found work at a print shop off Ontario Street, setting type and sweeping the floors. At night, he'd copy quotes into a leather-bound notebook, sometimes in English, sometimes Greek. He rarely quoted his father.

When George turned eighteen, he joined the U.S. Army. Told Evangelos at the breakfast table. Evangelos chewed slowly, then said,

"Write me when you've learned something worth remembering."

George left that afternoon.

By 1871, Evangelos had moved to Los Angeles, He was recruited to the new International Savings & Exchange Bank. This is where he met Isaias, his first Jewish friend. He lived with his wife and daughter in a house beside the old green, walked to work in a felt hat and long wool coat, always with gloves. Even in summer. He translated Pindar for a local journal. Wrote letters in quill. Dined alone.

Los Angeles suited him. Not for the sun, which he detested, but for its strange, fledgling civility. The city was new, but hungry. It wanted gravitas. He gave them Sophocles. He gave them syntax. He taught by candlelight. Refused gas lamps.

Over time, he opened a small deli near Olvera Street. Started by his German-Jewish friend, Isaias. Tiled floors. No sign.

He didn't know a thing about Jewish food. But he learned about the love and generosity of the Jewish people.

When George arrived—dust on his boots, grease on his shirt, the dog panting beside him—Evangelos didn't rise from his stool.

He just said, "There's a rag by the sink. Wipe your face before you speak."

George obeyed.

And thus began their apprenticeship.

Evangelos did not believe in inheritance. He believed in pressure. In boundaries. In the usefulness of being underestimated. When George came to him with blueprints—a rough sketch for a downtown taverna with a front patio and a narrow kitchen—Evangelos barely looked up.

"I need two hundred and fifty dollars to finish," George said.

Evangelos wiped his hands on a linen and looked past him, toward the street.

"The best help I can give you is none."

George didn't shout. He nodded. Took the paper back.

Evangelos watched him leave. Then turned back to the register and marked the day's receipts. Later, he sat alone in the shop's back office, rereading a letter from Athens. A cousin had written about the old church in Doxa—how the roof had collapsed, how the marble font still held rain. Evangelos folded the letter without finishing.

He didn't think of it as cruelty.

He thought of it as muscle—torn to build strength.

That night, he stood by the window and watched the wind shift the ivy along the back wall.

A neighbor's dog barked twice.

He said aloud, though no one was listening,

"If the door stays closed, he'll learn to pick locks."

And then, quietly,

"It's the Greek way."

Three weeks later, he passed the taverna—still unfinished.

George was on a ladder, shirt off, long hair waving, painting trim with borrowed brushes. Later that week, a supplier delivered a crate of cast-iron pans to the new address.

Unmarked.

Paid in full.

George never mentioned it.

Evangelos never admitted it.

That was their language.

Omission as bond.

Discipline as affection.

Not warm.

Not easy.

But binding.

George never buried Evangelos. Not properly.

The funeral was held in Los Angeles—closed casket, sparse pews, a priest who didn't know his name. George stayed in Miami, finished his shift, washed the walk-in cooler by hand.

But the real reckoning didn't come until years later, with a trowel in one hand and a blueprint in the other. Utah sky, bare mesa, Cynthia by his side. They were staking out what would become Balcony One.

That was when he felt it: the presence, the old gravity. Not grief—he'd lived through that. Not guilt either. Something denser. Like a muscle that had never properly healed.

He heard himself bark an order at the foreman. Sharp. Clipped. Evangelos's tone.

He paused. Stepped back. Tasted the silence.

Cynthia touched his shoulder.

He saw his father in every angle of that building. In the perfectionism. The demand for alignment. The refusal to use screws when dowels would do. Even in the way the spice shelf in the kitchen lined up flush with the edge of the backsplash—no flair, no drama, just order.

That's when he understood. The inheritance had always been structural.

Not in blood.

In the bones of the place.

Later, long after opening night, after Sam's death, after the storms, George walked the empty dining room in socked feet and whispered:

"You were never warm. But you were right."

The wind didn't answer.

But a shadow shifted in the glass of the back bar.

He left it be.

Once, during service, he caught Elizabeth slicing lemons with that same three-flick method Evangelos had drilled into him.

He almost corrected her.

Stopped.

Just watched.

Then turned back to the grill.

He never gave permission.

Only presence.

Not a blessing—but the weight of one.

And still, every fire George lit carried the shape of his silence.

Scroll

YIORWOS

Balcony One

George sat on a battered stool behind the southern wall of Balcony One, where the pinkish clay gave way to flagstone and a patchwork of weeds too stubborn to die. The back of the building faced south, toward the wide mouth of Zion. Most guests never saw this angle. They saw the front doors, the candles, the white tablecloths. But this—this was the real entrance. A turquoise metal door patched with paint. A trail of cracked chairs and orphaned frames. This was where things got fixed. Or didn't.

He looked up toward the sky, already rimmed with ochre. The sun was beginning to set behind the ridgeline, and the light slanted low, the way it always did before things changed. His fingers were dark with stain and lemon oil, his nails worn down from sanding the edges of a carved chair he'd found broken behind the feed store. Cynthia called it junk. But she let him keep the space. This was his domain. His cluttered reliquary. His way of staying still.

He didn't feel nostalgic. He never had. But something about that hour—when the heat let go and the wind finally came through the cottonwoods—always brought the old places back.

Cleveland.

The smell of slush and coal.

The heaviness of wet wool.

He remembered the basement kitchens and long winter walks with the Jewish boys who taught him how to survive—how to crack a joke before throwing a punch, how to open a deli, how to show up in a suit even if the shoes didn't fit. His father, Evangelos, was somewhere in California by then. A letter once a year. Maybe. But it wasn't Evangelos who taught him how to walk with dignity. It was Saul. And David. And Eli. Boys who became brothers, who vouched for him when he had no name that mattered.

He learned front-of-house first. Bowtie, clipboard, the whole show. They said he had presence. Said it like it was a compliment. He knew it meant they saw something exotic. Something clean-shaven and safe. He used it. Until he didn't need to anymore.

Then came Miami.

Then L.A.

Then Miami again.

It blurred. All of it. The kitchens. The cigarettes. The garlic oil burns that still lived in the grooves of his palms. Restaurants opened. Closed. Some his, some borrowed. There were women, too. But nothing stuck. Nothing held. He thought maybe Greece would.

He returned in his late thirties. Bought white stucco. Laid marble tile. Opened the Blue Parrot with a name full of hope. It didn't last. He was too American for the Greeks. Too Greek for the Americans. They called him foreigner in the village his mother died for. In the city where his father once swore love.

He closed the Blue Parrot after three years and came back west. First Las Vegas. Then eventually—almost accidentally—Utah.

Virgin.

He didn't expect to stay. But the Spendlove family fed him. Lent him tools. Introduced him to neighbors who nodded instead of stared. Cynthia showed up one day with a picnic basket and a list of rules. No kissing. No sleeping over. No bullshit. He fell for her immediately. She made him laugh without trying. Took him up Smith's Mesa, then into town, then finally into herself.

Cynthia was an artist and loved Sante Fe. So they had a small wedding there. They married when he was nearly sixty. And two witnesses stood with them. Evangelos, in his 80s and his wife.

They returned to Southern Utah and George immediately wanted to give Cynthia everything he had, everything he knew. So, he called up his go to wingman—Aris—and they built the Stage Coach Grille. After four years, they sold it and pretended to retire.

He thought his story had settled.

But Cynthia and George were not finished. They know they've been blessed and believe in their gifts and hiding them under a bushel would dishonor their faith. So they loved each other and conceived Balcony One.

And then came Sam Zitting.

Sam was the kind of customer you remember. Not because he tipped big—though he did—but because he listened. Every Thursday night, Sam brought his brothers. Sometimes his wife. Sometimes no one but his construction crew, red-faced and loud. They ordered everything. Shut the place down just for the hell of it. Sam loved Mateo's cooking. Loved George's stories. They talked about fathers. About building something that outlives your name. About sorrow. Quietly, always quietly. When Sam died of the flu, George didn't talk for three days. Cynthia thought he'd lost his voice. But it wasn't that. It was grief. The kind you don't show if you're a man raised without softness.

Still, George built.

He raised Balcony One from sand and grief. Not from blueprints— from memory. From texture. From need. That closet door? The one in the Zitting room with the grate? He built it to look like the door Evangelos' father slammed in his mother's face when she came to Athens, pregnant and unwelcome. Only this one opened inward.

He kept the ring his mother gave him. Wore it every day. The cracked mirror in the waiting room still catches its glint sometimes. He doesn't flinch anymore. He just nods.

Panagiota.

His mother.

His first reckoning.

She died before he could say thank you. But he hears her sometimes. In the creak of the stairs. In the weight of the copper tables. In the way the air thickens before the doors open.

He still works behind the building.

Still sands down the broken things.

Still believes in second lives.

The tourists never see this part. But if they did—if they wandered around the side and found him crouched over some ruined stool, eyes squinting in the light—they'd see something quieter than a legacy.

They'd see love.

Unpolished.

Unfinished.

Offered forward.

What outlasts the leaving is not legacy—

but love, made useful.

Bent back into shape, and offered forward.

Scroll

THE PSYCHIC ARCHITECT

Architecture is not what you build.
It's what continues—even after the builder is gone.

Some builders use blueprints. Some use their heart.

He listened—to the grain in the wood, the memory in the wall, the grief that had never been fully revealed. He knew what the building should be. It was conceived through him, and through her. Cynthia painted the soul. He built the ribs.

They called him practical, he may or may not agree. He was a gypsy. A keeper of stories. A man who built in silence and stained glass.

He was not haunted. He was filled—with love, and loss, and life.

He built more than a restaurant. He built a church. A temple. A cathedral that could carry its own weight.

He crafted a living building.

You are standing at the edge of it now.

He built with wood, stone, and copper.

He would have built with marble—if he was still in Greece. But here, in this desert, the pine came from Pine Valley. The cedar came from Cedar Mountain. Each board carried something he could not say out loud.

His memories inlaid the floorboards with turquoise—not literal, but psychic. Lines that shimmered inside the grain, lines he built around, not over.

He chose copper for its warmth. Glass for its brilliance. Velvet for how it comforted the soul, like a pew in a quiet chapel.

The copper inlays were his fingerprint. His rhythm. His offering.

When asked about the mirrors, he said,

"That's where I remembered her."

When asked about the blue glasses, he said,

"That was her."

The back of the building was his sanctuary. The patio—his music of worship. Every table had its own gravity.

The blueprints were never drawn.

They existed only in his mind.

And in his soul.

He built it because he loved.

He loved his mother. He loved his father. He loves his wife, Cynthia.

He also built it because—knowingly or unknowingly—his grief had no shape. He was not able to attend his mother's funeral. No casket. No ritual. No words spoken aloud.

He built it because love this large cannot stay invisible. Because memory with brilliance needs vast halls to echo within.

The rooms are not numbered. They are remembered.

Every beam was held in place to ensure immortality. Every fixture chosen with eternity in mind.

He built it because he was not there. But he could build a place where she might be found.

And she was.

And she is.

And some nights—just barely—he believes she's still building, too.

He built for the living—unaware that he brought the dead with him.

He built because he believed God had blessed him. And so, he honored that gift by building *Balcony One*.

The blueprints were physical. Emotional. Psychological.

Some rooms are smaller on the outside. Some disappear entirely— unless you know what you're grieving.

The building comes alive when light and shadow reveal its heart. Usually in the stillness of the night.

The pipes know him. The stage knows him. And the mirrors remember.

He did not call it magic. He called it preparation. The divine is not conjured. It's given a place to sit.

The building is not haunted.

It is alive.

And it lives for all those who step inside.

The building will remember you. It will remember your laugh. It will remember your breath.

When you walk these halls—the halls of *Balcony One*—and look at the mirrors, hear the songs played on the outdoor patio, when you've eaten at the tables, sat in the chairs, played at the chessboard—you didn't come here by accident.

He did not finish the design. He couldn't.

But if you touch the walls gently, if you listen closely at night, you might find the next room waiting.

And maybe this time—

you will be the one who builds it.

Where there is no shape, love builds.

Where there is no body, memory dwells.

Scroll

THE BUILDING THAT REMEMBERS

Balcony One – Before Dawn on the Last Tuesday

The light hadn't come yet. But something had shifted.

Not a noise. Not a draft or creak. It was deeper than that. Subsurface. Like a plate beneath the crust realigning after centuries of pressure.

Balcony One was quiet in a way it had never been.

Elizabeth stood behind the bar, her palms flat to the old walnut counter. Beneath her hands, she could feel the grain, the grooves where Cynthia had once laid out silverware, where George had drawn chalk lines before the final coat of sealant. The bar itself had been salvaged— something George had insisted on. Wood with history. Knots like memory. Her fingers moved without thinking, tracing a scar where a whiskey glass had shattered on opening night.

The mirrors watched.

All but one.

The oval mirror—the one that had appeared weeks ago, unanchored, unclaimed—stood by the pear brandy. It was not fogged. It was not cracked. But it no longer showed her face. Not truly. What it reflected now was… intention. Not shape, not color, but some kind of readiness.

She reached for the linen. Folded three times, simple cotton. The cloth had weight tonight—not just from thread count, but from meaning. From ritual. She unhooked the mirror gently, like it might breathe if jostled. Wrapped it without suffocating its surface. Not a burial. A cradling.

She crossed the bar, through the archway George had once widened by hand, into the heart of the restaurant. Past the Zitting Room, where copper bowls remembered grief and the bougainvillea still bloomed out of season. The light there was always slightly bluer than elsewhere. Cynthia had said it was the magnesium in the tile glaze. George said it was because Sam had never really left.

She reached the far wall.

It had held nothing for years. George had always left it blank. Said a space needed one true void to keep the rest honest. Tonight it hummed. Not audibly. But visibly. Like air that's been stirred by prayer.

She set the mirror there. Unwrapped it. Let it lean against the plaster. It didn't reflect her. It absorbed her. Like it had known she would come. Like it had been waiting for the soft pressure of her palm.

The chair behind her sighed.

One of the old ones. The kind that creaked when no one watched. She smiled—not at the sound, but at the *familiarity*. It was not haunting. It was residence. Something had returned to where it belonged.

She lit the blue glass candle.

The one that flickered out the night Sam died. The one that only burned true on Tuesdays. Tonight it caught instantly. A steady flame, no stutter. She placed it on the copper table without linen. Let its glow reach toward the mirror. A small axis of light. A silent acknowledgment.

Her body didn't weep. But it remembered. The ache in her throat was not grief—it was release. The sensation of something long carried finding its place at last.

She turned, slowly, a full circle. Bar. Stage. Zitting Room. Kitchen. Balcony.

Each space held a ghostprint. A resonance. Not as memory, but as presence. As if George had stamped himself into every grout line, every grain of wood, every breeze that passed through the vent above table five.

And each space had a mirror.

Some mounted. Some propped. One vanished the moment it was truly seen.

She whispered their names—not aloud, but through the mapping of her own hands, the sequence of her own care. She didn't summon them. She *remembered* them.

When she looked again at the wrapped mirror by the wall, it had begun to glow faintly. Not reflect. Glow. Not with fire. With recognition.

Not of her.

Of the building.

Of itself.

She didn't leave right away.

She stood in that quiet axis between wood, glass, wax, and wall—and let the hush wrap her. Not emptiness. Not silence. The hush of something sacred that has finished speaking. And now waiting to be heard.

Not still—never still.

The restaurant was never truly dark. Even before dawn, even with every switch off and every shutter drawn, there was always a glow—a faint radiance that didn't belong to bulbs or moonlight. George used to joke that it was just good insulation, holding on to the day's warmth. Cynthia had said it was the spirit of the place, rising early to set the tables.

Elizabeth had always thought it was memory. And now she was sure of it.

She walked the spine of the restaurant without turning on the sconces. No need. Her feet knew the floorboards like old lines of poetry. The boards beneath the bar dipped slightly, warped by foot traffic and wine spills. The hall to the kitchen still creaked in the exact same cadence George used to pace. Even the stone tile at the entrance kept the faintest scent of Santa Fe clay when the air turned damp.

But it wasn't just memory anymore. It was convergence.

Balcony One had become—permeable. Not to weather, or time, but to presence. To *George.*

She could feel him now—not as apparition, not as ghost, but as imprint. His will was layered into the bones of the place. His rituals. His griefs. His faith. The way he stirred the retsina with rosemary sprigs. The way he marked Tuesdays with copper. The way he never quite filled the last glass.

And in this hour before light, the building breathed him.

The bar remembered his laughter. The balcony remembered his arguments with his grandson—held not aloud, but in posture, in the way he leaned over the railing like his he might suddenly appear at the ridge. The stairs remembered Cynthia. The Santa Fe tiles, the color, the precision. And it still carried the smell of garlic and lemon oil. Even the windows bore the fingerprints of doubts—smudges wiped clean before service, but never truly gone.

Elizabeth reached the north wall.

No one ever sat there.

Not because the view was poor—it wasn't. It faced the slope, the stars, the sandstone ridges beyond the road. But that wall had always refused occupancy. Chairs moved away from it. Tables felt uneven beside it. Even Sam, who once rearranged the entire dining room, had left that space bare.

She touched the plaster.

Warm.

Alive.

Not metaphorically. It held temperature.

And—beneath her hand—a hum. A pulse. Not of electricity, but of *conviction.*

The same conviction George had carried for years: that this building was not just a restaurant. It was *remembrance.* A kind of embodied prayer.

Each wall a chapter. Each tile a footnote. Each beam a held breath from another life.

She looked across the room.

Every surface had softened. Not faded—just grown gentle, like skin after weeping. The grain of the wood, the dull sheen of polished concrete, even the metal lips of the barstools—everything appeared… resolved. As if the building itself had exhaled. As if it had made peace with its inheritance.

And in that peace, something settled.

Not closure.

Not erasure.

But integration.

This wasn't just George's last act.

It was his soul, housed in cedar and copper and glass.

And now, the building had begun to remember *her*.

Elizabeth lit the sconces, one by one. Not to illuminate, but to anoint. Each flame caught gently, slow to flare—as if recognizing the hour. As if reluctant to wake the walls. She didn't rush. This wasn't morning prep. This wasn't ritual. It was something deeper: consent. She was asking the building to allow this moment to happen.

She paused at the threshold of the dining room. The west wall, where the two-seat tables sat beneath framed art and votive shelves, was glowing faintly. Not from candles. From memory. From some layering of late summer light and old laughter. George had always said that space was liminal.

"It's where the dead come to see if they've been remembered right," he'd joked once.

Not a joke. Not anymore.

She moved through the space slowly. Past the kitchen pass. Past the host stand. Each step felt heavier, not from fatigue, but from awareness. This was no longer a place she worked. This was now a place she inhabited.

The room wasn't haunted.

It was *held.*

The sound changed when she stepped into the Zitting Room. No echo. No ambient hum from the icebox line. Just a hush, like she'd entered the interior of a cathedral. The copper table was set. The bougainvillea drooped slightly in the window box, its blossoms dry from the cold snap two nights ago. Elizabeth pressed a thumb to one petal. It crackled. She smiled. Even in death, it gave texture.

She remembered what George had said the first time they hosted a private party in that room:

"If a space doesn't carry a secret, it can't keep a promise."

He'd meant the architecture.

But it was true of him, too.

George had built Balcony One with secrets tucked into the bones of it. The blue candle that only burned true on Tuesdays. The slightly uneven beam over the stage—meant to echo a flaw in the Blue Parrot's back room. The pantry door that opened wider than the frame suggested. The corner near the kitchen where the temperature always dropped by a few degrees after 9pm.

None of it was arbitrary.

All of it was his way of encoding memory into material.

Elizabeth stepped toward the mirror she'd placed that morning.

It wasn't reflecting her.

It was reflecting *space.*

Room. Possibility. A shimmer of something not yet named.

For a moment, her throat tightened—not from grief, but from recognition. George had *transfigured* his life into architecture. Had written every exile and heartbreak and kitchen miracle into timber and light.

And she was not just witness to it.

She was one of many: its keeper now.

She touched the mirror's edge.

This was more than legacy.

This was *continuance.*

This was the soul made visible.

Behind her, a chair sighed. One of the old ones with joints that creaked only when no one was watching.

She smiled.

Not at the sound.

At the knowing.

She didn't light a new candle. She relit the blue glass one. The one that had flickered out just before Sam died. The one that only burned true on Tuesdays.

She struck the match.

To honor.

The flame steadied instantly.

As if it, too, had been waiting.

Elizabeth placed it on the copper table.

No linen.

Only the flame.

Only the mirror.

Only the hush that descended when something old had finally finished speaking. She thought briefly of Brooke. Of the bougainvillea. Of how some offerings are made without being understood, and only later reveal themselves as invitations.

To stay.

To descend.

To listen.

She wanted to cry. She hadn't in years. But her body remembered the shape of it—that sacred tremble in the throat that meant something had been held.

She stood in the dining room and turned, slowly—a full circle.

Stairs.

Bar.

Zitting Room.

Stage.

Sunroom.

Kitchen.

Balcony.

Each space held its own echo.

Each one had revealed something to her.

And in each, a mirror.

Some mounted.

Some lean-to.

One that had vanished the moment it was seen.

She whispered their names—not aloud, but in the order her hands remembered touching them. And when she looked back to the wrapped mirror by the wall—it was no longer reflecting her. It was reflecting light.

Only light.

Just the shimmer of morning, not yet arrived.

She didn't leave right away. She stood with the candle. Let the silence fold around her. Let the building settle—not with creaks or shifts, but with a quiet sigh too deep for architecture.

She touched the frame of the last mirror, the one still wrapped. For a moment, she imagined a woman's hands there.

Not ghostly.

Just layered.

As if time had chosen not to separate them completely. The linen had begun to take on the shape of it. Edges remembered. Corners softened. She wouldn't move it again. She would leave it just so.

The sun had not risen.

But the darkness had changed.

It no longer pressed.

It held.

She reached for the glass one last time—a clear impression. A mark not of ownership, but of witness.

Sophia did not appear. But something in the mirror deepened.

Not a face.

Not a voice.

Just a presence that no longer needed to hover.

Only to be kept.

Elizabeth stepped back. The candle flickered. Then stilled.

She did not speak.

She did not explain.

She only turned—

and left the room

exactly as it was.

The mirror had shifted.

Not dramatically. Just a tilt. A lean. As if it had adjusted its own gaze.

She stood at the edge of the copper table and waited. Not for a ghost. Not for proof. But for *alignment.* A confirmation that what she'd sensed in the Zitting Room, and again on the west wall, was not memory—but *structure.*

Balcony One wasn't reacting.

It was responding.

To her presence. To George's absence. To the culmination of something too layered to name. The restaurant *had taken him in.*

Not like a mausoleum. Not like a shrine. But like a story takes in breath before the final page.

The rooms spun around her—not with movement, but with meaning. She could *feel* them: the slight heat that came from the front doors after sunset, the creak in the second stair to the balcony, the echo that lived under Table Nine and only emerged during thunderstorms. She could feel the restaurant's memory like pressure behind her ribs.

It had *learned* him.

It had *learned* her.

In the stillness, she heard footsteps—not actual, but remembered. George's gait was unmistakable: a quick step of determination, a lightness on the pivot. She heard it. Or rather, the room offered it up. Like a language reemerging. Like the syntax of return.

Her breath hitched.

She spoke, not aloud, not in words. But something in her body formed the phrase:

"You are not gone."

And in answer, the blue candle flared. Not higher. Just brighter. Then settled.

She stepped forward.

And before her stood George.

The mirror still held light—but now, at its center, a dim outline had appeared. Not a face. Not even a shape. Just a *density*. Like breath against cold glass.

She didn't flinch.

Instead, she whispered—this time aloud:

"Thank you for building it."

The glass cleared. The flame stilled. And the air in the room became *whole*.

This wasn't a haunting.

This was a *handoff.*

Elizabeth turned toward the kitchen. Toward the front doors. Toward the world that would soon flood in with linen deliveries and breakfast prep and the hum of early guests.

But for now, the building held.

And so did she.

When the light came, it did not rush.

It slid.

Up the walls. Across the bar. Through the arches. As if Balcony One were exhaling for the first time in years.

She sat on the old chair that creaked beneath no one else, the blue candle still warm at her side, the linen-wrapped mirror at rest. Not silent. Not dormant. *Held.*

The mirror had not returned her reflection.

It had returned the room.

The first sound was not birdsong, nor the clatter of prep trays in the kitchen. It was the small settling groan of the west doorframe—George's favorite spot for watching guests arrive. It spoke not in grief, but in *familiarity.*

She let her fingers rest against the copper table.

No words.

Just touch.

Just weight.

Just the knowing that everything they'd built—he and Cynthia, Sam and Sophia, even the ghosts they never named—had been transmuted, spiral by spiral, into *space.*

This building did not trap stories.

It released them.

She would open the doors soon. Begin the rhythm again.

But for now, she let the hush linger. Let the light reach the high beams and catch in the old sconces. Let the mirrors breathe.

This was not a restaurant of grief.

This was the temple of continuation.

She stood. Smoothed her hands on her apron. Walked toward the front without looking back.

Not out of detachment.

Out of trust.

She knew what the mirror would show now.

Not a ghost.

Not a girl.

Not a man who built out of ache.

It would show *light.*

It would show *proof.*

It would show what remains when the story finishes its final breath—

and keeps *living.*

Not an ending.

An echo held long enough to become still.

THE WEIGHT THAT REMAINS

Zion, Not Seen

The light comes differently now.

Not brighter. Not softer.

Just more aware.

Balcony One does not speak.

But it listens.

It remembers not in language—

but in pressure.

In how the air folds around a chair just after someone has left.

In how a mirror leans slightly toward the room it loves.

In how the floor sighs once before dawn.

The Zitting Room knows what it held.

Knows the ache of inheritance.

Knows the weight of women who stayed not because they were asked,

but because they were summoned to remain.

Sophia was not the only one.

She was just the first the adobe decided not to forget.

Now Elizabeth walks the rooms with hands that carry lineage like sacrament.

Not loudly. Not for show.

But with that kind of reverence reserved for things half-buried and half-blessed.

There are no ledgers for what happened here.

No records for who hummed beneath the stairs.

But the building remembers.

And that is enough.

Zion, they once said, was a place.

Then a people.

Then a promise.

But sometimes—

Zion is just a room that still holds your breath

long after you've left it.

Some echoes do not fade.

They settle.

And they stay.

Scroll

THE SHARDS

A liturgy in twelve voices, remembered in wood, salt, and shadow.

There are twelve shards. Like ribs. Like apostles. Like doors left open after the dead walk through. I did not choose the number. The psychic architect did.

I am the building. I do not keep time. I keep what remains. And only touch the surface long enough to be felt—

and to feel.

SHARD: THE MIRRORS

Growth: Eternal

Known Properties:

- Do not reflect. They recall.

- Opened by a cracked ring.
- Appear in every room Sophia walks through.
- Show what the living refuse to speak.

ɵ SHARD: THE RING

Growth: 🏵 Fully Revealed

Known Properties:

- Inherited from George's mother.
- Originally came from John Trifili.
- Cracked the mirror.
- Created Sophia's return.
- Slipped once. Never again.

✷ SHARD: THE BLUE GLASS

Growth: 🌿 Emergent

Known Properties:

- Appears full without touch.
- Warps time and light.
- Turned blue after a girl saw the woman in blue.
- No one remembers replacing them.

✗ SHARD: THE COPPER INLAYS

Growth: 🏵 Fully Revealed

Known Properties:

- Hammered flat by George.
- Psychic Architect's fingerprint.
- Glows in truth.
- Shifts under lies.
- Each pattern unique. Some burn.

† SHARD: THE CROSS (BASEMENT)

Growth: 🌿 Emergent

Known Properties:

- Greek Orthodox.
- Once stolen. Now returned.
- Found by Elizabeth.
- Some walls bowed when it surfaced.

➚ SHARD: THE MOTHER OF GOD

Growth: 🌿 Emergent

Known Properties:

- Icon of Panagiota.
- Found in the basement.
- Revealed by Elizabeth.

▦ SHARD: CYNTHIA'S PAINTINGS

Growth: ❀ Fully Revealed

Known Properties:

- Painted from memory, not reference.
- Subjects are mythic.
- Guests change beneath them.

⇩ SHARD: THE POMEGRANATE

Growth: 🌱 Seeded

Known Properties:

- Rodinos. Ρόδινος.
- Crete.
- Appears in scent and symbol.
- Sometimes bleeding. Sometimes buried.

- Masculine. Ruddy. Optimistic.

⬩ SHARD: THE LEMON TREE THORN

Growth: 🌿 Emergent

Known Properties:

- Panagiota's memory.
- Beautiful. Bitter.
- Cuts even when pressed with care.
- Left behind.

⬤ SHARD: THE CHAIR AT TABLE SIX

Growth: 🌿 Emergent

Known Properties:

- Sam's favorite.
- Always warm.
- Guests skip it without knowing why.
- Once moved. Then moved back.

⬩ SHARD: THE SALT

Growth: 🌱 Seeded

Known Properties:

- Never passed hand to hand.
- Only placed.
- Greek superstition.
- Guests forget. George never did.

⊙ SHARD: TUESDAYS

Growth: ⬩ Eternal

Known Properties:

- Roses bloom.
- Glasses fill.
- Sophia presence.
- Night of the ghosts.
- No calendar explains it.

The shards do not speak. But they remain. They reveal what memories couldn't.

Twelve.

Enough to build a ribcage.

Enough to shelter a ghost.

Enough to remember you.

— *Balcony One*

Scroll

THE ONE YOU WRITE

Blank seal – the circle unwritten, open for the reader's breath

About the Author

Stone Eugene Clark crafts fiction shaped by psychological fracture, the quiet violence of belief and ancestral memory—spanning literary horror, magical realism, historical mystery, and the shadowed edges of crime.

Raised in the American West, he draws from buried archives, fractured faith, and inherited silence to craft stories that bridge myth and blood.

For updates and contact:

Email: stoneeugeneclark@gmail.com

Instagram: @stoneeugeneclark